THE BABY HUNTERS

JOANNA WARRINGTON

Joanna Warrington

All rights reserved

The moral right of the author has been asserted

Copyright 2025 Joanna Warrington

DISCLAIMER AND BACKGROUND TO THE STORY

This story is a work of fiction. Names, characters, businesses, places, events, incidents and the human experience are either the product of the author's imagination or are used in a fictitious way. Any resemblance to actual persons, living or dead, or actual events is purely coincidental.

This story is in three parts: 'Every Family Has One' is about Kathleen's life in a Magdalene laundry and her later struggles. 'The Catholic Woman's Dying Wish' is about her brother's search for her. 'The Baby Hunters' is about Kathleen's escape from the Magdalene laundry. You can read the books in any order. Here is the link to the complete series:
  UK : My Book
  USA : My Book
  Australia: My Book

This story begins in the autumn of 1974 after the birth of Kathleen's baby who died soon after birth. The story was inspired by my interest in the Magdalene laundries––institutions that existed in Ireland until 1996. Maintained by religious orders in the Roman Catholic Church, these homes were run by nuns for women labelled as 'fallen' by their families and society. There has been a great deal of interest in these institutions in recent years, immortalised in films like The Magdalene Sisters and Philomena and documentaries such as *Sex in a Cold Climate*.

'The Weeping Lady' Magdalene Laundry is a fictional institution and does not necessarily represent what happened within the laundries and industrial schools around this time. However, it may provide a glimpse into the life of the laundries that some people might identify with. Experiences varied.

The opinions and views expressed in this book are the opinions and views of the characters, and not mine, the author or any living person.

The story was also inspired by Hollywood star Jane Russell's adoption of an Irishwoman's child, Thomas Kavanagh in 1952. This was a controversial case and nearly ended the actress's career. News of the star's desire for another child reached Hannah McDermott. Reportedly Hannah offered her custody of baby Thomas on condition that Jane and her husband provided him with a good home, love, and education. Thomas was one of thousands of Irish children adopted by American couples. This practice continued right up until the early 1970s and unofficially potentially for much longer. Records were often lost and falsified.

Please visit my website at http://www.joannawarringtonauthor-allthingsd.co.uk
Joanna Warrington 2025

CHAPTER 1

SOUTHERN IRELAND

 ctober 1974
Niamh

'You're to leave this house and never come back, d'you hear me?'

Niamh was shaking; she'd never seen her dad this angry, and it terrified her. His face had turned a shade of purple, he had a crazed look in his eyes and as he waved his fist in her face, expecting a sharp blow to her cheeks, she cowered. He had never in all her sixteen years struck her, there had been no reason to, not until now.

'Fetch your bag.' He nodded to the stairs. 'You won't tell us who the father of your bastard is, so we've made arrangements. Father Joseph is coming to take you away.

He paused and glanced round at Niamh's mum who suddenly looked small and insignificant, her shoulders stooped, hugging herself as she trembled by the banister. He added bitterly, 'I would never have expected this of you, Niamh.' His mouth twisted into a snarl. 'What did you expect, a hero's welcome?'

Hot tears trickled down her face and she wiped her misty eyes with the back of her sleeve and looked over at her mum, silently pleading with her to intervene. She didn't want to go away, she wanted to have her baby at home and for her mother to help raise it.

Surely, her mum could understand this was the best solution, she adored babies, she'd had five of her own. But when Niamh saw the look of disgust on her face, she felt as if she were dog dirt. It was hopeless and all the pleading in the world was not going to work. 'You're a dirty little slut who allowed some scoundrel to take advantage of you.'

'That's not true,' she protested. 'None of this is my fault, but neither of you will listen,' she screamed as she climbed the stairs.

'Not your fault.' Her mother spluttered and let out a mirthless laugh. 'Whose bleeding fault is it then?'

'You're leaving,' her dad called after her. 'Pack your things, I won't have shame brought to my door. We'll never be able to show our faces around here again, let alone step inside the church. What will the parishioners think of us?'

Niamh headed for her room and the door juddered on its hinges as she slammed it behind her. She collapsed on the bed sobbing into her pillow. This was maddening, if only they'd hear her out. But she knew it was futile, her parents would always trust the family priest over her. They'd never in a million years believe her if she told them he'd assaulted her. The times he'd popped round for tea, spreading kindness and wisdom. He was the pillar of the community, trusted and looked up to for his moral and spiritual guidance. He helped run the Boy Scouts, gave scripture lessons at the primary school and he was on the village hall committee. It was just so unthinkable, so inconceivable; they'd accuse her of blasphemy and lies.

How little you ever really knew someone. Behind that gentle mask, was a cruel and ruthless man. And now she was going on a journey with him. She shuddered, sickened at the thought of what he might do to her. Where was he taking her?

When Father Joseph arrived, the priest looked at her through dark, triumphant eyes. A cold chill of fear trickled down her spine and her stomach dipped, the haunting recollection of that day lingering, visible in the throbbing vein in his neck, the creases around his mouth, his woody scent.

'It's time for us to go,' he said to her parents.

Outside, he threw her bags into the back of his Ford Cortina. She looked at her mum. She seemed tense, her face pinched and stiff. 'It's for your own good, Niamh. It's for the best. They'll give you good care and support.'

'Where are you sending me?' she screamed back at them as the priest guided her and opened the passenger door.

'Somewhere safe where girls like you are looked after,' her mum said.

Her dad was nowhere to be seen, and Niamh imagined he was back in his shed surrounded by his tools and lost in his own thoughts. Hammering nails was much easier than fixing the broken parts of his family. He spent most of the day in there.

Her mum, barely smiling, continued to stand rigid on the doorstep. Niamh suddenly felt like a criminal being taken away in a police car, condemned for a heinous crime, the crime of pregnancy. She glanced back at the house and her mum looked like a ghost. There was a horrible deadness about the place and about her mother.

FATHER JOSEPH SLIPPED in behind the wheel and drove off in silence. He had no desire to talk to the girl. As the car zigzagged down the country lanes, flanked by stone walls, the occasional farmhouse and endless emerald fields of cows and sheep, he thought back to that afternoon with her in the confessional box. It was his lunch break; he'd heard several confessions and was about to leave the booth when he heard the door open. Someone settled in and he'd sat back stifling a sigh. It was a rare free afternoon that day, the weather was perfect for a change, and he'd been looking forward to exploring the town by push-bike. There were so many penitents, she was just one of them, the whole village was awash with sin. Liverpool had been bad enough, thank goodness he'd moved to Ireland, but village life was also tainted. As a vessel of God's grace, he had to navigate the treacherous waters of human frailty, helping others to find redemption in the face of temptation.

'I've never done this before,' she'd said.

He recognised her voice but couldn't place her. There was something about her nervous voice, a certain vulnerability that he found alluring. He leaned forward, interested.

'Ah, there's always a first time for everything.'

She gave a nervous, stifled snigger which piqued his interest. He'd ordered himself to concentrate even though he wondered what she looked like and how old she was.

'First, we make the sign of the cross. In the name of the Father, the Son and the Holy Spirit...' He heard her echo the words with him.

She let out a long breath. 'Father, there are things troubling me.' There was that chink in her defences again and he'd been eager to exploit it.

'Are the things troubling you of a carnal nature?'

'Carnal.' She'd laughed. He wondered whether she was slender or curvy. Her voice was making him feel more man than priest. 'Do you ever have people who have done really bad things?'

He'd considered his answer carefully. 'We're all sinners in the eyes of God.'

'That's just religious claptrap. I did something bad, and I don't know what to do about it.' Her voice cracked and he had the urge to go to the other side of the booth and pull her into his arms. 'How can I live with myself?'

'That depends on what you've done.'

'I let my best friend's boyfriend kiss me and touch inside my bra.' She was whimpering.

He gulped, was silent for a few moments as he tried desperately to quell the rising desire warming his groin, threatening to overwhelm and crush him and even though he knew it was wrong, it was impossible to contain it. He had needs.

She'd cried; he could hear her pulling the Kleenexes from the box inside the booth. He'd wanted to take her in his arms, the need was so intense.

'I should go,' she simpered and when he'd heard the booth door swing open and her heels clack across the flagstones, his heart beating so fast, there was no time to think, he'd rushed out and grabbed her and taken her into the vestry, locking the door behind him.

He quickly put the memory out of his mind. Soon she wouldn't be his responsibility. He'd deliver her into the very capable hands of Mother Superior who'd set her to work and then when the time came, her baby would be adopted.

They arrived at the top of a hill and the car slowed as he turned into the long avenue leading up to the red brick and sandstone mansion. It was an obscenely beautiful warm day and as he looked around him at the straggly yews and cluster of old oaks, he thought to himself, *all is well with the world, praise to God.*

On the way up the drive, they passed a chauffeur-driven Bentley. He glimpsed a smartly dressed couple huddled in the back cradling a baby wrapped in a pink shawl. It was heartwarming to witness the joy on the couple's faces. He imagined they'd struggled for years to conceive and were so worthy of raising children.

'Here we are,' he said brightly, pulling up on the gravel drive.

She peered through the windscreen. She'd barely spoken during the two-hour journey but now she was firing questions. 'What is this place and why are there iron bars on every window?'

'Consider it a privilege to be here. This place is full of bad girls like you, but the nuns look after them with the goodness of their hearts, and for the love of God. If I hadn't brought you here, your parents would have chucked you out anyway, and you'd have ended up on the streets as a prostitute.' Part of him felt guilty, he was responsible for her being here, but every man had needs, and she had been in the wrong place at the wrong time. Who'd believe her over an esteemed priest, a man of God?

At the door they were met by a stout nun carrying a clipboard. As she beamed at him, he felt so appreciated, valued by the nuns. 'How lovely to see you again, Father,' she gushed. 'We do enjoy your visits, dinner will be served at six, your favourite, lamb roast followed by jam roly-poly, but before then, there's an urgent matter we need your help with.'

She glanced at Niamh, eying her suspiciously, and with a wave of her hand ordered her to sit on a wooden chair in the hallway and wait to be processed. 'What's your name, child?' she asked officiously.

'Niamh.'

She scribbled something on her pad. 'While you're here, your name will be Anne and your number is 1834.'

He was always impressed by the efficiency of the establishment. They were so well organised. They left the girl in the hall, and he was ushered through to Mother Superior's office.

'Father Joseph, am I glad to see you.' Red and flustered, she rose from her desk and bustled over to him letting out a big sigh. 'Kathleen's missing.'

He had to smile; there was always a drama at The Weeping Lady. Coming here gave him a sense of purpose and made him feel important. They were like a family to him, and the nuns respected him for his guidance and support. But it was also lucrative and right now, that was what he needed, money.

'The girl I brought over from Liverpool. Did she have the baby?'

'It died, but thank goodness you've brought a new lass in, I'm so grateful, our numbers are down, one has been dispatched today, another this evening. That will leave only fifteen girls, down by half on a few years ago. Numbers must rise and we must review our security, it shouldn't have been possible for Kathleen to escape, we've got to find her, Father, she must pay for her sins, will you help?'

'Yes of course, but first if we can settle my fee.' He shifted awkwardly in his chair. This was the most difficult part of their meeting, and he was always glad when the money had passed safely into his hands, he could relax then.

She took a small black box out of her desk drawer, unlocked it and handed him an envelope.

'Bless you, sister.' He folded his hands around the envelope filled with lovely notes and thanked God for this latest gift. Two thousand more pounds and there would be enough money to renovate his cottage and do the necessary work to modernise the church. The cottage came first though. The windows desperately needed replacing, they had old Crittall frames which were draughty, and there was no bathroom. Someone of his status shouldn't have to wash in a tin bath in front of the fire and use a privy at the bottom of the garden, he was the village priest, the most important person in the community. How could he do his job properly if he had to live in such conditions?

'What enquiries have you made so far with regard to Kathleen?'

'As you know, the girls are always trying to make a run for it, but they're usually caught by the guards and dragged back. But this time, it's been hours. There's no sign of Kathleen. The groundsman and the gardener have been out scouring the fields all around, there's nothing for miles and my initial thought was that she couldn't have gone far, not in her condition so soon after giving birth, and not unless she thumbed for a lift. She had a difficult birth; the baby had all sorts of complications, thankfully God took it because quite frankly Father, I really don't know what we would have done. Nobody wants to adopt a deformed child. And we don't have the facilities, it's not our responsibility.'

'Have you called the Gardaì?'

'Yes, they're making house to house enquiries down in the village, but it's only a hamlet, it won't take long and of course there's the pub. They've hidden girls in the past, that would be the obvious place to check but I don't think the publican would risk stowing another girl, too much is at stake. When we do find her, Father, she's going to get such a hiding. After all we've done for that good-for-nothing. If we don't set an example, more will try to escape.'

'I'm happy to help.'

'Thank you, I'd appreciate that, you have a stronger hand.' He'd used the whip on girls before. It was kept in Mother's Superior desk drawer.

Their conversation was interrupted by screams coming from the corridor and the thunder of feet on the stairs. Mother Superior swept from the room with Father Joseph following. Out in the corridor, a couple of girls were on their hands and knees scrubbing the floor. They carried on scrubbing and didn't look up. At the other end of the hall, Niamh was howling, like an animal brought to slaughter.

'I don't want to be here, you have no right to keep me here and I will not give my baby up.' It must have been explained to her what was going to happen. How did the little temptress not realise? He saw anger in her eyes, what an ungrateful trollop she was, the nuns were here to help and turn her life around.

He quelled the urge to slap her, but he could see that the nuns had already done that. There were cuts and bruises on her jaw and arms. Good, he thought, they'd shown their might. In a few days' time, she'd be defeated, there would be no fight left in her.

Mother Superior stepped towards her, grabbing her wrist. 'You can get that idea right out of your head. There are lots of respectable families lining up to take your child and it will be far better off without you.'

Suddenly, a new disturbance erupted from an upstairs room with raised voices and the sharp sound of a hand meeting flesh.

'Father, will you see to that?' Mother Superior gestured towards the disturbance. Then she grabbed Niamh roughly by the collar as if she were a stray dog. 'Come with me, I'm setting you to work in the basement laundry.'

He dashed upstairs and along the corridor to the room at the furthest end which was the nursery. A girl sat in a rocking chair next to an empty cot, tears streaming down her face as she clutched a pink baby's blanket and cried out, 'they've taken my baby, I want my baby.' He could see that a nun had slapped her, she had a red mark on one of her cheeks.

He stood in the doorway. 'It's no good crying like that, you have your future to consider too. Don't you want to get married and have a family of your own one day? You won't get a husband if you already have a child.'

'But I love my baby, she needs me, I don't want to abandon her.'

He remembered the couple with the baby heading down the drive in the Bentley. 'She's gone to her new parents, good people who have the means to give her much more than you can.'

She continued to howl.

'Excuse me, Father.' A nurse pushed past him holding an injection and a metal kidney tray, ready to administer a shot into her arm. She hovered over the girl, injected her, and moments later, she was calm. The fear and desperation he'd seen in her eyes disappeared, replaced by a haunting emptiness and hollow gaze. It was better this way, the sooner she let go of the past, the sooner they could set her on God's path to a more righteous future and that would also ease the burden on everyone around her.

He heard Mother Superior's feet on the stairs, and she came into view, hurrying along the corridor towards him, her skirts swishing on the wooden floor. 'Father, I've been trying all morning to reach yesterday's van driver to question him about Kathleen's disappearance. He's coming shortly. When you're ready, please return to my office.'

Every afternoon, a van brought soiled linen and exchanged it for fresh sheets and towels, which were then delivered to establishments in Cork.

Perhaps it was the van driver who'd aided Kathleen's daring escape.

CHAPTER 2

SOUTHERN IRELAND LATE SEPTEMBER 1974

Kathleen

Kathleen's heart raced; she'd been waiting for his arrival, it was gone 12:00 and now her eyes were fixed on the small window and the laundry van just pulling up. He'd already changed the time and day they were meeting. She glanced round. Nobody was about, but the supervisor would be back at any moment, she didn't have long, and the other girls were pressing sheets in the ironing room. This was her chance, it might be the one and only shot atshe couldn't let slip away. She grabbed the stack of fresh laundry and hurried up the stone steps, glancing in both directions to check the coast was clear. When the driver, Colin, spotted her, he swung open the van's back doors. Her pleas of a few days ago when he'd caught her alone had been heard, and today it was all falling into place. Where he'd take her and the fate that might befall her, she had no idea, but she was willing to brave the danger and her eyes were open to the consequences that awaited her if she was caught.

'Quick, get in.' He gave her a hard shove as she clambered in, the cold hardness of the metal floor slamming into her knees.

As she scrambled into the gloom of the van, he emptied a bag of towels over her head to conceal her. This was a huge risk for him, the sacrifice he was making for her, he'd lose his job if he was caught. Nestled in her hiding place, she was overwhelmed by a massive wave of gratitude mixed with guilt. He slammed the doors and moments later the engine fired and he accelerated away, crunching over the gravel. Pausing briefly at the end of the drive, he turned and sped off down the country lane, bumping and lurching through muddy ruts, grazing the hedgerow, and grinding the gears every so often, not caring about any damage he might cause the engine.

She peeped out from under the covers, taking a moment to size him up. His features were sharp, almost reptilian: long slender fingers, defined cheekbones, pointed chin and greasy, ash-coloured hair that hung limp around his face. The warmth he'd exuded the other day was gone.

'Keep your head down,' he called, 'we're not in the clear yet.'

'Where are you taking me?'

He didn't answer. Above the drone of the engine and her muffled voice under the laundry, maybe he hadn't heard her. His driving was awful, too fast one minute, then heavy braking the next, and now her stomach was performing somersaults and she could feel that morning's gloopy porridge rising in her throat.

She peeked from under the cover as the van slowed in front of a pub.

'Wait here, don't move. Just nipping in here a minute.' His tone was curt, or maybe it was nerves, there was a lot at stake for him.

Panic rose inside her as she watched him disappear inside the pub, and even though he wasn't gone for long, she was terrified about what might happen next. Was he going to leave her here in the pub where she'd soon be discovered as other women had been before her?

THE PUB HAD ONLY JUST OPENED, and thankfully it was too early for customers. Colin hovered near the bar waiting for Jim to appear. He heard his heavy footsteps on the stairs coming up from the cellar and then he appeared, his arms laden with a crate of beer.

He was puffed out from the steep climb and lowered the crates to the floor, mopping his brow. 'Hello, mate, what can I get you?'

Colin didn't have time for pleasantries, he just wanted to be rid of the girl. As far as he was concerned, he'd done his bit, someone else could take over, she wasn't his problem. Already he was regretting helping her and stopping at the pub was a further delay to his day. He couldn't be late to his next stop; it might arouse suspicion. Once they realised the girl was gone, he would be one of the prime suspects they'd consider. He realised what a fool he'd been, he couldn't risk losing his job, it was all he had, but the temptation of financial reward had been too strong.

Cutting to the chase, he blurted, 'I've got one of the girls in the back of the van.'

'Bloody hell, well done, I knew we could rely on you.' Jim slapped him on the back and strolled round to the other side of the bar. 'The way those nuns treat the girls, it's cruel and wicked. As I said to you the other night, the wife works there, she's seen it first-hand and Eddie the gardener, digging graves for those poor wee babies. The women are left to labour on their own, it's no wonder the babies don't survive the trauma of their births.'

Colin checked his watch and sighed. He'd been drawn into a conversation between several locals the previous week and Jim was only repeating everything that had been said during that conversation.

'Yeah well,' he said dismissively, 'I didn't do it out of the kindness of my heart, I need paying for my time and the risk I've taken.'

Jim blinked and stared at him, incredulous. 'This isn't about financial reward.'

'I don't care, I still need paying.'

'You can swing your hook, go on, clear off.' He waved his hand gesturing for Colin to leave. 'I've a pub to open.'

Colin stalked off towards the door calling over his shoulder, 'Fine, I'll take the girl back, shall I?'

Jim grabbed his arm, but Colin shrugged it off. 'No, wait, don't be doing that.'

'I can always bring her in here instead. Hide her in your cellar.' It was no skin off his nose either way.'

Seeing fear in Jim's eyes, he knew he'd be able to get something out of the old publican. 'This is the first place they'll look, the Gardaì will be swarming round, and I might even lose my licence. I've harboured girls in the past, I can't risk it again,' Jim pleaded.

'Suit yourself, you don't want her, I don't want her, she can go back.'

It worked. Jim dug into his pocket and pulled out a fiver. 'We're just a loose network trying to help the girls to escape, we're doing whatever we can. Here, take this.' He thrust the note into his hand. 'Don't come back for more. Just you remember this, lad, the most generous people in this life are those who silently help without the hope of reward.'

'What do you want me to do with her? She can't stay at mine, I live in a caravan with my old grandma.'

'Come back in a couple of days, I'll sort something.' He scratched his head and frowned. He hadn't the foggiest idea, Colin could see that. So much for an organised network, they were just a disorganised bunch of do-gooders.

'You make sure you do, she can't stay with me.'

'I need to speak to some folk. We'll try and smuggle her out of Ireland, I've got a mate who works on the ferries.'

Colin headed out of the pub to hit her with the news; she'd be coming home with him for a few days and if he couldn't get rid of her, he'd make good use of her.

CHAPTER 3

THE GRANVILLES, VIRGINIA, AMERICA 1974

Life should have been perfect for Robert Granville and his actress wife, the famous Janie Lee. They had everything they could possibly want: more money than they knew what to do with, a happy marriage, a beautiful home and successful careers. Robert was an entrepreneur. They'd found their dream home in the foothills of the Blue Ridge Mountains of Virginia, a grand colonial-style mansion with several acres of land and horses, a swimming pool, and a tennis court, and they were the envy of all their friends.

Except the reality was, their life was far from perfect, something that few of their friends appreciated. Their deepest longing was to have children and even though it now seemed out of reach after so many years of trying, it remained their greatest dream. Without children, who would they leave their fortune to? And rattling around in a huge house designed for a big family, it didn't seem right. Every successful couple had children, it completed the jigsaw.

The decorators had long since finished the nursery, and it was so beautiful, the décor and furniture inspired by the latest designs splashed across the pages of classy magazines. The door remained closed, a forgotten room that gathered dust and made them feel desperately sad.

As the years went by, they began to feel bitter about the injustice of their situation. How could so many undeserving people find it so easy, pushing out babies like a vending machine dispensing cans of drink, raising children they didn't even want while so many others never had that opportunity? It was like a bereavement, the loss of a dream, an assumed future.

The doctor in the hospital in Charlottesville said there was nothing wrong with the pair of them, and they should both relax. That was ten years ago. They were now pushing forty. It was too late. Janie's sparkly eyes had started to fade, her sweet smile became pursed, her lips puckered and hard. Now she was just his wife, who sat across the table with her hair pulled back into a tight bun, with a frown on her face. She used to gaze up into his eyes and promise to love him forever. He couldn't remember when he'd last bought her gifts when he went away on business, simple gestures that meant so much had now fallen by the wayside. He missed the squeals of delight; treating her had always been such a pleasure, he had felt he could achieve anything for her, but really, what was the point? She didn't need gifts, she could treat herself whenever she wanted. Most of the time she seemed so distant, in her own world and he had no idea what she was thinking. There had been a time when they'd lain in bed wrapped in each other's arms talking into the wee small hours, but now she turned away from him as soon as the light went out.

They'd come to accept that it was the one thing that could not be obtained with money––or so they thought. And then one day as Robert read the paper over breakfast, he stumbled across an article. It was entitled 'A Fairy-tale Come True' with the subheading, 'A Surprise for The Wife,' and beneath the article was a picture of two beaming children.

Two little Irish waifs, destined for a grim existence in poverty and despair have been rescued from a Catholic orphanage in Ireland by a wealthy New York benefactor who will offer them a bright future.

Witnessing this happy union made me think of a fairy godmother flying through the streets of Cork and through the convent gates waving a magic wand and whispering, "I grant you the greatest wish of all little children, to fly over the ocean to the land where the roads are paved with gold and all the toys and sweets you could ever wish for."

What a strange article, he thought, but he was intrigued and read on to discover the wealthy benefactor was in fact a business acquaintance of his, Niall O'Callaghan. 'Well, well,' he muttered.

Janie was at the kitchen counter making toast. 'What is it, honey?'

'Just an article about a business acquaintance.' He folded the paper and said nothing, quickly making the decision not to build her hopes. He kissed her on the cheek and headed straight to his office to phone Niall.

'You old son of a gun.' Niall gave a deep-throated laugh. 'It's been a while, to what do I owe this pleasure, how's business?'

'Great, thanks. I wanted to talk to you about a personal matter. I saw the piece about you in today's paper, you've adopted two children from Ireland. Congratulations,' he said trying to sound bright but feeling envious, 'Lovely looking kids.' He paused, his throat suddenly dry. Apart from the doctor, he'd never shared their fertility problems with anyone, it was private. A sharp pang of failure gnawed at him. He'd achieved huge financial success but had failed Janie. The inability to father a child with the woman he cherished so deeply was agonising. 'Janie and I have been trying for a baby for a long time, we've kind of given up, it's been so long and we're no spring chickens. But reading about you, how did you go about adopting them, was it easy?'

Niall took a deep breath. 'I know what you're going

through. Trying for a baby took over our life. It became a sort of mental torture, an obsession. It ruined our physical relationship and for years our lives were in limbo. It was a waiting game, for test results, sleepless in the middle of the night as we tried to come up with something that we could do. I have never felt so powerless, so inadequate, watching the physical and mental distress my wife was suffering, the anguish we were living with, not to mention having to make love to a time clock.' He roared with laughter. 'I looked everywhere for comfort, only how can you turn to the people around you who have not experienced this and expect them to understand? It's like grief. Your friends and family may be the most sensitive people in the world, but even if they are parents, especially if they are parents, ultimately they have no idea, unless they've struggled with it, what this kind of anxious, unrequited yearning feels like.'

He'd summed it up well. 'Yes, it's hard.'

'But look, mate, don't be downcast, get yourself over to Ireland, find yourself a kiddie. I went over on my own as I had some business in Ireland. I wanted to surprise the wife. It's nice to do that now and again. Better than surprising her with duty-free perfume.'

Robert found something intensely shocking about the crass comment, but he still wanted to know more.

'I expected to be over there for quite a while,' Niall continued, 'knowing that adoption, especially inter-country adoption, was likely to be a long, slow process. But just two weeks after arriving in Ireland, I returned home. I found the children at the first mother and baby home I went to, and they were the first children I saw. I liked the girl, Margaret, right away. Then Anthony came over and put his arms around me and said, "I like you", and he kissed me. He was so warm and affectionate, a great nipper. In a way, he adopted me.'

'What checks did they do?'

'I don't think there really were any. It was dead easy, those nuns are only interested in getting paid.'

How on earth, he wondered, had the whole business been conducted without his wife's involvement and knowledge? The more he heard, the more surprised he was. Those in charge of the children's welfare hadn't bothered to vet the would-be parents, they'd failed to conduct any inquiries or gather any information about their situation. But while he grappled with this moral dichotomy, feeling conflicted, it didn't take him long to see that this was a marvellous opportunity he couldn't dismiss.

'But what does the state have to say about all this?'

'Mate, why are you worried about the state?' He laughed and Robert felt intimidated. He couldn't just head over to Ireland without knowing the full facts, what he was up against.

'It's a pathetically poor and ignorant country, teeming with abandoned and desperate children just waiting to be scooped up by kindly souls like us and removed from a lifetime of misery. The government are reluctant to stop the babies-for-export business, they don't care, it's the Catholic Church's concern, that's the way they see it. The Church has the biggest influence over moral affairs, and they've always been determined to enforce a deeply traditional and conservative moral code.'

He tutted. 'That old chestnut. The bloody Church. My ancestors were Irish.'

'Fantastic, Catholic?'

'Yes.'

'You'll have no problem then, you'll be front of the queue.'

Nervous excitement fizzed inside him at the thought of what he was about to do.

He wondered about going alone and imagined getting off the plane with a babe in his arms, the look of surprise and happiness that would light up Janie's face.

'The country's changing though, just be careful, attitudes are shifting, this practice won't go on forever. The government has introduced an allowance for unmarried mothers. Strike while the iron's hot. More women are hopping on the ferry to England to get an abortion or popping the pill if they can get hold of it, although that's not easy. Either that or you could adopt from Vietnam or China. Don't bother trying to adopt here though, it's a nightmare. We've got a shortage of babies. I read that twenty American couples are chasing every available white American child.'

'We did try to adopt and gave up.'

'Of course, there's a black market of baby farms across the States run by dishonest doctors and lawyers only in it to make a fast buck.'

They talked for a while longer before Niall said, 'happy baby hunting, let me know how you get on, good luck.'

After the phone call, Robert dialled the number Niall had given him and a few moments later, he was put through to The Weeping Lady religious order.

A woman answered his call.

'Robert Granville Junior here,' he said in a husky voice. 'You may have heard of me, I'm pretty high up in the equestrian world and my wife is a famous actress. I'm in the market for a baby and I understand you may be able to satisfy this requirement. We're unable to have a child of our own so I'm forced to look elsewhere. Who do I need to speak to, to make this happen?'

'I'm the Mother Superior,' she replied curtly, 'everything goes through me.'

'Okay, look lady, I need to get a baby to satisfy my wife's desire, as soon as possible. How quickly can you get one?'

'Babies don't just grow on trees,' she snapped. 'And we do have a waiting list.'

'Lady, if it's money that's required to get us to the top of that damn list, then money is no object, name your price, I'm a wealthy businessman.'

There was a silence, just a slight crackle on the line before she said, 'There are no fees as such, but we do ask for a donation.'

He didn't bother to ask how much she was expecting. It couldn't be any more than the new car he'd just bought. 'Not a problem, lady.'

'Shhh, my baby,' she simpered.

'What?' Then he realised she was talking to a pet.

'Sorry, my cat gets anxious when I'm on the phone.' He imagined a cat curled on her lap. 'She's very troubled recently, the vet has given me some medicine for when she gets anxious.' She took a breath. 'Where were we?'

She was starting to irritate him. 'I was asking about fees, and you suggested a donation.'

'It wasn't a suggestion,' she snapped, 'more an implied requirement. We're not permitted to charge a fee, but we have substantial costs to cover.'

How she ran the home was of no interest to him.

'We can obtain a baby, but it's not just about how much you can pay, there are a number of requirements you must satisfy first, and it can take some time to complete the paperwork.'

He made a noise into the phone.

'Babies aren't made to order, this isn't a supermarket experience.'

He felt like laughing. She was such a tight-lipped haughty woman, full of her own self-importance.

'Things happen fast over here, I click my fingers, it happens, but I suppose things crawl at a snail's pace in your sleepy little corner of the world.' He let out a deep-throated laugh.

She ignored his comment. 'You may also need to wait for your chosen sex.'

'My wife would prefer a girl so she can dress it in pink and put ribbons in her hair.' He chuckled. 'You know how women are. And when my wife wants something, she gets it. Diamond necklaces, Gucci handbags, Prada shoes.'

'A baby isn't an accessory.'

He dismissed her comment. 'I have the money, why wouldn't I have the accessories? Let's get this done.'

'Why is your wife so desperate for a baby?'

'She gets lonely, I'm away on business a lot.' He shouldn't have to explain himself.

'Our babies don't come cheap. We'd be looking at a donation of around $3,000 for the perfect infant.'

'I don't care, I can afford it. Just you make sure it's not black or crippled. We want the perfect specimen, the prettiest baby girl with blue eyes and curly white hair. And make sure it's young, a newborn, so that my wife can bond with it and people won't be aware she hasn't given birth herself.'

'We don't normally hand newborns over.' She hesitated. 'But I could make an exception.'

'Now, do we have a deal? I can wire the money over, or if not then I'll go elsewhere.'

'Slow down. I have some pertinent questions to ask before we can proceed.'

'Huh, I'm sure my money can answer all the questions you have.'

'You'll be asked the same questions at every home across Ireland. I'm assuming both you and your wife are Catholic?'

'Yes. Isn't that a bit outdated and, dare I say, irrelevant?' Surely, she had more important questions to ask like their experience with children or if they had any criminal convictions.

'We only allow Catholic couples to adopt our babies. And mixed marriages are not eligible. You can prove you're Catholic?'

He tensed. It had been years since he went to church, they weren't religious. And he wasn't sure if he could prove it. What was she expecting, a baptism certificate? He doubted his mother still had it among her papers. It was no obstacle though, he'd pay for fake documents if he had to.

She pressed on, her voice clipped. 'You are fully initiated into the Catholic Church, Mr Granville, you have received the three sacraments of initiation: baptism, confirmation and the Eucharist?' He had no idea what the Eucharist was.

What a headache.

'And this is your first marriage, for both of you?'

Why was this even relevant?

'Yes.'

'Good, because divorce would present a problem.' She was silent before speaking again. 'You do understand I have a duty to ensure our children are raised in a good moral home, in the Catholic faith. You must uphold its values, beliefs and traditions and you will be required to sign a declaration to that effect.'

'Yeah, yeah, those are just formalities. We'll be better parents than most couples who walk through your door.'

'How soon can you come over? I have a young woman who is about to go into labour.'

'Okay, lady, I have some business to see to in Belfast, then I'll head down to you.'

CHAPTER 4

*K*athleen and Colin, the van driver

Colin got back into the van and without a word accelerated away from the pub in a furious manner. Caught off guard by the sudden motion, Kathleen lurched forward, slamming her head against the side of the van and yelping.

'Steady on.' She rubbed her throbbing head and peered out at him from under the covers. 'What's happening?'

'The plan's not quite worked out. You can't stay there. He reckons the Gardaì will come sniffing round as soon as the nuns alert them that you're missing. He's also got an American couple coming to stay next week. He thinks they're here for a baby.'

Probably here to adopt my baby, she reflected mournfully. They'd find out her baby had died soon enough.

'I'm lumbered with you until I can sort something else out. That wasn't part of the deal,' he said gruffly. 'There are a few things you'll have to do to earn your keep. My gran lives with me. I don't like leaving her alone all day, she's getting doddery and might have an accident. I need someone to watch her. And can you cook?'

'A bit.'

'We'll expect a bit more than beans on toast.'

Kathleen felt sick and hungry. It had been hours since she'd eaten, and with every twist and turn of the road, bouncing over treacherous ruts, she thought she'd spew her guts and he wouldn't be at all sympathetic if she did. In fact, she had the distinct feeling that he wasn't the nice person she'd originally thought he was. She clamped her hand over her mouth as bile rose to her throat. The van ate through the miles to their destination before turning down a bumpy lane. A canopy of trees overhead formed a graceful arch. The sun was fighting its way through the branches and Colin pulled the visor down to shield his eyes. Eventually the lane petered into a dirt track. She craned her neck as he pulled onto a grass verge in front of a wood. Her heart raced as she scanned the ominous woods. They were miles from anywhere, if she wanted to escape, how far would it be to the nearest town? A chilling thought crossed her mind––was he planning to harm her then dump her in the middle of the forest?

'Where are we?' she asked in alarm. 'I thought you were taking me to your house?'

He let out a mirthless laugh. 'I didn't say I lived in luxury. I live with my old gran in her caravan, my old man kicked me out years ago.' He pointed to a clearing in the wood and opened the door.

Kathleen eased herself onto her knees, wincing. They were sore from scrubbing floors morning till night. She could see smoke curling and a circle of trailers in a grassy glade. A couple of ponies were tethered between the caravans and laundry hung limply on makeshift lines swaying in the breeze. He opened the back door to let her out and they walked towards the encampment. Her gaze swept over the scene as they got closer. This was a life she could never imagine, cooped up in a caravan without modern facilities, but then she'd never imagined she'd end up at the laundry; there had been so much change in her life and in such a short space of time, how much worse could it get?

'Where will I sleep?'

'The only bed is with me, otherwise you're more than welcome to sleep in the woods, but I wouldn't recommend it, there are wolves roaming at night.' A dreadful sickening shiver swept through her. He looked at her, his eyes were bright and mocking. Was he teasing?

'What about your gran? Where does she sleep?'

'She's got her own bedroom. Sometimes she needs to get up for the loo in the night. I'll expect you to help her. I need my sleep, I can't have it disturbed, I need to work.'

'Can't I go somewhere else?'

'Got any clever ideas? Where do you come from anyway, why can't you go home?'

'Liverpool, but me mam won't have me back, she made that quite clear.'

'I don't see you have many options then, do you?' He smirked. 'You can either sleep under the stars at the mercy of the wolves or you can share my bed, I'll expect you to keep me warm. But whatever you do, don't get yourself knocked up again otherwise you'll be straight back where you came from. You don't know the trouble you've caused. You better keep your head down and do as you're told, you can't go out, you can't be seen out.'

'Are you gypsies?'

'Do I look like a traveller? You need to watch your mouth, girl, otherwise you'll find yourself on the wrong side of my back hand and show more respect.'

As they approached the encampment, scrawny children with dirty faces and grubby clothes were playing ball amidst a few scrappy-looking dogs. Piles of junk were mingled with a heap of bikes while a baby with a mucky face sat in a big old 1950s Silver Cross pram sucking on a dummy. An old lady with leathery skin sitting on caravan steps peeled potatoes with podgy hands, discarding the peel into a bowl. As they drew closer, she looked up and smiled at Colin before casting an eye over Kathleen with disdain. The way she tilted her head back and the twinkle in her eyes, made Kathleen think that Colin had brought a girl back here before. As the woman opened her mouth and made a clucking noise she flashed a row of rotten teeth. She leaned forward, peering at Kathleen, the roll of fat around her hips acting as a shelf for the bowl. Fat squelched out from her feet and arms. Kathleen stared at her legs, bloated and in a terrible state, purple and mottled and threaded with bulbous veins that looked as if they might burst. There was a grubby bandage on one of her legs. She didn't look very mobile, and Kathleen wondered what was wrong with her.

'Gran, this is Kathleen, she's come to stay for a bit, to help you out.'

She frowned and fiddled with her hearing aid. 'I don't need no bleeding help. I wish you'd stop interfering. If I wanted help, I'd ask. Bloody kids, you think you know everything.' Then she raised her voice and nodded. 'Ain't that right, Vera?' Kathleen looked round to see who the comment was for. A woman in a flowery apron was standing on her caravan steps mixing something in a bowl and observing the scene.

'It's hard enough feeding two mouths, let alone three, who's going to pay for it? You're supposed to be a man, but you can be so stupid.'

She looked at Kathleen up and down. 'You look a bit scrawny, child. Don't they feed you from where you come from? Are you one of them laundry girls, looks like you're wearing a uniform.'

Kathleen stared down at her ragged grey dress. How she longed to wear her own clothes again, and wondered how she might be able to buy new clothes, but in the scheme of things, that was the least of her worries. She had to figure out how to get away from here. He'd turn her into a skivvy, mistreat her and make her do whatever he wanted.

'Where you from, child? What's ya name? How old are you? Does your mother know you're here?' She rose to her feet and peered closely at Kathleen. 'You look undernourished, child.'

Before she had the chance to answer, Colin said, 'that's enough, Gran, you're supposed to be making her feel welcome.'

'I hope she's more use than that other lass you brought home. She spent all day crying.'

Colin ignored her and Kathleen wondered who she was talking about. 'What's for dinner?'

'I've only got enough dinner for two.'

Kathleen's stomach growled.

'I'll go without,' Colin said. 'The girl needs feeding.'

'Where's she going to sleep?'

'She'll be sleeping with me. The bed's big enough.'

'I don't want no hanky-panky in my home, and you can clearly see she's not old enough. You just behave yourself, boy. We don't want her in the family way, another mouth to feed.'

He barged past her, glancing back at Kathleen. 'Come on, let me show you where the cleaning stuff is.' His gran had wound him up and it showed in his snappy voice. 'You're going to have to earn your keep. One thing this place needs is a bloody good clean.'

They stepped inside the caravan. Kathleen glanced round horrified at the state of the place. The curtains were a mess and on the brink of collapsing because the sagging wire holding them up was drooped in the middle.

There was barely any room to move, it was so cramped. A grimy Formica table smeared with ketchup stains and grease was cluttered with rubbish and scraps of dried meat. The table took up most of the living area and there was a small threadbare navy sofa crammed into the corner. Littered with beer cans, crumbs and dirt, it didn't look at all inviting to sit on. Kathleen wondered how they managed to cook. The worktop, stacked with dirty pots, pans and crockery, was far too small, but there was a small oven.

He seemed fixated on getting the most out of her, leaning down and opening a cupboard under the sink to show her the bottles of bleach and Flash. It seemed a daunting task and she had the feeling that however hard she worked to make the place look nice, his gran would moan and criticise. She wasn't expecting a house guest, and probably didn't welcome any visitors to her home, she was that hostile. Kathleen felt very uncomfortable about staying and hoped it wouldn't be for long.

Colin dumped his keys on the table and glanced round with a look that told her he knew it was in a terrible state and he was ashamed of the place but wasn't prepared to admit it, and it was home to him. 'Let me show you Gran's room and go over her routine with you.' He made it sound as if he was her new employer.

She followed him to the doorway of another cramped and disorganised room. His gran's bed was tight against both walls with a tiny area to move around in front of a dressing table and wardrobe. The dressing table was cluttered with lotions, prescribed medication, bandages, and curlers.

'She's never had a carer other than me before, so it might take her some time to warm to you.'

She's made it clear she doesn't need help, especially from a stranger, and I don't have the experience, Kathleen wanted to tell him, but it was easier to say as little as possible. He gave her the creeps and his earlier words made her increasingly anxious.

'You can help her shower and dress, she really struggles with that. I can't remember the last time she washed. If she can get away without washing, she will. Dressing her is tricky, but you'll learn soon enough.'

When Kathleen smelt the dinner cooking, she thought she might pass out, it smelt so good. Her plate was piled with

THE BABY HUNTERS

mashed potato and half a sausage. It was more than she'd eaten in weeks, and she wolfed it down fast.

'Hungry, were you?' Colin laughed. 'I'm surprised. A young girl like you should have table manners.'

She was starving and her belly ached. She thought of the routine at the laundry. Up at dawn, sweep, scrub, eat, pray, rosaries, eat, sleep repeat. She had grown used to eating fast in the laundry canteen where all the women sat on benches, at the top of the canteen a row of nuns watching them. Slow eaters had their food pinched or a nun would come up behind and force them to eat it faster so that they gagged and vomited and then they were forced to eat their own vomit.

His gran was staring at her through intense eyes. 'You're one of them, aren't you?'

'What do you mean?'

'Gran means, are you a Catholic?'

'You're a bleeding papist, I thought as much, and you've escaped from one of them laundries or mother and baby homes. All that hailing Mary three times a day, priests are sheep shaggers, men of the cloth.' She turned to Colin. 'Where did you find 'er anyway, was she wandering the lanes, where did you pick her up? You've always been a mug for a pretty face, ya too soft, boy.' She pointed her knife at him. 'Don't you realise everyone's out to rob us, stitch us up. You're as much use as your father was. He couldn't keep his prick in his trousers. All men are the same.'

Kathleen grimaced. It was quite a tirade.

'You can't be more than fourteen, fifteen, got yourself knocked up, did you? Dirty girl. Bet ya mother wasn't too impressed. What happened to your fella then?'

'That's enough, Gran, let Kathleen finish her dinner.'

Gran made a huffing noise and speared a carrot with her fork.

During the first week with Colin and his gran, Kathleen

became introverted like she had been at the laundry. Her only saving grace was that she didn't have to get up early. She scrubbed the caravan end to end, cleaned the cupboards, the kitchen and tiny shower room and tended to Gran as much as she could. She hated providing personal care, she'd never seen her own grandma or mother naked, and she felt awkward and nervous. To begin with, Gran had protested.

'Go on, clear off, I don't want no help. I managed perfectly well on me own before you came along.'

Kathleen hesitated in the doorway. She could see her struggling. She wanted to make her clean and fresh because she smelt horrible, and she wanted to keep on the right side of Colin whose wrath she feared if she didn't assist in washing and dressing her.

Soon Gran started to relent, little by little, accepting the offer of dressing her bandage one day and pulling on her skirt the following, and slowly she came to see how much easier it was to have Kathleen there to help.

One day Kathleen washed her own dress and while it was drying, she walked round wrapped in a blanket.

'Where's your clothes?' Gran asked. 'You can't walk round like that, Colin will be back soon.'

'My dress is on the line.'

'It's not the only dress you have, surely.'

'It's all I've got.'

'Come on, child, why are you so silent, won't your mother be wondering where you are? You've obviously been mistreated because of those bruises of your arms. A child your age should be at school. Can you read and write?'

It was a rare display of warmth she'd not experienced in a long time, a gesture of kindness that tugged and made her think that somewhere deep in her heart, Gran cared about her. She wrestled with tears and the urge to embrace her but that wouldn't have felt right.

When Kathleen didn't answer, Gran grew agitated.

'I've got no family, no home,' she blurted.

'Everyone's got a family.'

'Me mam threw me out.'

'Well, I suppose you were a foolish child, promiscuous and the cause of trouble for men. You overstepped the line and you had to serve the time. We all pay the price for our actions. Your lot call it sin and there are harsh punishments for sinners. I don't believe in that nonsense meself, but I do believe young ladies should behave like young ladies and not put it about.'

There was no point in explaining that none of it had been her fault. Just like the nuns at The Weeping Lady, Gran was never going to understand and if she told her the truth, that the priest had forced himself on her and got her pregnant, and would she even believe her?

Gran shook her head and shuffled off towards her bedroom, each step requiring effort and accompanied by the sound of wheezing breaths. She heard drawers being pulled and a few moments later she came back clutching a woollen jumper and trousers. 'These don't fit me anymore, you're welcome to wear them.'

AT NIGHT, Kathleen slept hard against the wall and didn't dare stray into the middle of the bed and risk touching Colin. She lay rigid as a plank, her heart thumping, anticipating his wandering hands and only relaxing when he fell into a slow breathing pattern. When he started to gently snore, she knew she was safe. Gran had lent her a long winceyette, high-necked nightie which she pulled down around her ankles. She slept fitfully, afraid he might wake frisky. He'd told her that he wanted her to keep him warm at night but so far there had been no more comments, and she wondered if his gran had given him further stern warnings.

On a Friday night he went to the pub, returning smelling of beer and fags, and leery, but as soon as he'd tossed his clothes off and his head hit the pillow, he was away and snoring heavily. But one such Friday, he came into the room swaying drunkenly and climbed into bed naked, sidling up to her, throwing his leg over her so that she was locked and unable to move.

'I've got a task for you,' he said gruffly, breathing out a pungent odour, stale hops mingled with decay, a smell that made her want to retch.

When he clamped her breast with his big rough hand, she quickly pushed it away but knew that she couldn't fight him. She didn't have the strength. He was far too strong for her.

'Stop it, go away, don't touch me.'

'You frigid whore, you opened your legs for some other fella.'

'I didn't do it willingly.' Her voice cracked as tears gathered and she sniffed them back. A sudden rush of icy dread gripped her chest, accompanied by vivid images flashing through her mind, the memory of the ordeal with the priest in Liverpool all that time ago. It was like a nightmarish film reel. She couldn't go through all that again. A fierce determination rose inside her, she would resist with every ounce of strength she had.

'I'm not going to touch you, you bitch. But a man has needs and you can't expect us to support you for free, you need to pay your way.' Spittle landed on her ear and the bristles on his face grazed her cheek, he was so close. His voice had lowered to a hissed whisper, but his tone was menacing.

'But your gran said…' She was still facing the wall and didn't dare move.

'I don't care what Gran says, I'm the man of the house.'

'I don't want to be your plaything and get pregnant again, and you smell horrible, I'll tell your gran.'

'You do that, and I'll drag you back into that laundry by your hair.'

Her heart was racing. 'No, you won't, you'll get into trouble.'

'I don't care, you're the one they'll punish, you Catholics and your sins, or I might just dump you in the forest and the wolves can feast on you.'

Panic rose inside her; would he really do that?

'I don't want to be nasty, but there's no such thing as a free ride, so what's it to be, girl?'

She didn't answer and a few moments later, his breathing changed and his leg, still over her, went floppy. She waited, and when she dared to turn her head ever so slightly, she saw that his eyes were closed and he was lying on his back. She stared at him and waited until she heard his first snore. She had a reprieve, but this wouldn't be the last of it. She knew that he'd try again. She crept to the edge of the bed, curling her legs tight and quietly cried. How was she going to get away from here and where would she go? They were miles from anywhere and she had no money. Eventually she drifted to sleep, waking as the first light of dawn crept in. It was still very early, but she wanted to get up. The memory of the previous evening came crashing back, flooding her mind with fear, but if she disturbed him, he'd bark at her. Saturday was his lie-in.

Trying to be as quiet as a mouse, she sat up and swung her legs around, her feet on the carpet.

Barely making any noise, he woke, flinging off the covers and exposing himself. 'I need you to suck this. It needs milking.' He tugged on her arm, forcing her to turn and look at him. Fear swept through her when she saw it there in the gloomy light, hard and weaponlike. He wasn't about to forget his words just hours before. Her reprieve was over. Before she had time to act or protest, he grabbed her neck and forced her head towards it, ordering her to take it in her mouth. The smell, the taste, it was rank, and she gagged, bile rising to her throat. When it was over, he pushed her aside as if she was a dirty discarded rag and she rushed to the bathroom to be sick.

At breakfast, Gran peered at Colin through dark foreboding

eyes. Kathleen wondered if she guessed what was going on right under her roof, for her eyes carried a silent acknowledgement.

She finished her toast and slipped out of the caravan, staying within earshot, hoping to overhear their conversation.

'I heard the girl sobbing last night. What did you do to her?'

'Don't know what you're talking about, the girl's a nutcase.'

'Well from now on, she sleeps with me.'

Kathleen was surprised but relieved when Colin didn't protest but the thought of sleeping with Gran, while safer, was hardly appealing either. She had to work out a plan of escape. She still hoped the publican would help. Colin was supposed to return to the pub to find out what he could do. Leaving here couldn't come soon enough.

CHAPTER 5

LIVERPOOL, ENGLAND, LATE SEPTEMBER 1974

Kathleen's mother and the priest

In a bustling corner of Liverpool not far from the docks, Kathleen's mother Maria, with weary determination etched on her tired face, knelt on the cold cobblestones, vigorously scrubbing the doorstep of her Victorian semi until it was clean enough to eat dinner off. She'd always taken great pride in keeping the front of the house clean. Keeping up appearances was everything.

The neighbour's tabby cat regarded her lazily from its windowsill where it sat between two potted plants like a tiger surveying its domain. She glanced at her neighbour's grimy nets with disgust. Torn and ragged they needed replacing and the windows were so grubby it was a wonder the cat could see out. She stood up and rubbed her knees, smiling at her own pristine white nets fashioned into perfect pleats and her heart swelled with pride. Then she noticed the neighbour's bedroom curtains, still closed and gone eight. What was the dirty cow up to? she wondered. Her husband's body was still warm in the grave. Had she no shame?

Further along the street, front doors were slamming, children shouting their goodbyes as they left for school. Maria stood wistfully on the wet doorstep, a nostalgic smile tugging at the corners of her lips as she watched the children running across the road, their bags slung over their shoulders. The rhythm of the neighbourhood's morning routine was a reminder of her losses: her husband's tragic death and the painful decision to send Kathleen away.

Two young girls strolled towards her, draped in colourful ponchos and trendy bell-bottoms. Maria's eyes locked onto them with recognition, they were school friends of Kathleen.

'Morning Mrs O'Brien, heard from Kathleen lately?'

Maria bristled. She wished people wouldn't keep asking. Each time, her lies were becoming more elaborate.

'Not this week, she's too busy to speak to her old mum.' She gave a false laugh.

The girls stopped. 'We've not heard from her either. It's as if she'd disappeared off the face of the earth. We did write to her, at the address you gave us.' They were both frowning, and it felt as if they knew she was lying.

Uneasy, Maria avoided eye contact. She felt guilty for giving them a false address, telling them Kathleen had gone to the Hebrides to help her uncle on his farm. It was a complete fabrication, a lie, so easy to trot out, but the problem was, friends and acquaintances were too inquisitive, and she dreaded their questions and general nosiness and wished they'd all mind their own business.

To stop further questions about Kathleen, she asked, 'You two not going to school today? You're not in your uniforms.'

'We've got work experience today, at Woolworths,' the shorter one said.

'Will Kathleen be back next month?' the tall one asked. 'David Essex is playing at the Empire.'

Maria was quick to craft an excuse. 'I don't think so.'

'Is she going to school up there?'

'Yes.' This wasn't a lie for she was sure Kathleen would be attending classes at The Weeping Lady. Father Joseph had led her to believe that Kathleen's education wouldn't be interrupted. 'Now shouldn't you girls be getting on?' She swept her hand as if to shoo them on.

A hollow ache gripped her heart, amplifying the void left by their absence. Her life was forever altered by Kathleen's departure. Even Darius, her son, rarely visited. She realised she was spending too much time alone. Family had been her daily, central focus for so many years, maybe she'd taken them for granted, missing them now in their absence. She reminded herself that where Kathleen was concerned, it was for the best. The nuns were looking after her. But it was now early October, and she hadn't heard from Kathleen or the nuns and wondered if she'd had the baby.

She went back inside, chastising herself for allowing Kathleen space in her thoughts. The girl deserved all she got. The little madam. She started to clean the kitchen extra vigorously, not wanting to dwell on Kathleen's plight, but as she opened cupboard doors, the home seemed to be enveloped in a suffocating silence. The ticking of the clock above the cooker sounded louder than normal, marking the passing hours until her first winter alone.

As she was about to sit down, the doorbell trilled. Maria got up and peered through the front window, pushing the net to one side, surprised to see Father Joseph on the doorstep. She was glad she'd just scrubbed it.

DRESSED IN BLACK, he looked solemn and dignified. She hadn't seen him in months, she'd been told that he'd left Liverpool and taken a post in Southern Ireland.

She straightened her hair in the hall mirror and removed her pinny before opening the door. 'Father Joseph, nice to see you, what brings you here? I heard you were now in Southern Ireland.'

'Mrs O'Brien, may I come in?' He cast furtive glances up and down the street as if wary of prying neighbours, before stepping inside. 'That's if it's convenient to have a wee chat?'

'Would you like tea? I've just made a fruit cake, it's fresh out of the oven and cooling on the rack, looks as if you need feeding up.' She gave him a once-over and stepped aside to let him in.

'I'm looking for a new housekeeper, so I am, care to apply?' He chuckled as he politely let her lead the way into the kitchen and pull out a chair for him to sit on.

Once she'd poured the tea and cut him a generous slice of cake, she joined him at the table and asked, 'So, Father, as I was saying, what brings you here?'

'Well, I was wondering how our Kathleen is, have you seen her?'

'I haven't seen her since she left with you, I've had no contact at all since you took her to the mother and baby home, or laundry or wherever it is, The Weeping Lady? I would have thought you'd know. It's now October, she must have had the baby by now, I'm not anticipating seeing her again till next year, after she's completed her penance.'

'Well, that's the problem, she's absconded, we don't know where she might have gone, and had hoped she'd return here.'

Maria was taken aback and stared at him blankly. 'Absconded, why would she do that? She must be having a grand time. She'll be well fed and receiving a good education and new friends. I bet she's having a ball, why would she want to leave?'

'Indeed, but we are rather concerned, she's only just had the baby and wouldn't have regained her strength.'

Maria looked away, thoughtful. 'To be honest, Father, it's really none of my concern, I washed my hands the day she said she was with child. She got herself into trouble, she can get

THE BABY HUNTERS

herself out of it. I have enough of my own issues to worry about.'

'Yes, I'm sure you have, it can't be easy with your husband gone, God rest his soul.'

'I miss him terribly, Father.' A tear came to her eye.

'I'm sure you do. Are you keeping busy?'

'Yes, there's always a lot to do managing this house and I've had to take on a little part-time job.'

He took a bite of cake and commented on how delicious it was.

'That girl needs a bloody good talking-to. Opening her legs. No brain to work out the consequences, and no consideration for me. I needed her here, I have to struggle on my own, I have no sympathy for her.' Her heart remained cold and unyielding.

'Do you have any inkling where she'd go?'

'I have no idea and I don't care.'

'Any relatives she might have gone to?'

'I doubt it. I always knew she'd be trouble right from a young age and I was right.'

As he sipped his tea, she felt his eyes interrogating her. 'So tell me, Father, why have you travelled all this way just to be concerned for another problem child?'

'I was just visiting for my annual meeting with the bishop. And it's my responsibility to find out how my fallen flock are doing. As you can appreciate, we do not wish any of them to reoffend. The Virgin Mary only has limited patience.'

'But why are you interested, she's just one girl?'

She noticed his shifty eyes.

FATHER JOSEPH HAD a keen and special interest in this one particular girl. He didn't want her running home and crying to her mammy, sharing with her the events of that dark night in January in the church. He still remembered it well. Her tangled limbs, those young soft virgin breasts standing proud in the moonlight, her nipples like peaks and the tightness of a virgin soared through his mind, he was her first. The memory still stirred his groin and fired his belly.

'I'm interested in all my flock, Mrs O'Brien.'

The visit had been pointless, and frustration simmered inside, but it had been worth it for a slice of her delicious fruit cake. She'd always been good at baking. It was clear that she had no idea where Kathleen was, and now she was peering at him through suspicious eyes as if she'd caught him out. It was disconcerting, but he had to reassure himself, she couldn't read his mind and couldn't possibly know. And Kathleen had deserved all she got, dressed like a little slut.

'I've never forgiven the person who got my daughter pregnant. He's walking around as if nothing's happened whereas she had her childhood robbed, there's nothing I can do. After she went, for a whole week, I stood on the pavement opposite the school watching the kids go through the gate, trying to work out who it might be. But it was like hunting for a needle in a haystack, Father. For a long time I thought I was going mad, I looked at every male in the street with suspicion, but to this day I'll never know who it was, and I doubt the little madam would tell me. Let's hope the good Lord will deal His justice.'

A shiver went up his spine. 'Don't torture yourself.' He laid his hand over hers and gave it a squeeze. 'You need to put it all behind you.'

She got up and took her cup to the sink and stood staring out of the window.

'I don't want to alarm you, but she lost the baby.'

She didn't move for a few moments and when she turned, he noticed her eyes were wet. He could see the emotion so clearly on her face, he felt it echo through his body.

'In some ways, maybe it's God's will, a blessing in disguise.' She sniffed and in a prim voice, said, 'I hope she's had time to reflect and repent. It's a shame she never came to you, Father, for moral guidance, I've always admired what you do for others, you're a fine upstanding member of the community and I'm glad you came here today.'

Her words caused him to choke on his cake, and he sprayed the tablecloth with crumbs.

'Are you okay, Father?'

'I'm so sorry.' He took a hanky out of his pocket and coughed loudly before pushing his chair back to get up.

At the door he turned to her. 'If you do happen to hear anything that might help us find her, please do get in touch. You can speak to the Mother Superior.' Before he grabbed the door handle, he hesitated. 'I do feel I have an obligation to ensure that Kathleen's safe and well and being looked after. That was my promise to you.' He feigned sympathy with a smile.

He hoped she never found out the truth. He hated to think it, but he wished Kathleen was dead.

CHAPTER 6

BELFAST AUTUMN 1974

The O'Sullivans

Liam O'Sullivan stood in the courtyard of the slaughterhouse where he'd worked for the past ten years, his hands thrust into his pockets. It was the end of a long shift and his back ached and stomach growled. He made his way between the hanging carcasses, pushing them apart like pairs of curtains, his hands wet and slimy, his overalls caked in blood and stiff with cold fat. He was glad another day in this awful job was over. The stench of the place was intense-- sweet, and cloying. It was a smell he'd never get used to in a million years. Despite discarding his blood-splattered overalls in the slaughterhouse's laundry bin, he always took the smell home with him, met at the back door of their tiny back-to-back in Belfast by Sheridan, his wife, who always complained, pegging her nose with her fingers.

The slaughterhouse was the largest employer in the local area, but the pay was rubbish and the hours long. Over time he'd become desensitised to the gruelling sight of the queuing beasts, their low bellows a sign of distress and fear, but for a long time this and the blood-splattered white tiles had haunted him. He was grateful though for his lively and cheerful workmates who whistled and bantered all day to keep their minds from the task at hand. Their company overshadowed everything he disliked about the job.

On the way out, he was joined by his father who also worked at the slaughterhouse and lived close by on the Catholic side of the estate, having moved there a few years back when the Troubles kicked off. Liam, stubbornly, had stood his ground, ignoring every warning and every threat. He'd been adamant about staying in his home and not giving in to Protestant thugs and bullies. He liked it there and felt an emotional connection to the house. There were so many memories woven into the very fabric of those walls. Tender moments like carrying his bride over the threshold, decorating the place together when she was expecting their first baby, the birth of their five children, upstairs in the tiny front bedroom. Every corner of their home held a precious story. But it wasn't easy now they had a baby and needed more space, and not a day went by when he wasn't aware of the ominous bomb threats that loomed over them. Every evening Sheridan begged for them to move.

Liam watched his father put his hand in his trouser pocket, hoping to be offered a ciggie.

His father pulled out a packet of Silk Cut. 'Go on, son, take a couple, times are hard for you.'

Liam took four with a cheeky grin and fumbled in his own pocket for a lighter. 'See you tomorrow,' he said, walking away in the opposite direction.

He lit one of the cigarettes and inhaled deeply. Almost immediately he felt the hit and relaxed. He drew the smoke to the bottom of his lungs and exhaled, each time with a heavy sigh. The cigarette hung from his mouth, and he stuffed his hands into his pockets. It was autumn and the sky was a dismal grey with faint drizzle falling and mirroring his grey thoughts.

He meandered his way around the labyrinth of lanes set

around a boggy park. Approaching home with each step along the cobbled paving, he contemplated the same question that always preyed on his mind. How was he going to feed another mouth? The responsibility of supporting a family of seven weighed heavily and was a constant worry. They often had to go without, making do with knackered shoes, worn trousers or shirts that no longer fitted. They stole coal from the yard late at night when they wouldn't be spotted, and as for a television or a bathroom, they were luxuries they could only dream of. Sean, at fourteen, had a hearty appetite, followed closely by Aidan at thirteen, who seemed destined to eat even more. At least little Aisling was still a baby and breastfed, but that would all change soon. How he wished he could earn decent money. All they could do was cut back, trimming costs here and there. He'd asked for a rise, but his boss adamantly refused to consider it.

As he crossed the road, The Blue Anchor's warm lights spilt onto the cobbles, and the laughter and chatter drifting through the open door beckoned him in. Most days it took a great deal of willpower not to dive straight into the boozer, but that only made matters worse and wasn't fair on the family, so he limited it to a couple of times a week and stuck to halves.

As he rounded the corner into his street, a sense of being watched overwhelmed him as he felt unseen eyes peering at him from behind curtains making him quicken his pace. He couldn't bear to look at the Union Jacks in the windows. Lately there were more and more of these appearing in the estate. It was a menacing sign; the Loyalists were getting angry. The flags should have been down months ago because the Twelfth of July was long past. It was sheer bloody-mindedness that they were still up and a display of support for the Unionists in the recent general election. He stared down at the kerbstones; even they were painted in red, white, and blue. It felt as if this was aimed at his family because they were the only Catholic family left in the whole street. Fear had driven the other families out, but

Loyalist bastards weren't going to drive him away. But the stronger the Protestant sense of community grew, the more isolated and excluded he and his family felt.

He arrived home, slipping through the narrow entry between the terraced houses cluttered with bikes--their tyres long stolen--strewn against the dripping red bricks, and felt a sense of impending doom. He pushed through the back door into the kitchen and despite his fond attachment to the place, he thought what a miserable existence this was. He wanted so much more for his family.

Sheridan was sitting in the armchair by the coal fire feeding the baby. His youngest daughters, Roisin and Maeve rushed into his arms, enveloping him in warm hugs and excited chatter, thrusting handmade drawings into his hands. They were twins and had their mother's beautiful blonde curls and bright blue eyes.

'Let your dad get through the door.' Sheridan adjusted the baby in her arms and smiled at her husband. 'Dinner won't be long, love, it's a fry-up.'

He sat down on the other armchair by the fireplace. The girls eagerly climbed onto his lap, each vying for his attention and a comfy spot to settle in. Their voices rose up and over each other, rising in volume. He kissed their damp heads, breathing in their little-girl scent.

After a time, they lost interest and clambered off. He looked at his wife and knew by her downcast expression that she was about to start her usual rant.

'I'm sick of living round here, we need to move. Don't you care about the kids' safety? What will it take, Liam? For one of us to be badly injured, a tragedy before you take it seriously? You're living in a goldfish bowl. If anything happened, there's not one neighbour we can rely on.'

'Fear's driven the others out, it won't drive me out. I will not move.'

'You're as stubborn as a mule. It's more than fear, they fled in terror, burnt out of their homes. It'll be us next.'

'Calm down, love, we've been here for years, we're not in a position to leave, and besides, I've put a lot of work into this house. Things will return to normal, remember how things were before '69?'

She scoffed. 'What planet are you living on? You're completely blinkered. You're out at work all day, you don't see half the things that go on. I've got a cold feeling that something's about to happen, they're taking over, greedy lot, they'd steal everything from us if they could. There's another stack of firewood and crates just up the road, more bloody bonfires.'

'Give it a rest, love, all this ranting ain't gonna help.'

'I hate the lot of them. Paisley, he's a bloody disgrace, he's no better than Hitler or Idi Amin, I'd love to see that bastard dead. I don't want my kids growing up with the way things are. I heard about a Catholic landlord who had all his houses petrol-bombed. His only crime, was his faith.'

From the corner of his eyes, he saw the girls cowering behind the table. They were always scared when their mother went off on one.

'There's not much we can do about it, just got to keep our heads down.'

She finished feeding the baby, roughly putting her back in the crib as if she was to blame for their troubles.

She banged her fist on the table. 'God help us, we could wake in the night to the smell of burning and that's all you've got to say? Grow some balls, Liam.'

It was useless, he might as well talk to himself. He went over to the kitchen sink and washed his hands with strong soap, splashing water onto his face, making loud spluttering noises.

'Towel,' he said, his eyes clenched tightly.

She threw a towel at him. She didn't say another word and

started the dinner, tossing bacon and black pudding into the frying pan.

Still drying himself, he went to the window in the front room, moving the net aside just by a fraction as he peered out. Several youths were leaning against a wall across the street. One of them wore a red, white, and blue scarf knotted at his neck, and was looking over at their house. Seeing Liam, he pointed. The others turned to look. The big one, wearing Doc Martens swung up his hand, giving Liam the two fingers and jeered at him.

'Lay the table, Liam, would ya?' Sheridan called through.

The children all lined up to wash their hands at the kitchen sink before sitting down to eat. Liam speared his bacon with a fork and spread out the newspaper on the table near him; he liked to catch up with the news while he ate. He flicked through the pages, his brow furrowing. It was full of doom and gloom, the usual violence and unrest across the region. A Catholic father of four had been stabbed to death. The police said there was no known motive for the killing. A number of huts in the Maze Prison had been destroyed by fires which had been started by Republican prisoners. He sighed with the futility of it all. How was it all going to end?

'Any jobs in the paper today?' she asked.

His jaw tightened; he didn't need her constant reminders, the irritating digs she made. If a job came up, of course he'd apply.

'I can work in the slaughterhouse or join the dole queue, which would you prefer?'

She straightened her back and stared straight at him. 'Don't be sarcastic. I can barely put a meal on the table, Liam, you don't realise how hard it is, making the housekeeping stretch to seven of us.' She had a way of making him feel diminished, half the man he should be.

When they'd finished eating, the kids were allowed to play.

'Stay in the backyard,' she told them as they headed out. 'No wandering into the street.' How different things were now. There was a time when they chatted to neighbours on the doorstep and kids ran in and out of each other's houses. Not anymore.

Sheridan cleared the table while he continued to read the paper. About to check the football results at the back, he turned the page, and a headline caught his eye.

Millionaire Hollywood actress, Janie Lee and equestrian entrepreneur husband, Robert Granville arrive in Ireland to adopt a child.

The article went on to explain that British adoption law prohibited them, as foreign nationals, from taking a child who was not a relation from the UK to the US for adoption.

They are not deterred by this and told our reporter that they will not be going home empty-handed. They were advised to try Ireland and have been staying in a hotel while they wait to adopt a baby upon its birth at one of Ireland's mother and baby homes.

'Here, Sheri, come and look at this.' His wife had always been a big fan of Janie Lee and had seen all her films. She looked up from the sink, dried her hands and came over. He pushed the paper towards her, and she looked down at the smiling Janie Lee, in a green dress, her tousled curls escaping a wide-brimmed straw hat.

'Oh my,' she drawled, 'isn't she just so beautiful, and so talented. I can't believe she can't get pregnant. Such a shame, and so sad, all that wealth, and they can't have children of their own.'

'You know, love, it's a reminder that even though we're not rolling in dosh, we've hit the jackpot with five beautiful kids who are all ours. Money doesn't buy happiness.'

'Maybe, but we've got the opposite problem, I fall too easily,' she said. 'If I have to go through another pregnancy, it will finish me off.' Still peering at Jane's photo, she said, 'What a fantastic opportunity they'll be giving a child, the chance of a much better life, to want for nothing. America.' Her eyes brightened as she continued to gush. 'The land of opportunity.'

'And what about the real mother?'

She stared at him. 'What about the real mother?'

He shrugged.

'What's the alternative, growing up in poverty in this godforsaken country? I know which I'd prefer for my child.' She made a harrumphing noise and went to pick the baby up from its cot before sitting beside Liam at the table. The baby flailed her arms, fidgeted, and protested before grabbing the newspaper, and patting Jane's face. She made a cute gurgling noise and smiled at the picture.

'How the hell could a mother consider giving up her child after carrying it for nine months and bringing it into the world? I'd never give one of my children away.'

'Yes, that's Jane,' Sheridan said to the baby while ignoring her husband. 'You agree with Mammy, don't you?' She continued to bounce the baby and made cooing noises.

What was going on in her mind? 'Just because they have pots of money,' he said, 'doesn't mean they can swan into our country waving a cheque book and expect to buy a kiddie.' The whole affair irritated him.

'It's not like that, love. These women are desperate, they must be to give up their most cherished possession, their baby. It's an act of love, I totally get that. They don't have much choice, they want them to have a brighter future, I know it's a huge sacrifice to make, but I can totally relate to how they must feel.'

'What about the fathers? They need to step up to the responsibility.'

She stared at him with that look of hers that told him how inadequate he was. 'They don't though, that's the point. They get them up the duff, then disappear. Every child deserves stability.'

'There are plenty of couples in this country that can't have a baby and would love to adopt, and some of them are wealthy too. That's the problem with wealthy people, they think they can buy anything or anyone with just a flash of their cheque book.'

She turned to baby Aisling and blew raspberries on her cheek. 'Just imagine if it was you going to America. They'd love your blonde curls and blue eyes, the perfect wee baby, you'd be treated like a queen and would want for nothing, you'd be dressed in the prettiest pink dresses and have all the toys that money can buy, then when you're older, you'd marry a handsome rich American. What a wonderful life you'd have.'

'God woman, you're talking drivel, thank God she's too young to understand what you're saying. Have you gone mad? Not sure what you're thinking, but I'm off to the pub.'

'That's right,' she said, 'do what you always do, bugger off to the pub while I put the kids to bed. For every pint you piss, you're depriving your kids.'

He couldn't bring himself to tell her that it was her that drove him to the pub. Angry and frustrated, he slammed the front door, lit a cigarette and headed up the street. With every step he felt sorrier for himself. Whatever he did, it was never going to be good enough. They were poor, life was a struggle, but they had each other, why couldn't she be happy and see that?

CHAPTER 7

Southern Ireland
Kathleen

Kathleen continued to work tirelessly in the caravan, scrubbing the floor, washing clothes, and pegging them on the line. She cleaned the bathroom, cooked, and lugged heavy shopping bags up the hill from the local grocery store. The days turned into weeks, trapped in endless labour, with little respite or appreciation. She'd escaped from the laundry, but she was still incarcerated, imprisoned instead in the outside world. Her life had been reduced to that of a skivvy, at the beck and call of others, and more scarily, at the mercy of men. It frightened her that Colin might pounce on her one day unexpectedly. She wasn't as strong as him and wouldn't be able to fight him off. Overall, though, she felt safer here compared to the laundry where one wrong move could result in a brutal beating.

Colin was a dirty, lazy git. He dumped his clothes on the floor, his bed was a mess. The toilet was always disgusting after he'd used it, and it was down to her to clean it. Twice a week she had to fill an old tin bath for them to share. She boiled and filled, boiled, and filled with water heated on the stove. It was back-breaking work. Afterwards, she stood against the table to recover as Colin lowered himself into the hot water. He always bathed first and took his time, then his mother would get in, and she was always last. By the time it was her turn to get into the water, it would be cold, and grey from their dirt and skin and swirling hairs from their bodies would float in it and stick to her skin.

It was now mid-November and Kathleen had just been into the village. She puffed her way back up the winding lane, flanked by ancient stone walls until she reached a weathered gate at the hill's crest. Pausing to breathe in the crisp late autumn air, she looked back at the village below, the weight of the old pram laden with shopping she had pushed up the hill now a memory. November had stripped the trees bare, their skeletal branches reaching towards the overcast sky heavy with the threat of rain. She sighed and looked up feeling the first drizzle on her face. Irish rain, it came so often. It was the wettest type of rain and made the fields lush and green. It was both a blessing and a curse, and she liked to watch it from the caravan window. It was one of her rare pleasures as well as being able to listen to the radio again. The rhythm of the whip and lash of the rain against the glass was hypnotising as it hit the ground with the velocity of artillery fire, quickly forming big muddy puddles, the type of rain that took no prisoners.

She was reluctant to rush back to the caravan despite the drizzle, fearing more chores and tedious conversation with Colin's gran. A simple woman who repeated her questions and comments like a broken record, she bored Kathleen to tears, having nothing of interest to say, all she did was carp. Kathleen wondered if she'd ever been happy. She knew nothing about her past and why Colin was living with her, and she didn't like to ask.

With the rain now coming down harder, she resumed her walk back, soaked to the bone by the time the caravans came into view, her hair dripping, her thin dress clinging to her skin. She threw off her coat and unloaded the shopping bags before filling the kettle.

'There you are, child, did you remember to drop into the chemist to pick up my prescription?'

'It wasn't on your list.'

She was exasperated. *Bloody woman with her constant demands.* There was never any thanks for trudging up and down the hill, and no sympathy when she returned wet and bedraggled. How much more of this could she take?

I feel so unappreciated.

'Well, you'll have to go back then because I need more ointment and bandages,' she snapped. 'I don't know where your head is half the time, you're up in the clouds with the fairies.'

'But my clothes are all wet and I need a hot drink to warm up.' As she began to peel off her coat, she shivered. The cold had seeped into her bones. 'I need to get out of these sodden clothes.' It was ridiculous because even if she sprinted down to the village, she didn't think she'd get there before the chemist shut up shop. It was early closing on a Wednesday, and she was exhausted.

'I need, I need,' Gran mimicked in a whiny voice. 'The world does not revolve around you, child,' she said sternly.

How lovely it would be to feel special, the centre of somebody else's world. It doesn't seem likely that will ever happen.

Gran didn't care, the woman was heartless. 'Once you've picked up my prescription, you can clean the toilet and then read the newspaper to me.'

'But I only cleaned it this morning, how can it be dirty again?' Kathleen said in despair.

'Stop your backchat, child. Do not question me, when you get to my age, you have to use the facilities frequently and I am not always in full control of my functions.'

She sneezed loudly, and remembered the time when her

grandad got caught in the rain and fell gravely ill and died three days later of pneumonia.

She hesitated before opening the door, hoping Gran would take pity on her but knowing she was too cold-hearted for that.

'Keep your sneezing away from me, I don't want to catch a cold. Now go on, get out.' She gave a sweep of her hand as if ridding the caravan of dirt.

Kathleen set off down the hill feeling thoroughly miserable. The rain sluiced her face, her hair hung in limp wet strands, and she didn't bother to push it away, there was no point. A short way down the hill, a car approached from behind and she almost considered thumbing for a lift, but it was going too fast. Its tyres smacked into a puddle, drenching her with muddy water.

It was the last straw. She let out a sob and was suddenly wracked with great heaving sobs that only the cows in the field could hear.

How was she ever going to get her life back?

I feel like a caged bird. I can't believe how much my life has changed and in such a short space of time. A year ago, she was happy at school studying for her O levels, hoping to get onto a secretarial course at college with her friends.

Sandra and Lois.

She got a stab in her chest as she thought of them now, and felt desperately sad and lonely. All the good times they'd spent together, clothes shopping, school discos, afternoons at one of their houses listening to music, chatting about the boys they fancied, trying on make-up and different outfits, collapsing in fits of laughter. It had been so long since she'd laughed or had any fun. She wondered what they were up to and if they missed her.

Father Joseph had stolen everything that she was and replaced her life with this miserable existence. He'd been wicked, yet they'd made her out to be the sinner who should be put to work to pay for her sins. She was a fallen woman in their eyes, promiscuous and the cause of trouble for men. Nothing else could explain any of it. She thought she'd continue her education in the laundry, but it had become clear that she wasn't there to have her baby and continue her studies, she was there to serve time, for the crime of getting pregnant.

She'd give anything to return to Liverpool and pick up her old life, but she had no idea how that was possible. She didn't imagine her mother would welcome her return, especially if she knew she had escaped, shirking her duty to stay and complete her penance. Would she even forgive her for getting pregnant? Probably not. She was a difficult child in her eyes, she'd marked her card and because of that, there was no return. If only she could turn back the clock. How she wished that night had never happened. She should never have gone into the church with Father Joseph. But she hadn't known what he was like, he was the family priest, someone to look up to, the person that everybody respected and relied on.

How can I ever trust another man? Are they all like that?

She thought of Colin and the move he'd made on her. She shuddered, realising it was only a matter of time before he tried it on again. She had to get away, the last thing she needed was another pregnancy. At the very least, she had to have her wits about her.

Reaching the village, she found a note on the chemist door. It had closed early due to staff sickness. She turned and trudged back up the hill, panicked at the thought of another backlash. Arriving back in the field, she spotted Gran standing on the caravan steps chatting to a friend and felt a surge of fear as she anticipated the confrontation ahead.

The friend wandered back to her caravan as she approached. Gran's hands were planted on her hips as she eyed Kathleen, a scowl on her face. 'Well, child, where's the package? You've come back empty-handed.'

The chemist was closed.'

'Closed? She glanced at her watch. It's not even five.'

'There was a note on the door. They had to close due to staff illness.'

'You don't have an ounce of common sense in your blood, silly girl.' With a hiss of anger, she suddenly struck her across the ear. 'You didn't think to thump on the door, there's always someone in the back room, it's a chemist for goodness' sake.'

Shocked by how aggressive she was, Kathleen reached to protect her ear. This was the last straw. She couldn't take anymore. She darted past Gran, rushed into Colin's room slamming the door behind her, and flung herself on the bed, burying her face in his pillow. Confused and frustrated, her body heaved with great gulping sobs.

Crying loudly, she didn't hear Gran quietly open the door until she spoke. 'Pull yourself together, you've a lot to learn, child.'

'I hate it here, I'm just your skivvy, I don't want to be here, I want to go home.'

'Well go home then, that's if you still have a home to go to,' she said maliciously before cackling.

Kathleen let out a loud sob.

'You ungrateful little madam. No one's keeping you here against your will. You'd be in the gutter now if it wasn't for us. We've fed and clothed you, this is the thanks we get.' She plonked herself on the bed and Kathleen eased herself up, her back to the wall as she wiped her nose with her sodden sleeve.

'Now you listen to me, young lady,' she said sternly, 'pull yourself together, life has many knocks and falls, it ain't all plain sailing, I should know.'

She drew her knees up and hugged them.

'No point in dwelling, child, I moved on.'

'I don't know what my future holds. Nobody cares, nobody loves me, they all use me, the nuns did, and you're no better. I've got nothing to offer any employer, I don't have qualifications, I've missed the last year of school. How could God be so cruel? Why does Mary never listen?'

'Enough,' she bellowed. 'Stop wallowing in self-pity, child. You will face far greater challenges across your life and you need to be ready for them.'

How true this statement would turn out to be, but she didn't realise it then. Time would tell.

CHAPTER 8

C olin

Colin's final call of the day was to a grand private residence near Cork, an imposing Georgian mansion of creamy white stone. He approached the tall black gates topped with a row of spear points and recessed into a high stone wall, got out and opened them before entering. He followed the gravel avenue flanked by towering trees down to the house, driving slowly as he glanced at the beautiful manicured lawns. Every fortnight he made a visit to collect soiled sheets and clothes and provide freshly laundered items. He had no idea who lived here––anyone with wealth was a pompous toff, and self-entitled as far as he was concerned––but he did have a soft spot for the pretty young maid who worked here and always welcomed him at the door. Last time he was here, she'd invited him into the kitchen for tea and cake. She liked him, he felt sure of that. He hoped that his luck might be in, maybe this time he'd pluck up the courage to flirt with her, see where it led.

He parked the van by the tradesmen's entrance and opened the van's rear doors to unload the sacks. He whistled to himself, a happy feeling of anticipation welling inside him. He lifted the brass knocker and let it fall against the sturdy door, imagining the rich deep sound reverberating through the long staff corridor.

He was surprised by how excited he felt. He realised how different the maid was to Kathleen. More self-assured and full of fun. He stood a much better chance with this lass. Kathleen was cold and frigid and with Gran's watchful eye, making a move on her had become impossible.

The door finally swung open after what felt like an age. When it did, he was taken aback, his hopes dashed when a woman he'd never seen before met his gaze instead.

She was stunningly attractive, tall with tousled blonde Botticelli curls, and her face had a glow about it, like one of those supermodels who shone without the use of make-up. He guessed she must be about ten years older than him. She was obviously not a servant, which meant just one thing.

Shit, the lady of the house. Lady Eleanor herself.

It wasn't usual for the owners of the house to open the door to tradesmen. Something didn't feel right, perhaps he was in trouble for something, but he couldn't think what. It was her clothing though that unsettled him. She was scantily clad, in a nightie that didn't leave much to the imagination. This brazen woman didn't seem to care, and the way she was looking at him, a seductive smile playing around the corners of her mouth and reaching her eyes, she knew it had unsettled him and seemed to enjoy the power she had over him. He quickly looked away.

'Come in, young man.' Her voice was deep, and husky and he had the sense that this was put on for his benefit.

He bent to lift the sacks of laundry and headed into the corridor before waiting for further instructions.

'Where's the young maid today?'

'I've given her the day off. Leave the sacks there, will you.' She gestured towards the end of the corridor which wasn't where he normally put them. He took the sacks and after putting them down, turned around to find her standing so close he could smell her floral scent. He quickly headed to the door to bring in more sacks.

'You've got strong muscles, young man,' she said as she watched him go back and forth to the van. Every time he entered the house, he noticed she was revealing a little more of her cleavage.

After dropping the last of the sacks, he was about to head for the door when she took him by surprise and slipped her negligee from her shoulders, letting it fall in a puddle at her ankles. He stopped in his tracks, staring at her in shock, mesmerised by her beauty as his heart hammered in his chest.

What the hell is happening?

She's way out of my league, I can't believe my luck. And to be handed it all on a plate.

But no, I cannot take this risk.

As if she could read the hesitation in his eyes, she said, 'don't worry, there's nobody around.'

This could get him into a lot of trouble, trouble he could do without. His head was screaming for him to turn and be on his way. He could end this now and save himself a lot of bother, but it was as if a force had rooted him to the spot as his gaze trailed over her body. His groin stirred to life. She was an attractive woman with a fine figure and an ample bosom, and it had been a long time since he'd enjoyed the pleasures of the flesh. He coughed. His mind was in turmoil. The rhythm in his blood was a chant.

I shouldn't, but I'll enjoy this.

This was a very bad idea, but she was so close now that he could feel her breath on his neck. Her hand reached out and stroked his cheek. 'Are you married, a girlfriend?' He realised he was inching away from her, his back now hard against the cold brick wall. He was afraid of compromising his job, if he rejected her advances, she'd make a complaint. He couldn't afford to lose this job.

'You wouldn't want your boss to be disappointed now, would you?' she whispered seductively into his ear while reaching to unbutton his shirt. He didn't protest.

'I haven't done anything wrong.'

'I'm sure he would want his customers to be happy.'

She glanced up at him, her eyes dancing like a flame of a candle as she held his gaze, casting a spell over him. Was she playing, was she serious or just toying with him? His body was consumed with a raging lust he couldn't control.

'You're a very attractive woman, but I'm not sure I should be doing this, and I really should be on my way. I have more deliveries to complete.'

'That's okay, young man, I'm sure you don't mind working a little later if you have to.'

She took his hand and led him along the corridor, through a door into a grand hallway and up an ornate staircase.

Her bedroom was elaborated decorated, fake Louis XIV style furniture, white with gold beading. She pulled him towards the four-poster bed, pushing aside a mound of coats, leather jackets and dresses. He guessed she'd been sorting clothes and having a clear-out.

Hours later, they lay in bed, limbs tangled, her head in the crook of his arm as they basked in the warmth of their release.

She'd drifted to sleep, but he lay there staring at the ceiling feeling massive regret and guilt. It had been a wonderful experience, as if an itch had been scratched, but now he had to get out, he couldn't linger, he had no idea when her husband would be returning. But if he rushed away, he was scared she'd consider it a snub and accuse him of using her.

He gently lifted her head and sat up. She looked so beautiful lying there, but this was all wrong. He got up and hurriedly dressed, a pang of fear taking hold. He was caught in her spider's web, she had a hold over him. One wrong move and she could damage him.

She stirred and stretched her arms. She'd just cheated on her husband but didn't seem to care. 'Not bad for a first time, I shall expect the same service next time.'

He'd enjoyed it, but how could this work in the future?

'You will be useful as a handyman, there's lots of jobs that want doing, I'll expect you to provide an all-round service.' She winked at him, teasingly pulling back the sheet and giving a tempting glimpse of her long slender legs.

'Your husband won't be too happy if he finds out.' This greatly unnerved him.

She gave a dismissive wave of her hand and sat up, propping the pillows behind her head. 'Don't worry about him. He's always away on business.'

'And your staff, won't they get suspicious?'

'You worry too much. You need to relax. Come back to bed,' she said, patting the sheet.

'I've got to get on.'

She looked offended, forcing him to promise he'd be back, which made him cross with himself because he hadn't wanted to do that. As far as he was concerned this was a one-off, but now she was dragging him into a liaison, which he knew he'd bitterly come to regret. No good could come of it.

He was about to go when she got out of bed and went to her wardrobe. 'Before you dash off, I'd like you to take a couple of sacks of my old clothes.'

'What would you like me to do with them?'

'I don't care what you do, they're old and in my way,' she said swinging open the wardrobe doors and pulling bags out.

When he got back to the caravan, he was starving. Gran and Kathleen had long since eaten dinner.

'Where have you been?' Gran scolded. 'Dinner was hours

ago. You'll have to go hungry now, it's your own fault. I'm not running a hotel.'

He dumped the bags on the table.

'What's this lot? I hope you're not going to leave them there in my way.'

'Women's clothing.'

Kathleen had her back to him. She was in her own world, staring out of the window but at the mention of women's clothes, she turned, looking interested.

'Did you nick 'em?' Gran opened one of the bags and pulled out a cheesecloth blouse, holding it up to inspect.

'They were given to me.'

'Who by? And why?'

'Just some posh lady at one of the houses I visit. She wanted me to dispose of them.'

Gran tutted and shook her head. 'Some folk are rolling in it. These are good clothes, they'll fetch good money.'

'May I take a look?' Kathleen asked reaching towards one of the bags. 'I desperately need some clothes. I've been wearing the same dress for weeks.'

Gran fired back, 'If you want any of this lot, you'll have to pay me.' She jabbed her chest with her finger. 'Or you can do some extra chores. These clothes are not free.'

'Come on, Gran, they were given to me not you. I decide what happens to them. I want Kathleen to have them. They must be about her size.'

Gran put her hands on her hips and stared at him through eyes as cold as a February morning. 'What's it to you if she dresses nicely? We're not a charity, and these clothes are far too good to work in,' she said, examining a red frock. 'I don't want her attracting any unwanted attention. She doesn't need any nice clothes to do the cleaning.'

'Be kind for once, would be lovely for her to have something nice to call her own. She's had a hard life.'

Gran scoffed. 'Hard life.' She laughed. 'She's barely a child. You want to know about hard life, I have some stories for you that would make your toenails curl.'

While they talked about her, Kathleen was busy delving into the bag excitedly and holding items against her. One particular dress had taken her fancy. They looked at her aghast. Gran drew breath and said, 'wow, that's fit for a princess, what a beautiful gown.'

'Please can I have this one? It's beautiful, I'll do anything if you let me have this.'

'Yes, but you'll really have to work hard for that one.'

'Perhaps she can wear it on Saturday to the barn dance.'

'Barn dance? She ain't got time to come with us. She'll be doing her chores. Everyone will want to know who she is and where she's from, best she stays here, out of sight, out of mind.'

'Blimey, Gran you are a battle-axe. The girl could do with a night out. You were young once.'

'Don't you talk to me like that. If it wasn't for me, you wouldn't have a roof over your head. When I was her age, I didn't go out swanning around enjoying myself. You would never have coped if you'd lived back then, you youngsters don't know you were born, you've got no idea how hard life was.'

'Well she's coming, that's the end of it, it's not up for discussion. And if she's coming, she'll need something nice to wear.'

CHAPTER 9

Kathleen

The day of the barn dance arrived, and all the families were getting ready. Kathleen was excited because she'd get to wear the beautiful dress, a chance to escape the rags she'd worn for weeks.

She put on the dress and admired her reflection in Gran's mirror. The colour looked just right on her and complemented her skin tone. It hugged her waistline and the tucks at the front accentuated her breasts, giving her a small cleavage. She puffed the sleeves and admired the overall effect, feeling grown up and older than her years. As she twirled in front of the mirror and watched the skirts swirl around her knees in a pleasing way, it occurred to her that her mother would never have allowed her to wear a dress like this. The thought made her smile. Tonight was going to give her a sense of freedom she'd not felt in so long.

Gran barged in. 'That's totally inappropriate for a child of your age,' she barked.

Her heart sank and she slumped on the bed. When was her life ever going to feel like her own?

'You're not going in that, and that's the end of it. I won't be shown up,' she said, turning to Colin who was standing in the doorway behind her. 'This is all your fault. Look at the ideas you've put in this girl's head.'

He sighed. 'I'll deal with Kathleen, Gran, you go and wait outside.'

He pushed Gran out of the caravan to wait with the others, before returning to speak to Kathleen.

'Gran's right, you're not going out like that.'

'What's wrong with it? I want to wear it. You said I could.' It felt as though she was pleading with her mother. She was suddenly overcome by a wave of sadness, longing to be back home even though she'd despised it at the time.

'It's far too revealing, it'll attract too much attention, you've already got yourself into trouble once, we don't want you getting into trouble again. You don't know what the fellas are like round here, they're simple country folk who won't think twice about taking you round the back of their tractor and giving you one. Don't say I haven't warned you.'

'Well, what shall I wear then?' she screeched in despair, feeling like a spoilt five-year-old. 'I'm not wearing my dirty laundry dress.'

He disappeared and came back with one of the sacks of clothing and emptied it onto the bed before rummaging through. 'This one will do.' He passed her a simple cotton dress, brown with a green pattern around the trim and a high fringed neck. He turned away from her while she slipped the dress off and put the new one on, staring in the mirror in dismay.

'This is horrible,' she said turning to see him frowning. 'And you know it. I look like a frumpy old maid.'

He threw his hands into the air. 'It'll keep Gran happy though. Come on, we don't want to be late.'

'I think I'd rather stay here.'

He gave her arm a tug. 'You are coming, I need a dance partner. You look okay in that.' He shrugged. It didn't matter to him how she looked, but it mattered to her. She was sick of looking a frump. 'No, it's not the nicest of dresses, but it'll do.'

They joined the throng of families heading up the hill under a star-spangled sky to the barn at Meadowbank Farm. As they reached the barn, there was a wonderful buzz in the air. People were laughing as they danced in lines, some half-heartedly prancing around, not focussed on getting the moves right, or focussed on getting them wrong as they enjoyed making fools of themselves. Others watched on, smoking, drinking and chatting.

A band had set up along one side of the barn, two men were strumming guitars, and another played a flute. Kathleen smiled. She thought how typically Irish this was. It a completely new experience for her. She had attended a comparable event in a church hall, but it lacked the atmosphere. This looked much more exciting.

As she gazed at the scene, she noticed how the women were dressed, in cowboy boots, pretty three-tiered skirts and flouncy blouses and chequered shirts. Immediately, she felt conspicuous and self-conscious in her hideous brown dress. How could she shine when she didn't look her best? It niggled her because this was after all the first time she'd been to a social event in a very long time, and it felt important to look nice.

The aroma of burgers and hotdogs wafted through the air, mingling with the sound of guitars strumming in the background. Haybales were stacked along the sides of the barn and the floor was covered in straw, creating a rustic atmosphere. Laughter and chatter blended with the twang of the guitar. Despite her dress, she was determined to enjoy the evening and put all thoughts of her miserable life out of her mind.

Everybody had brought their own drink, and plenty of it. Colin cracked open a bottle of Guinness for himself and a bottle of pop for Kathleen. She hated the way he treated her like a kid, she would have liked to try a Guinness. Even Gran, who'd gone off to join a gaggle of older women drank it.

Halfway through the evening, Kathleen went to find somewhere she could squat for a wee. She headed into the darkness towards a cluster of trees and bushes, leaving behind the brightness of the lanterns that were strung across the barn's beams. As she trampled across the tall grass, the music and laughter faded, replaced by the sound of whispering trees and the hoot of an owl. She pushed aside a few branches and crouched down.

Afterwards, as she stood up and pulled up her knickers, she heard the crack of a branch. She froze, her heart missing a beat. Then another crunch and the sound of heavy breathing. She spun around, scared, her eyes scanning her surroundings. Had she been followed? She strained to listen as she stayed stock still. The crunching of wood, then a shadow. Quietly moving a branch aside, careful not to make a sound and still holding her breath, she spotted a small pony. Her hand flew to her chest with relief, and she chuckled to herself.

She trudged back through the damp grass, standing a little way off on a bank so that she could enjoy the scene from a distance in the quiet of her own company and without the pressure of joining in.

As she gazed out, she suddenly became aware of somebody standing very close to her. Looking up, she realised it was one of the camp lads. His name was Wayne. He was in his mid-twenties.

'You all right, love?' he said, slurring his words.

Before answering, she noticed him swaying from side to side.

'You look lonely, love, do you fancy some company? I could do with a pretty face to liven up my evening.' He gave a loud belch.

She could smell the beer on his breath as it travelled the short distance between them.

'Haven't seen you at one of these shindigs before and have to say, you're the most attractive one here. You fancy a jig? I'm younger than some of those old farts.'

'Thanks for the offer, I'm okay, I just like sitting here on my own taking in the view. Not really into drinking and these big social events.'

'Yeah, I like a nice view too, and from what I see your landscape looks pretty good. Nice pair of jugs you've got, shame they're all covered up.'

A feeling a revulsion came over her. He was a typical drunken slob.

'There are plenty of good views at the party, so I suggest you go back and take a look.'

'Oh dear,' he jeered, 'you normally this prickly with your neighbours, or just playing hard to get?'

'No, I'm just not interested in anyone. I just want to be left on my own. Go on, get back to the party, there are loads of girls there.'

'But I like you though, you're different in your fancy dowdy dress, you look like you've stepped out of a storybook. You think you're too good for us?'

'Would you just please go away.'

'You can wallow in your own company, Miss Snooty, I'll tell the others to stay away from you, you're going to have to change your attitude if you stick around here.'

'Piss off, you jerk.' He was really starting to wind her up.

'That's a fine way to speak to me.' He had a sneer on his face and spat into the grass inches from her before stalking off.

On his way back she noticed him speak to Colin who seemed to respond in an aggressive manner towards him. This slightly unnerved her.

Colin wandered over. 'You okay, love?'

'Why won't people just leave me be?'

'It does seem a bit odd that you're sitting over here.'

'I've had enough now. I want to go back to the caravan.'

'You can do, but if you want to walk back in the dark on your own, so be it.'

'I'm used to being on my own, why should you care? I'm nothing to you, just a skivvy.'

'You ungrateful little cow, be like that then, I thought you'd enjoy a night out, next time I won't bother inviting you.'

'I thought you were supposed to be sorting something out, I've been trapped here in your miserable little caravan for weeks, it's not much fun sharing a bed with your gran and I'm definitely not sleeping with you because you can't keep your hands to yourself.'

As she stormed off down the hill, she noticed the other chap watching them from a distance. A few minutes later, she was aware of someone following her and turned to see him.

'Not you again, I told you to leave me alone.'

'You shouldn't be walking back in the dark, so I thought I'd keep an eye on you.'

'I'm fine, I don't need you or anyone else, I'm going home to bed.'

'So am I. We could slip into bed together, keep each other warm. It's a cold night.' He chuckled.

When he laid his arm on her shoulder, she knew he needed to steady himself. He was the worse for wear. His arm was heavy, and she stooped under the weight. He moved in close, his legs wobbly like a calf. She smelt the rank beer breath mixed with sweat and glanced at him, noticing his ruddy cheeks and glassy eyes. It was a wonder he could stand up, let alone walk.

It wouldn't take much for me to push him over and into the ditch.

In one swift move, she flung his arm off and gave him a hard shove into the ditch before running for her life back to the sanctuary of the caravan.

CHAPTER 10

The O'Sullivans

It wasn't safe for the children to be out on the streets alone, not with trouble at every corner and living in enemy territory and so Sheridan took them to school and fetched them at the end of the day. Aidan and Sean always kicked up a fuss. They didn't like their mother mollycoddling.

'For God's, Mam, you're showing us up, making us look really silly, it's embarrassing, we're not kids anymore, it's hard enough to fit in around here as it is,' Sean would say, but she always insisted. She couldn't bear the thought of anything bad happening to them.

She came to an abrupt stop on the pavement as she stared across at their house and gasped. A gut-wrenching jolt surged through her as she struggled to take in the scene. The splattering of brightly coloured paint daubed in large letters across the front of their house sent a wave of shock and disbelief through her very core.

They all stood in silence, a battlefield of emotions rising inside her––anger, betrayal, and a raw, primal fear clawing her insides. The children began asking questions, but she was so choked she couldn't speak.

BASTARDS OUT.

'What's Da going to say?' Sean asked.

'The Lord only knows.'

'Whoever did it, needs their bleedin' head kicking in.'

'That's enough, Sean,' she snapped. The Troubles were affecting her boys, shaping their outlook, filling them with hate. She could see the bitterness starting to grow in both of them, and these days they were getting into more fights. She knew there wouldn't be much she could do to stop them getting involved in the violence, not least because it was right there on their doorstep, just there, all the time. She imagined other communities where mothers met in the street and gossiped about what had been going on as they swept the bottles and stones that littered the ground. But living here, she was isolated from her own kind.

As they crossed the road, Sean stalked off in the opposite direction. 'Where are you going?' she called after him.

He turned his collar up and waved her away. 'To get whoever did that,' he screamed.

She rushed towards him. 'No, Sean, you'll do no such thing.' But it was hopeless, he'd legged it up the hill and she had the younger ones to think of.

Inside the house she appeared calm, not wanting to alarm the kids, but she was consumed with anxiety. She poured the children glasses of squash and as they sat around the table she tried to distract them by creating a semblance of normality.

'What was your favourite lesson today?'

'Don't know,' Aidan replied, slinging his coat on the sofa. 'I hate assembly. It's always about the news. I hate the news.'

Her heart sank. Why couldn't they learn about happy things? Bombs and violence and hatred were part of their miserable existence in this city of malice they called home. School should be about forgetting and escaping and being a child.

Booby trap. Internment. Rubber bullets. Petrol bomb. Gelignite. This was her children's vocabulary.

She nipped to the loo and when she came back, the room was empty apart from the baby still in her pram.

At first she thought they were playing a game, but the house was so tiny, there weren't many places to hide, and it took her under a minute to look.

Panic rose inside her; they'd been told not to go outside, not even to play in the backyard, not without her permission. Frantic, she dashed out of the back door, nearly tripping over the trailing hosepipe strewn across the slabs. Liam had left it there in case they were firebombed. Too many houses had suffered that fate in the past few years. Even though Liam had his head in the sand, stubbornly refusing to move, he wasn't completely unprepared for trouble.

She breathed a sigh of relief when she saw them playing in the yard.

'Get in, the lot of you,' she screamed, grabbing Maeve's collar. 'You know you shouldn't be out here. And where's Aidan?'

'He went out the back gate to find Sean,' Roisin said.

Suddenly, the fence panel shook, and raucous shouts and laughter rose from the alley. 'Who's there? Sean, Aidan?' She flung open the back gate just as the fence panel collapsed into their yard and a spray of stones were hurled over. Her children were screaming and crying, and, in the commotion, she saw a group of teenagers darting down the alley.

She started to run after them but realised how foolish that would be. Turning and dashing back into the yard, she was met with the sight of the collapsed fence panels and shards of wood scattered across the ground, the children hysterical. A piercing scream cut through the chaos as she noticed Maeve clutching her face and blood trickling through her fingers. Rushing over to the injured girl, she screamed at Roisin to get inside. Her trembling hands gently prised Maeve's arm away from her tear-streaked cheek. With her arm around her, she guided her into the kitchen. Blood oozed from a gash just an inch to the side of her eye.

Jesus, Mary, and Joseph, she could have lost her eye.

Maeve was still sobbing as she quickly assessed the wound, her mind racing with worry. She grabbed a nearby tea towel and as she applied pressure to the wound to stem the bleeding, she silently cursed Liam. If he'd listened to her pleas, this wouldn't have happened. All she'd wanted was for her children to be safe, and now this.

'You're going to need a couple of stitches, poppet.'

Deciding what to do with Roisin while she raced to the hospital with Maeve was the next problem. Leaving them with a neighbour wasn't an option, and where were Aidan and Sean? She was worried sick.

They didn't have a telephone or a car and both sets of their parents lived a twenty-minute walk away. As a snap decision she decided her best bet was to take Roisin too. With Aisling in the pram, they set off to Liam's workplace to persuade his boss to let him leave early to take his daughter to hospital. It wasn't ideal and as she dashed down the street, the girls clutching the sides of the pram and still crying, she was also frantic with worry for Aidan and Sean.

As she veered off down a shortcut, she crossed her fingers that Liam's boss would be understanding and maybe even order a taxi for them.

Dusk was moving into darkness and the streetlights were

glowing. She was alert, watching gardens, houses, feeling on edge. A short way ahead of her, seeing three youths, her heart jolted as sheer panic swept over her. They were standing on the pavement watching her. It had been a terrible mistake to take the shortcut, whatever had she been thinking? There was no doubt in her mind; they were the same youths she'd seen in the alley beside their house. She kept her head down and kept walking at the same pace, glancing up as casually as she could to check on the group. Making a sudden turn, she darted to the other side of the road holding the pram's handle tightly, aware they were now following. She breathed deeply, aware she might need to run or confront them. As she quickened her pace, they overtook her and surrounded them.

'When are you getting out?' asked the biggest one, 'to let someone decent into that house?'

'Leave us alone, can't you see, my child is hurt?'

'Fenian bastards.' The spotty one spat in her face.

Scared out of her wits, she zigzagged around them, expecting to be grabbed any minute and beaten to the ground, but they just stood there laughing. She hurried away, wiped her face, listening over her shoulder and above Maeve's sobbing to hear if they were following.

'Feckin' bastards, we'll get you next time,' they called out.

She knew they would. Liam might not believe it, but she did. What they'd done so far was tame compared to what they were capable of. Next time it would be knives, clubs or worse.

As soon as they were out of view, Sheridan began to run. Her legs were jelly, and the children were struggling to keep up but finally they arrived at the slaughterhouse and headed straight to the boss's office.

She might have got away from them, but had they done something to Aidan and Sean? There had been no sign of them out on the streets.

She knocked on the boss's door and as she waited, she thought about the youth's parting words as she'd hurried away. In her panic, she'd not processed them but now she realised what they'd said.

'Your sons will make good target practice.'

A coldness swept over her.

CHAPTER 11

The O'Sullivans

'You shouldn't have let them out of your sight,' Liam said, screaming at Sheridan. 'You're their mother, you're supposed to protect them.'

Liam and Maeve were back from the hospital and Sean and Aidan had just walked in. Sean was black and blue. Trembling, he went to the mirror. His waxy face was covered in scratches and bruises and his lips were swollen. Ignoring Liam, she followed her son to the kitchen sink where he leaned over and spat blood and saliva before splashing water over his face.

'Open your mouth, son,' Liam said. Sean winced and let his dad check his teeth. They were all still intact, but his gums were bleeding.

Sean's knuckles were bleeding too, and he turned his hands over to show Sheridan his cuts.

'What happened?' she asked, stifling back the tears.

'I got a hammering.'

'Jesus, Mary and Joseph.' Liam was scrutinising his face. 'Who did it?'

'I don't know.'

Liam was about to touch his face, but Sean twisted his head away. 'Don't fuss, I'm okay.'

'For the love of Jesus, why did you let him go out and after dark? You know the dangers,' he scolded Sheridan.

'Don't have a go at Ma, she tried to stop me. I wanted to find out who graffitied the house.'

'It's just paint, son, it'll wash off.'

'And sticks and stones will break us,' Sheridan said letting out a mirthless laugh.

In bed much later, Sheridan turned to Liam in the darkness. Neither could sleep. The events of that day were churning round her mind.

'What sort of life will our kids have?'

He had his back to her and gave a heavy sigh. 'Go to sleep, Sheri.'

'Sleep?' She sat up, furious, and leaned over him. 'Maeve could have lost her eye today, and that's all you've got to say. And Sean, beaten black and blue by those thugs.'

He sighed, turned onto his back, and swept a hand through his hair before staring up at the ceiling. As usual, he had nothing to say.

'I don't think you realise, I'm living on my nerves, frightened out of my wits.'

'Calm down, love, it'll get easier.'

Did he honestly believe that? She still felt sick to the core, the sight of little Maeve earlier on and then, and while waiting for their return from the hospital, worrying where Sean and Aidan were.

'We need to move. I keep telling you. It's not safe round here anymore.'

'When did you last go down to the council?'

'I go to the council every bloody week. Why's it always me that has to go down there? They don't listen to me. It's all right for you, you're out at work all day, you don't have to live with this.'

'Woman, you're neurotic.'

'What's bloody wrong with you? Are you oblivious? You try staying at home all day, the constant knocking on the door, bricks over the fence, the chanting. The police won't even do anything, they won't come round here and when they do, the kids just laugh at them. Even the priests are afraid. Have you not noticed, they never come after dark? If you don't do anything, I'll take the girls and you can stay here with the boys. I'm not putting my baby at risk. Sean and Aidan do their own thing, they don't listen to me. That's why they got into trouble this evening. Are you happy to watch them used as target practice? I don't want to sit here grieving when they're dead. The way our Sean's going, I can see him getting mixed up with the IRA.'

'Actually, that might not be a bad thing. They might protect us. They wouldn't stand for this.'

'Don't be feckin ridiculous.'

He sighed.

'This isn't a home anymore, it's a prison. I'm going to go and see me mam tomorrow, you can rot in hell, so you better start making plans.'

'You can't do that to me. You can't take my girls. We're supposed to be a family, you want to break us up.'

'No, I want us to be a proper family, safe. We're the only ones left round here. All the other Catholic families have been driven out. Every time I step outside, I don't know if a bomb's going to go off, we're trapped, we can't leave. People blowing each other up, shooting each other, living round here is a war zone. I never know if I'll come back to find a pile of cinders. I thought I'd married a man not a mouse, start thinking about your family first for once.'

She hated it when he had nothing to say. His silence made her angry and provoked her more than his words.

'We can't give the baby a life, you don't care about your baby, perhaps it's better to give her to someone who can, I can't cope anymore. Maybe I can sell her to that actress, I could buy something away from here. I'd go anywhere that's safe. You can do what you like, you obviously don't care about us.'

'You'd sell our baby? What kind of woman are you? What happened to the caring gal I married? Don't talk stupid.'

'You haven't been listening to a word I've been saying, it doesn't register, does it?'

'You're neurotic.' He got up and pulled on his trousers.

'Where are you going?'

'Out, till you're asleep, I'm not putting up with this. I'm going downstairs. You're stopping me sleeping, babbling in my ear. I need a clear head. I've got to work tomorrow. Last thing I need is a screeching banshee giving me earache.'

'Sod off then, leave me alone. I'll find a solution because you obviously won't.'

After he'd gone, she curled her legs to her stomach and sobbed uncontrollably. Eventually, exhausted, she fell sleep. Sometime later, she found herself wide awake, Liam was back and snoring softly beside her. The room was bathed in an orange glow from the streetlights. Was someone outside?

A sudden noise jolted her, the click of the letterbox's metal spring. She slid out of bed, her bare feet touching the floorboards. It was chilly and she grabbed her dressing gown, loosely tying it around her, and quietly padded down the stairs. At the bottom of the staircase, she found a folded note in the letterbox. She switched on the light in the hallway and took the note.

GET OUT YOU TAIG SCUM OR WE'LL BURN YOU OUT. THIS IS FINAL WARNING, THERE WILL BE NO OTHER.

UVF

Her heart was thumping, and hands were shaking as she

switched out the light and tiptoed into the darkness of the front room. She peered through the crack in the curtains.

The street was empty, and the only movement was the rain cascading at an angle under the orange glow of the streetlights.

She stood back from the window as fear, like icy tendrils, tightened its grip with every beat of her heart. It felt suffocating and she realised she was trembling. She kept expecting the window to burst into a shower of glass and flame, but she knew that it wouldn't be tonight. They'd given their warning. It would be some other night.

It was that last sentence, 'THERE WILL BE NO OTHER', that really panicked her. This was the last straw, with or without Liam's support she couldn't stay. It was time to take these warnings seriously. He wasn't going to take charge, not until they were burned out of their home.

She went into the kitchen to make a brew and sat at the table. As she wrapped her hands around the cup, trying to gain comfort from its warmth, anger rose inside her. People who didn't even know her, hated her. They hated her children too. Even her innocent tiny baby. The hate was for what she was, what she stood for. To be despised for just being a Catholic, it sent a chill down her spine.

She wanted to go back to bed, wake Liam and show him the note. But something stopped her. Maybe it was the sense of hopelessness she felt that it wouldn't make any difference. Soon it would all be too late. He never listened to her. The first threat had been posted the same way and written with a red biro. Liam would load the gun he kept under the floorboards and tell her to sleep in her shoes in case they needed to jump from the window. The presence of the gun in the house made Liam feel safe, but it worried the hell out of her, it would be all over for them quicker than Liam could reach for his gun. They'd be bleeding into their mattresses before he could load the bullets.

Tomorrow she'd go back to the council. She made a weekly

visit to check the housing waiting list status. She didn't hold out any hope though, she expected the officer to repeat the same thing, that with the baby, it would be more challenging to relocate them. She found this reasoning perplexing; shouldn't they be a high priority now?

Next to the fire, in the kindling basket, she noticed the folded newspaper with Janie Lee's smiling face gazing out as if pleading with her. She stared at it for several moments. Her smile would soon be reduced to ash in the fireplace. She snatched it up and tore out the article, folded it and thrust it into the pocket of her coat which was hanging on a peg in the hall. Her heart was racing in her chest, and she had to clamp it with her hand and take a nerve-steadying breath. Sitting down and taking stock, she was shocked at the thoughts running through her mind. The thoughts were propelled by a deep and fierce love she felt for her children. It was relentless and burned bright in the face of adversity. In her heart was a love so deep and unwavering that she would literally move heaven and earth for them. She'd walk the fiery path of sacrifice. She'd do whatever it took to keep them safe and give them a better future.

Her heart pulled in conflicting directions; dawn might bring a different mindset. The decision, the toughest she'd ever had to face, was now a race against time and dwindling choices. Whatever choice she made would seriously impact their lives forever.

CHAPTER 12

*K*athleen
It was Sunday, the day after the barn dance. After cooking lunch for the three of them and clearing up, Kathleen went for a walk around the site and up into the woods beyond. Pines wound like a ribbon up the valley. It was a rare treat to enjoy this time to herself, to stand between the trees watching them sway as if the branches were conducting an orchestra, or to listen to the sweet fluting of a blackbird, the cascading trills of its song reaching her soul.

The path along the hedgerow was slick with mud and sucked at the soles of her thin shoes. She watched every step, careful not to slip. Emerging onto drier footing, she looked up to see Wayne several metres away, standing in the field watching her with an amused smile. Her heart jolted. It was as if he was waiting for her, and she wondered how long he'd been there, as if stalking her. He was casually flicking the braces of his brown trousers. She approached him cautiously, having no idea if he remembered the events of the previous evening. Did he realise that she'd pushed him into the ditch?

Drawing closer, he said, 'I'm glad I've bumped into you. I

must say, you are a feisty young lady with a lot of spirit, I like that in a lass. Sorry if I overstepped the mark last night, I had a little too much to drink.'

They'd started to stroll back towards the caravans and Kathleen stopped suddenly, realising that if Colin saw them, he'd think they'd been out walking together and that something had started to develop between them. It would only cause an argument. She turned in the opposite direction, back towards the woods. 'No worries, I'll let you get on,' she said over her shoulder hoping he'd take the hint. She quickened her pace.

He ran to catch up with her and grabbed her arm. She shook it off. 'I do fancy you though. Perhaps we could go for a drink so that we can get to know each other better and maybe, who knows, you might not push me in the ditch next time.'

'I'm not interested, sorry, I won't be around for much longer, I'm moving on,' she said politely.

They'd reached the brow of the hill and the woods loomed ahead. She stopped a short way in, uncertain which way to turn. It wasn't a good idea to go into the woods with him, but at least they were now out of view of the caravans, while still close enough to call for help if she needed to.

He reached out and took her hands in his. They were huge around her tiny delicate hands and felt rough and calloused, worker's hands. 'All the more reason to have a bit of fun then, while we still can.'

He startled her by suddenly pulling her towards him, and forced his tongue into her mouth. She squealed and tried to push him away, but he was too strong. He was clamping her hand. 'Get off me,' she shrieked, eventually able to push him away when he loosened his grip.

A minute later though, he came at her and grabbed her by the hair and twisted her arm behind her back. Pain shot up her arm and she yelled out for him to stop.

'Okay, little Miss Tease, I will teach you a lesson you will not forget.' He yanked her into the bushes. Brambles and gorse grazed her face and neck as he shoved her to the ground and lay on top of her, trying to pull her clothes off and unbuckling his trousers at the same time.

She screamed at the top of her voice as hard as her lungs would allow and tried to wrestle him off.

He clamped a hand over her mouth, threatening her with violence if she made any more noise. She screamed again in desperation when she felt a hard slap across her face. She was helpless, he was too strong for her, and she realised there was nothing she could do to make him stop.

She lay still, forced herself to relax and play the game. She flung her arms out, his head was near her midriff, and fumbling beside her, she felt something hard in her hand. Wood, a rock, she didn't know. In desperation she picked it up and smashed it into his face as hard as she could. He reeled back in pain, and she hit him again. He slumped beside her, and she prised herself from under him and was eventually able to push him away with her legs.

She was in a terrible state, shaking and crying and trembling. Her clothes were torn, she was splattered in mud, her skin grazed and bleeding as she got to her feet and ran on wobbly legs back to the caravan. She banged on the caravan door and when she saw Colin she pointed to the woods and told him to come quick.

They reached the woods, but Wayne wasn't there. They glanced round, calling his name. They heard the rustle of leaves, and Wayne stumbled out of the undergrowth clutching the side of his head. Trickles of blood coursed down his face.

'You wanna keep that bitch tethered, she's out of control.'

'What did you do to her? Kathleen wouldn't harm a fly.'

Nursing his head, he snarled at Colin. 'What's she to you? You pervert, she's much too young to be in your bed.'

'Watch your tongue, you little shit, I wonder what your

father will have to say about this. Attempted rape of a juvenile is one of the sickest crimes that you can commit. You bastard.'

Conor looked at Kathleen and smirked. 'The bitch led me on, said she needed a good seeing-to, and then changed her mind and hit me in the face.'

Kathleen stood there, still shaking, tears running down her face.

They stopped talking when they heard Gran calling. Kathleen and Colin turned and wandered back, with Wayne limping behind them still nursing his head and calling expletives behind them.

Gran was standing between the caravans, hands on hips, with a face like thunder. 'What's been going on, why do you men always end up in a brawl? You're like a bunch of kids. You're both in your thirties, you should know better. What's it over this time?' She looked straight at Kathleen. 'There's always a woman behind any trouble. I saw you were trouble first time I clapped my eyes on you. You're nothing but a brazen hussy.'

Then she turned to Colin. 'The girl's got to go. And besides, she ain't no use to me. She can't cook or clean. Next time you bring a woman home, make sure she's older.'

'If anyone should go, it's Wayne. All he thinks about is what's between his legs. Just wait till I tell his family what he's been up to, he will be out on his ear,' Colin said.

'Oh no you don't, young man.' Gran was angry, and reached out and clouted him. Colin yelped. 'He is one of us, I have to live here, and I don't want you upsetting the apple cart. She will be long gone, and I am not having *her* disrupting my life whether it is her fault or not. Good riddance is what I say, just get it done and soon.' She turned and sailed back into the caravan.

Wayne stalked off and Colin just stared at the ground, hands shoved into his pockets, head stooped, not speaking. If he was embarrassed by Gran's words, he didn't apologise or try to comfort her. Instead, he turned tail and headed back to the caravan.

Kathleen felt utterly wretched, a piece of dirt on the bottom of a shoe. Her future was an expanse of emptiness and she had to confront the harsh truth: she had no home, nobody wanted her, not even as an unpaid skivvy.

CHAPTER 13

The O'Sullivans

The morning after the threat, Sheridan was still terrified. She marched the kids to school, with Maeve taking the day off to recover from her injury. She didn't linger for conversations with the mums at the school gate. Bumping the pram down the pavement, and clutching Maeve with her free hand, she looked both ways, and hurried across the road to the bus stop, flagging the next one to take them into the city centre.

Her heart raced with dread at the prospect of what could lie ahead. This was a war zone, and it was hard to ignore the reports of buses going up in flames or being seized in violent hijackings. To take two young children with her was foolish, reckless, even she knew that. But she had to get on with it, life went on despite the Troubles. And Liam wasn't going to help. She'd grown used to the fear, this was a risk she took every single week because this was how it was, and Liam never objected. In fact, he seemed completely indifferent to the perils.

On the bus she took Aisling out of the pram, holding her close, enjoying her warmth and the smell of her baby scent. These were desperate times calling for the most desperate of measures. Her heart was quietly breaking, but her head screamed sense. Aisling wouldn't suffer, she wouldn't remember her Irish family.

She glanced along one street, seeing it was empty and there was a single parked car. A sense of unease crept over her; the scene felt wrong, it was as if something was about to happen. As she stared at the car, it bulged and exploded into a great ball of smoke and fire and its doors somersaulted away from it, glass from the houses next to it raining down like hail onto the tarmac.

She stared out of the window through teary eyes, immune to such horrors but also traumatised. How she wished for better times, a better future for her kids, a chance to escape this apocalypse.

The bus trundled towards the city centre, passing whole streets that had been burned to the ground or streets where there were gaps in the terraces like knocked-out teeth, just piles of bricks and rubble remaining. Heading to the shopping area, they passed Burton on the corner. There was scaffolding around the building and a sign in large capital letters which said, 'Army Control Ahead.' Everywhere across the city these days, it seemed as if there were barricades and army check points. Makeshift units with gun turrets that looked like Portacabins were a familiar sight, army ambulances parked up, the occasional burned-out car reduced to ash and spare parts, armed soldiers, a mesh of barbed wire across a road, Saracen personnel carriers moving at slow speed. But there were also streets and corners that looked like any other city across Britain. They passed the Bradford & Bingley Building Society, where a couple of women in chequered coats were huddled in discussion, their hair freshly permed. Men in suits carrying briefcases were hurrying past the Cheltenham & Gloucester Building Society and crossing the road at the traffic lights, ladies tripping along the pavement carrying little handbags browsed department store windows. Cars trundled along, spewing thick clouds of smoke.

She got off the bus at the offices of the Housing Executive. There was a housing allocation system for council housing, and on previous visits she'd been told it was based on need and with a points system to ensure fairness and equality.

Fairness, they don't know the meaning of the word.

Equality. All I want is for my children to be safe in a place called home.

Pushing through the heavy swing doors, she found a long queue ahead of her. A disgruntled man was leaning over the Perspex partition arguing with the clerk behind the counter.

'Are you saying you won't do anything? You lot are fucking useless, you should try living in our slum.' Aggressively, he shoved a piece of paper towards her.

'Mr O'Dogherty, I understand your frustration.'

'No, you don't, none of you do, you haven't got a clue.'

Sheridan noticed a man in the office behind the counter look up from his desk and frown. She recognised him, he was the manager, a crusty older fella with thin grey hair who looked like he should have retired long ago.

'Could I please ask you to be more courteous otherwise we won't be able to help you. Our staff are doing a difficult job in exceptionally difficult times and deserve to be treated with respect.'

The man hurled more abuse and stormed out of the office.

Sheridan parked the pram and sat Maeve on one of the chairs at the side of the room, before she joined the queue. She jiggled the baby in her arms trying to stop her from crying while they waited, and eventually, she was seen after a good forty minutes. By the time she spoke to the clerk her feet were aching, the baby getting heavy in her arms.

The offices were very hot and stuffy, and she couldn't wait to get out into the fresh air. Maeve kept getting up and tugging her skirt, asking how long they were going to be there.

The clerk looked down a list on the desk in front of her, scanning each line with a finger. A few moments later she looked up.

'Nothing for now. Come back next week,' she stated, her tone disinterested as she casually dismissed her and shifted her attention to the next customer.

Maeve was sitting at her feet. 'Get up, darling and show the lady your wound.'

'Look, this is what they've done. She's only six. She could have lost her eye.' Her voice was wobbly and threatened to break.

The clerk's face was expressionless. She shifted on her chair and craned her neck to look at the next customer. 'Look we can't help, there are no homes.'

'There's also this.' She fumbled in her pocket, shifted Aisling to her other hip as she pulled out the note posted through their letterbox. 'It came last night.'

The clerk stared at the note as if it was merely a shopping receipt.

'We've had bricks thrown into our backyard, graffiti and my son was attacked last night, beaten black and blue. We've got to get out. Please, I'm begging you. I've got five children to think of. We can't go on like this.'

'Come back next week,' she repeated in a flat tone.

'There might not be a next week.' She was aware of her voice rising but couldn't control the desperation and frustration rising inside her. 'You'll have blood on your hands, lady, if you don't do something,' she screeched.

The manager stepped forward. 'You heard my colleague, we can't help this week, come back next week.' Then he looked at the person behind her. 'Next.'

Out on the pavement, she felt like a deflated balloon. She

looked up at the sombre sky which reflected her own emotions at her. The overwhelming sense of hopelessness felt crushing.

    She hurried across the road, not wanting to stick around for longer than was necessary. What she needed right now was to see the one person in her life who she could rely on, the one person who truly cared. Her mum. Her mum would know what to do, she wouldn't even have to ask to stay, she'd offer to take them in. She didn't want to impose, of course she didn't, and it was far from ideal going back to her parents, particularly when they only had one room to spare, but beggars couldn't be choosers, she reminded herself. What choice did she have?

CHAPTER 14

The O'Sullivans

Sheridan's parents lived in the heart of the Catholic area. Her dad was a fitter up at the shipyard and her mum did the odd shift behind the counter of the local grocery store. As she walked towards the home where she was born and raised, she felt instantly calmer and more relaxed. Home wasn't just bricks and cement, it wasn't just somewhere to rest the head or pour boiling water over tea leaves, it was a feeling, a starting place for love and hope and dreams.

She turned the corner by the pub where she recognised a few old chaps milling outside and draining pints. The road swept down a steep hill with red-brick terraced housing straddling the hill on either side. The front doors opened right onto the pavement and when you stepped inside, wiped your feet on the mat, the stairs rose ahead of you. What she loved most was the perfect symmetry of the little red chimneys, like divers at the Olympics. They stood serenely against the skyline. She stopped to take it all in, gazing across to Harland & Wolff and the two great yellow-painted twin gantry cranes, Samson and

Goliath, then in the other direction towards the Mourne Mountains.

She was glad not to bump into any of her mum's neighbours idly chatting on doorsteps, not wanting to face a barrage of questions about Maeve and her injury.

The street was quite obviously Catholic, with most of the houses displaying framed pictures of the Virgin Mary, rosary beads, or candles on their windowsills. Some displayed Sinn Fein posters or slogans of independence such as 'ourselves alone.'

When she came to number 40, she stopped and gave the door a hard knock.

There was a squeak as it opened. Her dad had never got around to oiling the hinges.

'Oh hello,' her mum said, startled, before peering down at Maeve. 'Oh my goodness, what's happened to you, poppet?' Then she looked up at Sheridan quizzically.

'I don't really want to talk about it on the doorstep, can we come in, Mam?'

She left the pram outside and carried the baby in.

'This is a lovely surprise, you're lucky you caught me in though, I'm usually out on a Tuesday.' She followed her mum through the front room to the tiny kitchen at the back of the house.

'Maeve, do you want to watch TV?' Sheridan looked at her watch. 'Andy Pandy will be on in a tic.' The little girl nodded, put her thumb in her mouth and went to curl up on the sofa.

Her mum bent down and kissed her granddaughter on the head. 'Nanny will bring you some squash and a biscuit. I've got some of your favourites, Jammie Dodgers.'

Maeve's eyes lit up and when she was settled in front of the TV, they closed the door, their voices falling to whispers. 'What's going on? You look awful.'

Her mum took the baby, who'd just woken. She jiggled her

on her lap as they sat at the small table in the centre of the kitchen and Sheridan handed her mum a bottle of milk.

Sheridan started talking and it wasn't long into the conversation when her voice broke, and tears trickled down her face. Soon she was sobbing and looking around for a tissue to blow her nose on.

'How awful, I had no idea things were so bad, love,' she said in a soft, caring voice, the one that had soothed her as a little girl. Finally able to pour her troubles to a sympathetic ear, she couldn't stop crying and this made her realise just how dreadful things really were.

'I feel desperately sorry for you, love, I really do. Have you been to the council?'

'Yes, I go up there every week. There's nothing.'

'Well,' she said pausing, 'don't give up hope, something will turn up, it always does.'

She's not going to offer a bed. Can't she see how desperate I am?

Her heart quietly sank; the moment had passed, if she was going to offer to help, it would have happened by now. She sniffed back more tears, got up and stuck her head around the door to see if Maeve was okay. The little girl had fallen asleep. She went in and stood over her. How peaceful, how safe she looked. This was where she wanted to be, back here with her mum and dad in the heart of the Catholic community where she belonged.

She went back into the kitchen where her mum was filling the kettle. 'It was a really nice surprise, you popping round, love. I miss you all and the baby's growing so fast.' She glanced over at the baby, now back in Sheridan's arms. 'She's grown. Every week I notice a difference.'

'I'm really worried, Mam, for the baby's safety and we desperately need a bigger house.'

'Well dear, I do understand, maybe you should have thought

about that before you had five kids. That's why your father and I just settled for two.'

'It's hard.'

'I don't know how you cope, love, it would have driven me mad having five screaming kids running round. I'm glad I'm not a young mother again.'

'But, Mam, I'm not coping, that's just it. I'm at my wits' end, I don't know what to do.'

'He needs to keep his pants on, or you need to shut the shop, girl, otherwise you'll have more problems, you could really have done without this one. You need to put some bromide in his tea.' She laughed. 'There aren't too many large council houses available, so you might have a long wait. The rate you're going, you'll need a farm.'

'I don't need a farm, I'm thinking of splitting the family up, leaving the boys there with Liam and taking the girls somewhere for safety, just till we're rehoused. We only need a room, I'm happy to share with the girls and the baby doesn't take up much space. You've got a spare room, Mam. Couldn't we come here for a while? I wouldn't ask if I wasn't desperate, and I am really desperate.'

'You know I'd help if I could, but your father needs his peace and quiet after a day at the shipyard. We're not as young as we used to be, and your father certainly wouldn't be happy if he had to pack up his trainset in that room. It's set up on the floor. And I use that room for my sewing.'

'Is Dad's bloody trainset more important than your family's safety?'

'What's Liam doing about it? What's he got to say? It's his job to provide for you. He is your husband after all.'

'He's out at work all day he doesn't know what it's like and he's not taking these threats seriously.'

'Well maybe you're overreacting. You could be suffering from post-natal depression. They mentioned it on *Woman's*

Hour the other day. Said it's a nasty illness. Have you seen the doctor? He might be able to give you something for it, something to calm your nerves. You always were a worrier. Thought you would have grown out of it by now.'

'There's nothing wrong with me. I don't need a doctor.' She tried to stay calm, but her mum was beyond irritating. 'It's okay for you, you're safe here.'

Is it going to take a death before people realise the danger we're in?
If my own mum won't help, I'll have to do something drastic.

'You made your bed, love, you've got to cut your cloth accordingly I'm afraid. You kids, your generation want it all. Look at me and your father, we've had to struggle to get what we have.'

She started crying again. This was supposed to be her last resort, she'd hoped her mum would offer a bed, even just for a few weeks to get them out of imminent danger. 'I've even thought of splitting the family.'

'Why on earth would you do that?'

'I was hoping I could come here.'

'Huh, last thing we need is screaming kids.'

'Perhaps it's best I give the baby up for adoption. Everyone thinks the baby is the problem.'

'Well,' she paused, 'if you hadn't had the baby, there would be more options. How long has all this been going on?'

'About three years.'

'If it's been going on that long, why have another baby? That's just bad planning.'

She said nothing.

'Well then, you've only got yourself to blame, I would have thought it was bad enough coping with four kids, but you've added to the problems.'

'Everyone has a big family, we're not any different.'

'You'll just have to go and investigate other options. Knock on a few more doors.'

'Don't you think I already have?' Irritation simmered inside her.

'Maybe talk to Auntie Maud. She's got a big house.'

'Oh God, no way, not that old trout. She's the last person I'd ask. Can you imagine it and why would you even think of her? She wouldn't cope with all the noise. How can you tell a five-year-old to stop? And her precious roses, her plant pots if they break them.'

'At least you'd be safe. I thought that's what you wanted. Beggars can't be choosers.'

She had to leave. If she stayed here any longer, a falling-out was inevitable. There were no more words to win her over. Her mum couldn't see the danger they were in.

She trudged back up the hill, her heart quietly shattering.

If I can't get my own family on board, if I can't look after my own baby and guarantee her a safe future, I'm going to have to make some hard choices.

On the way home, on a whim she popped into the newsagents and grabbed a copy of the newspaper. Perching on a nearby wall, with shaking hands and a horrible sickness swirling in her stomach, she scanned the back page for the phone number for the editorial team. Then she went to the nearest phone box, yanked open the door and dialled the number while Maeve waited outside with the pram.

The gravity of her plan shocked her to the core, horrifying her so much that she had to pinch herself to check she wasn't stuck in a dreadful nightmare.

CHAPTER 15

Colin 'Where are you off too?' Gran asked Colin, a knowing grin on her face.

'It's Wednesday, Gran, I'm going to work, like I do every Wednesday.' He finished the last mouthful of his cornflakes and wiped his mouth.

Gran took her time grinding the butt of her cigarette into the ashtray as she peered at him. She was a wise old bird, and little escaped her.

She sniffed the air like a bloodhound. 'I've noticed you always wear aftershave on a Wednesday. That horrible cheap stuff from down the market. And you always look smart as if you've made a special effort.'

'And what do you notice about me on a Thursday, or a Friday and let's not forget Monday and Tuesday too. Are you spying on me?'

She smirked then winked at Kathleen who was sitting beside him munching on toast. 'He scrubs up well, doesn't he, child?'

'Can't say I've noticed.' She turned to stare out of the window.

The girl was constantly lost in her dreams, noticing him would be wishful thinking. The sooner she was gone, the better.

'You got a woman?'

'Don't be stupid, Gran, who would fancy me?'

'They might not, but some women are desperate.' She opened her mouth and laughed, revealing her decayed teeth, an unwelcome sight at breakfast.

After his initial doubts about continuing with Lady Eleanor, Colin had started to look forward to Wednesdays. She satisfied his urges. He wasn't getting it anywhere else and wasn't going to turn her down. He had to admit she was rather good in bed and knew exactly what she was doing. He cringed at the thought of her and her husband. When he was with her, the world disappeared, spiralled down to nothing except his lust and her need. And the chores she asked of him were easy enough.

Approaching the house, he felt a pang of desire, his groin stirring to life. She always made sure that nobody was about when he called round and today was the same. She greeted him at the back door, a playful glint in her eye as she took his hand, gently squeezing it and ushering him through the hall and upstairs to her boudoir. She had a fine taste in lingerie, it was getting more adventurous, and he was getting adept at taking it off and sometimes he didn't need to take it off at all. They hurriedly undressed and tumbled onto the bed, laughing at their shamelessness.

Afterwards she invited him to join her in the main kitchen for coffee. He gasped at the grandeur. Elegant crystal lighting cast pretty patterns across the emerald-green cupboards, and marble worktops. The floor was covered in a lino of geometric designs which matched the colour of the cupboards. The thought of living in a mansion existed only in his wildest fantasies. It was another world.

'Take a pew,' she said, pulling a stool from under the island in the middle of the room before going to fill the kettle.

He sat down and glanced at the headlines of the local newspaper lying in front of him. He pulled it towards him and read the story.

'You okay?' she asked, holding two steaming mugs of coffee. 'You look like you've just seen a ghost.'

She put the mugs down and leaned over to see what he was reading. She tapped the picture of Janie Lee beaming out. 'Of course, you visit the laundry, have you seen the famous actress up there? Isn't she beautiful?' She gazed at the picture for a few moments.

'No, can't say I have.'

'A girl's also escaped, there's a small picture of her down the bottom there.' She indicated to the grainy photo of Kathleen which looked like a prison mugshot. 'It says if anyone's seen her to contact the Gardaí. I wonder if there's a reward.'

She glanced at him. 'You know something, don't you?' Her eyes were bright and there was an excited tone to her voice. 'I can see it in your demeanour and you've gone pale. One minute you look ashen, then at the mention of a reward, your eyes light up.' She laughed. 'So, come on then,' she coaxed, 'spill the beans. Has she been sharing your bed, keeping you warm at night?' She winked and nudged him.

'No, it's nothing like that.' It didn't seem to bother Eleanor if he had.

'Ah, so you do know her?'

He hesitated, tempted by the relief he knew he'd feel once he'd unburdened the secret. 'Yes, but you've got to keep it to yourself.' He was going to regret this. The sooner he could get rid of the girl, the better. She was becoming a liability.

'It depends, what's in it for me?' She gave another of her playful smiles.

He ignored the question. 'I found her wandering the lanes, I didn't help her to escape before you start accusing me.'

'I was only teasing. Actually, I think it's rather sweet, the idea of you rescuing a poor damsel in distress.'

'That may be, but I've now got a problem on my hands, she can't stay with me.' He looked up at her, an idea forming.

She read his mind. 'Oh no.' She shook her head and looked alarmed. 'She definitely can't come here.'

'Oh please,' he pleaded. 'She's good at cleaning and cooking and won't give you any bother. And you wouldn't even have to pay her.'

She scoffed. 'Colin.' She huffed in a haughty manner. 'Paying the girl is the least of my problems. Do I look like I'd struggle to keep a maid?'

'What am I going to do with her? She can't go home to her family and she has nobody else.'

'She should have kept her legs closed, we all have to learn the hard way,' she said primly.

'You sound like you speak from experience.'

'I'm not saying anything.' She flapped her hands then picked up her mug and took a sip of coffee. They were quiet for a few minutes. 'I do have an idea though. One that might work.'

He was all ears, intrigued. So, this woman could be of use beyond the bedroom.

She looked at him. 'If I were to help you, you would be forever indebted to me, and my price does not come cheap.' She winked at him. 'The juices of my mind are working, but other juices are flowing too so you'd better not disappoint. Make sure you clear your diary, so I'm satisfied, in every way.'

Somehow she had a hold over him, one he could not turn away from and the more demanding she became, the more it turned him on. His groin was starting to feel warm again.

CHAPTER 16

*K*athleen

It was a cold, crisp morning with frost-laden trees all around. Kathleen hadn't been out in days. Every time she mentioned going for a walk, Gran would quickly come up with excuses to stop her. She knew it was because of the business with Wayne and couldn't imagine her motivation was to keep Kathleen safe from him, more likely she was protecting her own interests and reputation.

Gran was asleep in bed and not feeling well, so Kathleen slipped out, closely the door quietly behind her. She stepped into the cold bite of the morning and rubbed her hands against the chill, watching the misty cloud of her breath as she sighed up at the glorious sun in a faultlessly blue sky the colour of denim. These days were halcyon, the best, and made her think how wonderfully beautiful Ireland was. She circuited the caravans, her long shadow streaking the white grass, already thawing in patches.

She headed for the pathway that skirted the woods. The sun was flickering through the branches and creating sparkles on the frozen ground. She marched on; it was good exercise walking up the hill. At the top, she saw the church down in the valley peeking over the treetops like a prying neighbour.

While making her way down the hill, she noticed a figure leaning against the gate, gazing at the scenery. Dressed in a stylish maroon fur coat and matching boots, the woman seemed out of place and too glamorous to be standing in a field. She was groomed to within an inch of her life.

'Morning,' Kathleen said brightly.

The woman turned, startled. 'Oh gosh, you took me by surprise, it's so quiet and peaceful out here, I wasn't expecting to see anyone.'

'You sound American.' Kathleen was sure she recognised her from somewhere, so much so that it was uncanny.

'Yes, is it obvious?'

She laughed. 'Of course.' She saw the gleam of her perfect white teeth between her parted lips.

'What a beautiful view and a beautiful morning, makes you glad to be alive, doesn't it?' But more beautiful than the view Kathleen thought, was this woman. *Where have I seen her before?*

Her cheeks were fresh peach, and her hair gleamed in the sun. But there was something about her eyes. They looked haunted, strained with either tiredness or stress. She sensed that tension hovered just below the surface. Kathleen found herself wanting to know about her life.

'Why do I recognise you?' she asked.

'I'm an actress, you've probably seen me in films, and now my picture's all over your papers because I'm here on a visit.'

'Oh wow,' Kathleen said. 'I can't believe I've met an actress and, in a field full of sheep.' She laughed. 'I wasn't expecting that. Are you a famous actress?'

'I'm Janie Lee, I guess you could say I'm famous.' She gave a shy laugh.

'Oh, my goodness.' Kathleen clamped her hand to her mouth and felt herself blush. 'If I'd known I was going to meet a famous actress in a field I would have bought pen and paper for your autograph.' It was her turn to laugh. 'But it doesn't matter.' She giggled, feeling childish and silly. 'What brings you to Ireland?'

'My husband and I are looking to adopt a baby.'

Kathleen's heart skipped a beat. 'Where from?' She fixed her gaze on the church, no longer wanting to look at this famous woman who was about to cause untold anguish to one of her friends.

'One of the Magdalene laundries. The Weeping Lady.'

She felt the blood drain from her, suddenly feeling sick as she mumbled her next question. She didn't want to have to think about the next poor girl forcibly separated from her baby. 'Is there a mother, have you met her?' She shuddered.

'There was a mother, we were collecting the baby back in September, but she lost it, so we're sticking around until another is born. It's easier for me to take digs than return to the U.S. It just means my filming is on hold for the time being. Bit of a pain.' She shrugged. 'This means more to me. I'll wait forever if I have to.'

Christ Almighty, maybe she was going to take my baby.

'I must get on, nice talking to you,' she said curtly.

'Wait, I can give you my autograph,' she said fumbling in her bag.

'It's okay, it doesn't matter.'

She gave a strange look and Kathleen guessed that being turned down was a first for her.

'You look pale,' Janie said, looking at her in a curious way. 'I'd get something to eat if I was you, something warm inside you.'

Kathleen turned away and headed back up the hill feeling numb and didn't look back.

CHAPTER 17

Janie Lee

Janie Lee asked the taxi driver to drop her at the end of the driveway so that she could savour the tranquil views as she walked up to the house. It was an obscenely beautiful crisp day; the sun was dappling through the trees lining the avenue, but a cold breeze buffeted her face, whipping strands of hair across her cheeks.

She was enjoying her stay in the Emerald Isle. This unexpected time out from her demanding acting commitments was much-needed respite. But they'd come here for a purpose, to find a baby and now that she was here, she was determined not to return home empty-handed. It was disheartening though, just when they were on the brink of realising their dream of becoming parents, there was another setback. The baby they were anticipating had died.

She was meeting with the Mother Superior this morning to explore her options and discuss delivery schedules for other babies. Reaching the brow of the hill, she stopped to sit down on a bench and looked down towards the house conjuring images of life within those walls. She found herself slightly envious of the girls. The fun and laughter those girls must have during their confinement, a shared experience and welcome escape from their overbearing parents who'd sent them here. Most, she believed, were from poor and oppressive homes, otherwise cold and hungry, they were probably glad of a good meal, the love and support of caring nuns and a warm bath. There was something idyllic and romantic about this set-up. It reminded her of boarding school––midnight feasts, sharing a dormitory, secret friendships and flirting with the gardener. Not that she'd been to one herself, they were a typically British experience. But she had watched the TV series, *St Trinian's* in her hotel room, about a boarding school for wayward girls run by an eccentric headmistress. She wondered if the girls here played pranks on the nuns and what their reaction would be.

She rose from the bench and continued the short walk to the house, pausing to check her lipstick in the big brass knocker before giving it a hard rap. There was some sort of commotion going on inside, she could hear raised voices, then shouting and wondered what was going on, but then the door was opened by a stern-looking nun wearing a loose habit to her feet, a white wimple covered with a black veil that fell over her shoulders.

'Enter,' she said robotically and without a smile or pleasantries before turning and pointing to a row of wooden chairs lined against the wall. 'Wait there, please.'

As she turned tail the rosary beads, adorned with a metal cross dangled from a thick leather belt swayed gently. She strode off down the corridor, the heels of her sturdy black men's shoes clipping on the floor and her skirts swishing like curtains. Janie imagined those revered cloaked women coming together for evening prayer, a line of sombre silhouettes resembling black sacks.

As she waited, she looked around her. The cream walls were decorated with images of the Virgin Mary and there was a table with leaflets on it, a figurine of a saint and a vase of dusty silk flowers. The floor smelled of fresh wax, and where the sunlight streamed in through the stairway window, it illuminated patches of gleaming wood.

Just then, a door opened, and the Mother Superior appeared. She was a rotund, tall woman with a rope around her middle which would have been most unbecoming if she'd been wearing a dress. Janie's heart jolted in her chest. This woman was nothing like the person she'd imagined but her husband had said very little about his initial visit. Janie noticed a presence about her, a formidable figure of authority and immediately knew that she was somebody you didn't challenge or mess with. This stood in complete contrast to the woman she'd imagined--gentle, kindly, and meek.

She was invited into her office and offered a chair. As Mother Superior pulled out a sizeable book from a drawer and laid it open on her desk, scanning it first before putting on a pair of small wire-framed glasses that made her eyes look twice the size. Janie attempted small talk with a comment on the weather, only to be met with frosty silence.

'There's a slight problem, two of our babies died during childbirth.' She kept her head down as she looked at the writing in the book.

'Oh, I am sorry.'

She glanced up and gave her a look of cold businesslike indifference before moving swiftly on. 'I need to discuss this with the nuns who work in the baby unit.'

It shocked Janie that two babies had died in such a short space of time, and she wondered what the birthing facilities and care were like.

'There are a couple of babies who are ready to be released. They're fully weaned and thriving. If you can wait in the corridor for ten minutes, I need to speak with the nuns who work in the baby unit.'

Janie followed her into the corridor and, without being

offered tea or coffee, she sat on the wooden chair and watched the nun disappear upstairs. She opened her handbag, taking out a small vanity mirror, and was just checking her makeup when she heard the piercing scream of a woman's voice coming from somewhere along the corridor.

Without thinking, she quickly got up and tiptoed along the corridor to find out what was going on. She came to a dark recessed area where coats were hung and slipped into the shadowy corner, melting into the darkness so that she could observe what was going on.

A woman was on her knees in the corridor and two nuns were standing over her. Janie couldn't work out what she was doing and wondered if she was praying. It appeared that a bowl of food had been overturned. A tray lay nearby, as if it had been accidentally knocked over. A nun was pushing the woman down and forcing her to eat the food from the floor like a dog. Janie stifled a gasp; she'd never ever seen anything like it. The poor woman was crying and trying to eat it, but she kept falling forward, causing the food to end up in her hair and eyebrows. The nun who pushed her down kept shouting in a thick Irish brogue, 'eat that, now eat it.'

She backed up, feeling her way along the line of coats, trying to stay out of view and peering into the gloom. She noticed a further corridor that shot off into another part of the building. Mother Superior had made it sound as if she would be a while, so there was time to explore. There was a humming noise coming from somewhere. The corridor was covered in chequered lino and she crept towards a door at the far end. She could hear swishing machine sounds.

Being naturally nosey, she pushed open the door and her eyes were met with the stares of about thirty others. It was a steam-filled room full of almost corpse women and they were dressed in the same outfit, a grey dress and cardigan and they all had the same short, bobbed hair. Some had a clip in it, a few had shaved heads. They were all ages. Some were elderly but every one of them was thin and malnourished. They stared at her, open-mouthed and frowning and not one spoke, not even to say hello. Their sleeves were rolled up and Janie noticed their red chapped hands.

Had she stumbled across the laundry? All she could see were sad grey women washing and scrubbing and nobody talking. There were all sorts of pulley systems and ropes crisscrossing the ceiling. Tubs and buckets and vats and baskets were hanging. Washing machines rattled against the walls. It was so hot, it was stifling.

Hearing the voice of a nun, she quickly pulled the door towards her so that it was still ajar, and she was able to peer in while staying out of view. The nun was roaring at a painfully thin elderly woman whose skin clung to her bones. She looked like the walking dead and Janie noticed she was toothless. She watched as the nun raised a hand and whacked the old lady hard. She was horrified. What kind of a place was this where nuns were angry and mothers and elderly women were hit? The reality of this place contrasted starkly with the idyllic image she'd had in her mind.

She quickly retraced her steps and heading back to where she was supposed to be sitting then paused and peered up the staircase to where the Mother Superior had disappeared. She thought it strange not to be invited into the baby unit. Surely, they wanted their clients to be more involved. She would be very disappointed if she was offered a baby without being able to choose. After all, they *were* making a substantial donation. These orphanages and homes had more babies in their care than they could cope with, that's what she'd been led to believe, and were only too happy to have fewer mouths to feed.

There was a white stone saint standing in a niche built for it at the bottom of the stairs and another at the top. Checking that nobody was around, she padded up and ahead of her saw a dormitory with beds lined up against the wall. Beside each bed was a small wooden locker. Next to the dormitory was a bathroom where basins stood on wooden plinths in rows and there were several old Victorian baths. It all looked so sterile and soulless and reminded her of a hospital. She glanced round. There didn't seem to be any privacy for these women. They bathed and dressed in full view of everyone. She shuddered, hating that idea. But it was a temporary way of life, not the nicest of places and certainly not the one she'd imagined in her head. She reminded herself these women would soon return to their old lives, their families would welcome them back with open arms as if nothing had happened, the memory of those babies they'd delivered now behind them.

What a convenient and ingenious little scheme they're running.

Janie headed downstairs and returned to her chair just before the Mother Superior reappeared.

'Right,' she said with efficiency. 'If you'd like to follow me, I'll take you up to the baby unit.'

She was led up the stairs and along the corridor to a room at the end. She could hear babies crying. She followed Mother Superior and was shocked by the icy and unwelcoming feel of the room. She glanced around, stunned. She had anticipated pastel walls decorated with cheerful nursery rhyme posters and shelves brimming with baby toys. The room reminded her of a ward in a Victorian hospital long overdue for refurbishment. Tired-looking iron cots were crammed along both walls. A few mothers, dressed in drab grey frocks, cradled their infants on the bare floorboards feeding them with a look of exhaustion and malnourishment etched on their faces. Not a single mother glanced up with a smile or greeting. Instead, she observed a couple of them scowling and holding their babies closer in suspicion and turning away from her.

Janie was horrified by the number of babies and wondered how many women came here.

'How many women do you have?' she asked.

'We take them from all over Ireland. There will always be girls who get into trouble.' She broke off and marched over to one of the women. Janie was shocked by her brutal manner as she watched her yank the woman by her arm, forcing her to get up. 'Time you went back to other duties, you've had long enough in here.'

After the woman had returned her child to its cot, she padded to the door in bare feet. Mother Superior turned to Janie with a bewildered look on her face. 'They'd spend all day lazing around here if they could, there's work to be done.'

'Yes, I saw a woman cleaning the floor downstairs. Don't you have any modern gadgets instead of having them scrub on their hands and knees? They'll end up with housemaid's knee and bad backs.'

'As we are a charity, money is very tight, and we desperately need donations to improve the situation for everybody. We try to instil a work culture among everybody here, it may seem harsh, but they need to learn, and nothing in life is free. Hard work never hurt anyone as I'm sure you will agree.'

As Janie looked around, trying to grasp how this institution operated and the ethos behind it, Mother Superior coaxed her, 'Come on then, don't be afraid, the babies don't bite, take a look.' She gestured towards the row of cots near the window.

Janie peered at each baby. They were dressed identically in long white gowns and each cot had a numbered tag attached to it. Hovering over one cot, she took a step back in horror, taking an instant dislike to one of the babies because it was ugly with a thick mop of jet-black hair and a furrowed brow. She immediately thought of her uncle. The next had a scalp of flaky cradle cap and another reminded her of a worm the way it wriggled on the sheet.

She was shocked to see a black baby. It stood out it in the bland whiteness of the room.

'That one will be the hardest to place,' Mother Superior said. 'You can take it as well if that would work. Two for the price of one.' She chuckled. 'Could be nice company for your child and useful for jobs around the house when it's older.'

Janie thought how beautiful it was. Its face was perfectly formed, its hair was curly and it had gleaming ebony skin and wide brown eyes that smiled up at her. It was older than the others. But there was no way she was going to adopt a black child, and her husband and family would be horrified, so she quickly moved on to the next cot.

There was a frail-looking baby in the next cot, its tiny body twitching restlessly as it turned its head from side to side. Leaning closer, she noticed a birthmark on its forehead which contrasted against its pale skin.

'That should be easy to remove, when its older,' she mused envisioning a skilled surgeon expertly correcting it.

The nun looked alarmed. 'No, you might remove the mark, but once Satin's child, always Satin's child.'

The nun scoffed and Janie shivered then laughed. 'Surely you don't believe that twaddle.'

'Well, you've been warned. Take the child at your peril.'

She moved on and as she peered at each face, she didn't know how she was supposed to feel or if she was supposed to feel anything. Was she being too harsh with herself, expecting a rush of unconditional love? The sight of these innocent, vulnerable babies should have triggered a primal instinct and encouraged an emotional connection and desire to love. Perhaps she felt this way because the babies weren't dressed in pretty clothes. There was a blandness, it was like looking at a row of carrots in a greengrocer. Nothing jumped out at her. The babies weren't selling themselves to her. The nuns had a lot to learn about presentation. If they'd been dressed in pretty clothes with gorgeous bedding, she might have felt so differently. But this wasn't Macy's nursery department. She'd had such different visions of this place, but it wasn't this. There should have been a buzz of excitement, coming into the world, not this stark whiteness. This was like a car production line. She remembered the famous quote of Henry Ford's in his autobiography, when he referred to the Model T. "Any color the customer wants, as long as it's black."

'How do I know my baby will come from a good family? I don't want a child that comes from simple parents or the rough end of town.'

'There are no guarantees.'

'And I want a girl.'

'Well, I'm afraid you'll have to wait if you want a girl. The girls we have are still very small and need at least two months longer so that they're bigger and stronger. You wouldn't want me to hand you a little scrap, now, would you? Not with the money you're donating.'

'I don't want to wait.'

'I can reserve it for you, come and have a look at the babies that are ready to go, see which you like.'

'You must get attached. Must be hard to let them go.'

'Don't have time for that, the sooner they're gone the better,' she said primly and without feeling. 'There will always be another to take its place. I have two babies available, both are boys.'

'But I *want* a girl,' she insisted. The sense of disappointment was beginning to overwhelm her. She'd put her career on hold, flown miles, lodged in hotels for weeks, only to end up with a boy, this wasn't the plan.

'As I said, you'll just have to wait, none are old enough yet. If I had my way you could have the lot, they're nothing but trouble and cost us a fortune.'

Just then, a young woman entered the room, dressed in the same drab grey linens. She looked excited, as if visiting the nursery was the highlight of her day, and was breathless from running up the stairs, but when she saw Janie, her eyes widened in terror. She hurried over to the cots, scanning each, a sense of desperation on her face before identifying her child and then there was a look of relief. She picked up the ugly one with the mop of black hair, clutching it tight to her chest protectively as if it might be grabbed from her arms at any moment. The woman's panic over the imminent loss of her baby was glaringly evident, but she needn't have worried, Janie had no intention of taking that one.

'Slow down, Theresa, over here, please,' Mother Superior commanded in a sharp tone with a gesture of her finger and a mocking expression on her face. 'Allow this nice lady to hold the baby, she's here to choose one.'

The woman was reluctant to pass her baby to Janie until Mother Superior raised her voice and insisted.

Janie held the baby for a few moments, all the while conscious of its mother within close range like a fierce lioness guarding her cub.

Back in the office downstairs, Janie said to Mother Superior, 'That girl looked like she wanted to keep her baby. She was very defensive when I held her child.'

Mother Superior scoffed at the suggestion. 'I've no doubt they'd all like to keep their offspring, but we don't always get what we want in life, do we?' She peered at her, and Janie wondered if this was a hint that she shouldn't be adamant about wanting a girl.

'There are lots of respectable families like yourselves, lining up to take the children. They will be far better off with them. Those girls deserve what's happened to them, they sinned. They'll never make anything of themselves if they keep the baby. No man will ever marry them, and they'd have to resign themselves to never having a family.'

'I suppose you're right, it's for the best.'

The girls' plight was of no concern of hers, this was a business transaction, she couldn't allow herself to feel sorry for these girls. Mother Superior seemed as if she had their best interests at heart even though at times she came across as harsh. Her sole focus now was to find a pretty little baby girl and return to America. The film director and her manager were growing impatient and calling every day to ask when she was coming back. She'd signed a contract and if she stayed over here much longer, she'd end up breaking deadlines and commitments. There was no way she wanted to jeopardise her career, but her desire for a little girl was so intense. Was she prepared to wait, or were there other options? She was sure there were other homes to contact. She wouldn't be rushed quite yet.

CHAPTER 18

Kathleen

Kathleen cradled her mug of tea, watching the steam rise into the chilly air. She'd packed up the few belongings she had, including the dresses she'd acquired, and her bags were now waiting by Colin's van. He'd told her to be up and ready early and not to tell Gran she was leaving.

Dawn was peeking over the horizon, orange tendrils tinting the dark. A delicate blanket of frost draped the world. Kathleen often rose at dawn, time alone she welcomed and looked forward to. This was the chilliest dawn she'd experienced during her stay in the caravan and soon, as the sun rose higher, the trees would shimmer casting a sparkling light like scattered diamonds over every blade of grass and every branch of tree.

Even with the hardships of life here––Gran's endless demands, and Colin's treatment of her––she would miss the peace and beauty of the countryside. What a contrast it was to the hustle and bustle of Liverpool, a city that held no place in her heart particularly after the traumatic events that night when she'd endured the unfathomable horror of being assaulted by the priest. Perhaps rural life was where she belonged even with

Wayne creeping around her. As her grandma used to say, better the devil you know than the devil you don't. She could do a whole lot worse. But she hadn't been given a choice, she was on the move again.

She heard the caravan door click, the slightest of noise so not to wake Gran, and then Colin emerged from around the corner, his breath a misty cloud as he strolled towards her. She had no idea where he was taking her, he'd kept the plan a secret, only telling her that arrangements had been made.

She gulped the rest of her coffee and wandered over to his van, her stomach churning. What if he was taking her back to the laundry, would he be that cruel? Many times he'd threatened to do just that. Or what if he was putting her on a ferry back to Liverpool? Gran had often said that she should go home to her mam. "No matter what mischief you're guilty of, child, remember that a mother's love always comes with forgiveness."

Deep down, she felt her mother's forgiveness was out of reach. She recalled a quote, *to forgive is to set a prisoner free*. She'd always be that prisoner because home would never welcome her back. A captive of the outside world, she roamed with a caged heart, and this was how it would always be.

They set off across the field, the headlights of Colin's van twin golden orbs cutting into the darkness. Kathleen glanced round to look at the caravan site one last time, with a strange mixture of relief and nostalgia, but it was steeped in darkness. As they bumped and lurched on the dirt road before joining the lane, she braced herself before asking him where he was taking her.

'One of my clients has a brother who owns a hotel in Wales. They need a maid.'

'Really?' She couldn't quite believe her luck. This *was* a surprise.

'I've not been there myself, but my client says it's beautiful. It's an old, converted castle with grounds and a lake.'

'Oh my God.' She couldn't contain her excitement as tears filled her eyes. Despite his harsh behaviour towards her, he had a kinder side, he meant well even if it didn't always show.

'Work hard, and do not let them down, as it will reflect poorly on me.'

'Course I will.' This was her chance to shine. Then her heart sank as a sudden thought struck. 'Will I be paid?'

'It's a job, of course you'll be paid.' He threw her a look. 'What did you expect, to work for nothing?' He laughed. 'And you'll have board and lodgings.'

She wanted to remind him that was all she was used to, being a skivvy, expecting nothing more, but she stayed quiet, not wanting to jeopardise this new opportunity he'd secured for her.

'So, what else can you tell me about it?' She wanted to know everything, where she'd be sleeping, if she'd have days off.

'How should I know? I've got you a job, and with a roof over your head. Now just shut up and be grateful and let me drive. I'm not a morning person, I don't like talking. Won't be long before we're in Rosslare where you'll take the boat to Fishguard. Someone will meet you at Fishguard and drive you to North Wales.' And with that, he turned the radio on and 'When Will I See You' Again by The Three Degrees blared out and seemed strangely poignant.

At the ferry terminal, Colin cut the engine. 'Well, here you are, kiddo, good luck.' As he turned to her, handing her a ticket for her passage across the Irish Sea, his smile radiated the most warmth she had ever witnessed from him, and she was taken aback and felt strangely emotional. 'Just remember, girl what I've done for you, I'm not the heartless git you think I am.' He took her bags out of the back and there was an awkward moment as they said goodbye. Suddenly her guard was down, and she flung herself at him. 'Thank you so much and thank your gran too. I don't know what I would have done without your help.' She wiped a tear from her cheek.

He pulled away, held her shoulders with his hands and grinned. 'I know my gran can be an old dragon and I'm a bit of a cantankerous old sod, but it's been nice having you around. I'll miss you, kiddo.' She had the sense that he was struggling with his last words, they weren't said with ease, but she appreciated them all the same. Her time in the caravan hadn't been all bad.

He didn't linger to wave her off and when she glanced back, he'd already gone.

Once the boat was in motion, Kathleen stood on the deck watching the land she was leaving behind before turning her gaze out across the serene sea. Just like the seagulls soaring above, their cries echoing through the air, she felt a sense of freedom. There was something dreamlike about the space that straddled sea and land, like a mystery unfolding, a sense of anticipation, travelling to a new start. But she also felt a bit scared, her stomach was knotting, and she had no idea what it would be like at the hotel. What if she disappointed them and if they ended up sacking her, where would she go? She felt an inner determination to succeed.

It wasn't long before land came into view, the gentle undulation of the green cliffs looking so untouched. In her dreamy state, she imagined pitching a tent on the unspoilt beauty of those cliffs, living out her days alone without a single soul to bother her.

As she stepped off the ferry, her gaze trailed over the line of people waiting at the rails. A few taxi drivers were holding name boards, but her name wasn't on any of them. She stood in the middle of the throng. People were barging past and were greeted by loved ones with welcoming hugs. An old man not looking where he was going knocked into her but didn't apologise. Everybody seemed to know where they were going, nobody else looked lost. As the crowd slowly dispersed, there was still no sign of her driver.

Alone at the docks and aware she had no money, no contact number for the hotel––she didn't even know the name of it or where it was––panic washed over her and doubt crept in. What if Colin had deceived her? What if this was just a way to get rid of her? Maybe even Gran was involved. What if there was no job waiting?

What a fool I've been, getting all excited, building my hopes, it was too good to be true.

What now?

She stepped outside, glancing around, checking if anyone was just arriving before dashing back into the terminal. She remembered her mum telling her to stay put if they got separated while shopping, and she would come back to her. She plonked herself on a bench and watched as the last passengers left the terminal, trying to stay positive, thinking there must be a legitimate reason for being held up. But when the hands of the clock showed she'd been waiting for a whole hour, she got up in a panic and went over to a member of staff.

'When's the next ferry due in?'

'Not until this evening, lass. There are only two a day. Are you waiting for someone?'

'I was supposed to be picked up, but they haven't turned up.'

'There's a phone box outside.'

'I don't have a phone number or any money.'

He frowned. 'Don't worry, come into my office, I'm sure we can help. The operator will get you the phone or I've got the phone book for the local area.'

'No, you don't understand.' Suddenly she was shaking, and tears rolled down her face. She wiped her cheeks with the back of her hand as she struggled to explain her predicament. 'I was supposed to be going to work at a hotel in Wales somewhere but that's all I know, and I don't have any money. All I can do is wait here. Maybe they think I'm coming on the evening ferry.'

He rubbed his chin and looked doubtful. 'It's a long wait, lass. I expect you're hungry. Come into my office, it's warm in there. My colleague, Lenny, will make you a pot of tea and toast.'

The man held the door open and called to Lenny, an overweight man in his fifties wearing a tight t-shirt emblazoned with the company logo. 'Fix this lass up with tea and toast, will you? She's got a long wait till the next ferry.'

The man went back to his duties.

Lenny eyed her up and down before taking a sip from his tea, a half-eaten sausage sandwich lying on top of a paper wrapper on his desk.

'Morning, darling. What's a pretty girl like you doing all on her own?' he asked in a gruff voice before wiping the corners of his mouth to remove blobs of ketchup.

The office was warm and cosy after the draughty terminal building, and she tried to ignore the calendar on the wall that showed a topless woman lying in a field of buttercups.

'I was expecting a lift to my new job, but my employer hasn't turned up.'

'Here's a phone.' He picked up the receiver and passed it to her. 'Be my guest.'

He took another bite, chewing it slowly as he continued to eye her up.

'I don't have a phone number and I'm not sure where the job is. I don't have any money either.'

He leaned back in his seat, peering at her as if she were an oddity, his t-shirt riding up around his waistline, exposing some of his bulging belly. *Too many sausage sandwiches*, Kathleen thought to herself.

He laughed. 'You can't be that daft, coming all this way with no money and you must know where you'll be working. You look an intelligent lass.' Suddenly he looked suspicious, a lightbulb moment sparked in his eyes and her heart sank. She'd been rumbled.

'You've escaped, I wasn't born yesterday.'

Her heart was pounding, and she stepped towards the door, instinct telling her to bolt before he called the police.

'You're one of them girls.'

'I don't know what you're talking about,' she said, her face flushing. 'My friend Colin sent me over here.'

He chuckled. 'Don't worry.' He tapped the side of his nose. 'Your secret's safe with me. I could help you,' he said, brushing crumbs from his clothes. 'But what would be in it for me? I'd be taking a big risk helping a Magdalene.' She watched his eyes move up and down her again and she took a deep breath, trying to stay calm in the presence of this grotesque man.

'I'll be clocking off soon. I could help you,' he went on, his eyes lingering on her chest area even though it was wrapped beneath a coat. 'But I'd need something in return.'

'I don't need your help and I think I'll wait outside.' As she reached for the door handle, her stomach growled. Remembering the promised tea and toast, she decided she'd rather go cold and hungry.

Kathleen glanced back. The creep was watching her from the office window, a smirk on his face. He sent shivers down her spine, she had to get away from here, but where to go, she hadn't a clue.

With the excitement of landing a job fading, a pressing question now consumed her; how was she going to survive?

CHAPTER 19

Kathleen

As Kathleen sat on the bench in the cold and windy terminal, her head bent as she stared at the ground trying to reassure herself there'd been a mix-up and the hotel's representative would soon be along, she heard Lenny come out of his office and lock the door behind him. She looked up, worried. His shift had ended, but she was adamant she wouldn't be taking a lift from him.

There had been people milling about, but the terminal forecourt was now empty. He strode over to her, his hulking body closing the space between them and leaning down grabbed her arm and yanked her up.

'You're coming with me.'

'Get off me.' Terrified, she tried to free herself, but he was a strong man, and his grip was tight.

Just then, a woman swept into the terminal, her heels echoing around the concourse as she clipped towards the bench.

'Are you Kathleen?'

Lenny released his grip and stared at the woman, a disgruntled look on his face.

'Yes,' she said with relief, turning to pick up her bags.

'I'm so sorry I'm late, I got the wrong time.' Flustered, she reached over and took one of Kathleen's bags. 'Is this all you've got, a couple of bin liners?' She looked surprised.

'Yes.'

As they headed out of the terminal, Kathleen turned to see Lenny glaring in fury. The relief of getting away from him was huge. She hurried to keep up with the woman as she strode across the road to the carpark, and she called over her shoulder, introducing herself as Margot. She had a posh accent, like the Queen. Kathleen guessed that Margot was probably in her fifties. Her hair was dark and gleaming and shaped like a pudding basin, not a hair out of place. She knew how to dress, looking immaculate in a perfect-fitting rust suede coat cinched at the waist, and a Paisley scarf around her neck, adorned with a floral brooch pinned to the lapel. As she bent to unlock her rather nice pristine white Triumph Stag, a collection of bangles around her wrist jangled. Kathleen's heart soared. Her luck had turned. And she'd managed to dodge a bullet with the creep. She shuddered to think what could have happened had Margot not arrived at that moment.

Margot filled the silence with chatter about how she and her husband, Arthur had inherited a Welsh castle from an old uncle and turned it into a luxury hotel. It had taken ten years to renovate. Kathleen found it interesting to begin with, but the longer the conversation dragged on, she grew bored. Why she needed to know all about the planning applications and the dredging of the lake, the felling of the trees in the wood and the antics of the builders, she didn't know. It was a long journey and soon she found herself staring ahead, her eyelids drooping, and then she fell asleep.

'My dear.' Margot tapped her on the knee. 'You can sleep when you get there. You don't need to start work till Monday.'

'Sorry, I've been up since the crack of dawn.'

'I'm glad you're used to early mornings. You'll be up at five, to prepare breakfast and complete your kitchen duties. As I was just saying--until I realised you were asleep--we have very exclusive guests, staff must be always on their best behaviour and neat and presentable. Bert, the staff manager, will sort out your uniform.'

Her long manicured fingers played piano keys on the steering wheel while they waited at traffic lights. Kathleen wanted to comment on her gorgeous nails but was afraid of being told not to wear polish at work.

'Do you have any interests?'

'I like to sing.' She'd sung around the campfires at the caravan site.

'It's always good to know about other skills staff have.'

She hoped she wouldn't be roped into singing. It was one thing to sing in the church choir or round a campfire, but quite another to be expected to perform in front of the well-to-do.

It was a long journey and eventually the car slowed and turned into a gravel driveway bordered by neat grass verges. On one side stood a sign displaying the name of the hotel.

Brodwin Hall Hotel.

As she reached the brow of the hill, the shape of the castle came into view and panic set in. It was enormous. Would she be expected to clean the whole hotel, and what if she couldn't meet the standards set?

She had very little idea of what would be expected of her and where she was going to sleep.

Getting closer, she saw the beautiful gardens and beyond, the lake. Drawn in by the scene, it felt as if she'd arrived in heaven.

'What do you think?' Margot asked.

She was lost for words. 'I don't know what to say. Wow.'

'You'll be fine,' she reassured her. We'll get you settled in your room, and don't worry, you won't be sleeping in the dungeon.' She laughed. 'I'll give you the guided tour, you can meet the other staff and then I'll pass you over to Bert.'

The absurdity of her life, it was amusing. From a caravan to a castle, how incredible, who would have believed it? The irony was, she felt out of place in both the caravan and a castle.

As the car came to a halt in front of the hotel, she smiled to herself. So many changes in her life, in such a short space of time, but arriving here at this new and intriguing setting felt like the beginning of an adventure.

What challenges awaited her? Would this new chapter in her life lead to kindness and stability? Would she at last be valued and respected?

The butler came out to the car to collect her bags. When he saw the bin liners, he looked bemused. 'Where's your luggage?'

'Just take the bags to her room while I show her around.'

CHAPTER 20

The O'Sullivans

Sheridan lay in bed, her eyes fixed on the cot, just staring, as she faced away from Liam who was pulling his trousers on, getting dressed for work. She couldn't bring herself to turn over and look at him, fearing the guilt would overwhelm her and make her reconsider.

Had she discussed it with him, this wouldn't be happening. He'd never agree to it, however bad things were, and they would be stuck, their situation unchanged.

It was just another ordinary day in their lives, in this city trapped in a cycle of violence and unrest where the streets whispered tales of fear and wounds ran deep through every home and every family. The day could pass for any other, except that it wasn't. Today was monumental, it would be seared on Sheridan's mind forever, an anniversary, a dreadful reminder of the day that changed their lives. She knew she'd remember every tiny detail of the day as if the events were in slow motion, because if this was hard now, what would it be like later on, and how would it be for the rest of their lives?

Was it possible to sever yourself from your child, your own

flesh and blood, forget and move on? It didn't seem humanly possible.

'Love you,' she murmured, peeking out from the covers as Liam opened the bedroom door. Because he always left so horribly early, he never kissed her goodbye; not wanting to disturb her, he'd creep out of the room and be gone.

His hand rested on the door handle. 'That's nice, you don't say that often.' He didn't turn to look at her, and for one dreadful moment she thought he'd guessed, but that was probably her paranoia playing havoc with her mind, the guilt she couldn't shake. 'Things will be okay, love, I promise.'

'Yup.'

It wasn't too late to back out. This was her child. She didn't have to do this. No amount of money was worth this.

And yet if I don't...

After he'd left, she crept out of bed and lifted the sleeping baby into her arms and returned to the warmth of her sheets to enjoy her. She didn't take her eyes off her, didn't want to miss a single minute. Every last moment was precious. As she looked at her six-month-old baby, she felt completely numb, as if her mind and body were trying to protect her from the impending trauma. It felt like a surreal situation, as if she was floating above her body and above the baby, strangely detached from herself, disconnected. She was surprised by her calm acceptance.

Is this really happening? Have I dreamed the last few days? Getting into a taxi that was paid for, meeting Janie Lee and her husband in a remote country hotel, the actress she'd always admired and idolised, the woman she'd chosen to raise her child.

Am I being flippant? Like throwing magical confetti as if this was a simple solution. She knew it wouldn't be, and yet something deep inside her was propelling her along, she couldn't back out.

As she dressed and prepared the children's breakfast and walked them to school, she reminded herself over and over that this was for the best. It was a mantra and became hypnotic. But how would she know it was for the best? There was no way of knowing. Was it better to be poor and grow up with family than have everything with non-biological parents? Such a heart-wrenching dilemma. And was she selfish to keep it from Liam?

As she began the journey in the taxi back to the country hotel to meet Janie-Lee and her lawyer, she willed herself to be strong. It was incredible to think how easy it had been to make contact with her. All it had taken was a phone call to the editor of the newspaper and he had put them both in touch. In many ways, she wished it hadn't been so easy.

Aisling was smiling and gurgling up at her the whole journey.

'What an amazing chance this will be,' she whispered through a fog of tears as she struggled to be positive. 'Mummy will always love you.' She kissed her on the forehead and breathed in her scent. 'I'll never forget you, but I can't give you the life you deserve, I wish I could, I wish things were different.'

A sudden realisation hit. Aisling was being sacrificed for her other children's future, but sometimes the hardest choices led to the greatest outcomes. She touched the cross hanging from her neck, rubbing the cold metal between her fingers, closed her eyes briefly and prayed for God to understand.

She kissed Aisling. 'I wish I could be a better mummy. I love you with all my heart but it's just not enough, and one day I hope you'll understand that and forgive me.'

Tears quietly plopped onto the baby's cheeks, and she tried to imagine that wonderful life and all the opportunities that awaited Aisling.

As the taxi drew up in front of the hotel, her heart was thumping so much, she thought it would escape her chest. This was now the second time she'd met Janie and her husband. That first meeting had been surreal, as if she wasn't present, but floating above herself in some kind of out-of-body experience. She couldn't remember what had been said or promised.

She got out and paid the driver, glanced round at all the Porches, Daimlers, and other posh cars, and then up at the whitewashed hotel. Then she noticed the couple standing in the portico-ed entrance, arm-in-arm, smiling at her, and that's when everything hit her at once.

I don't have to do this.
She's my baby.
What am I doing?

With each hesitant step towards the couple, her legs trembled beneath her, threatening to buckle at any moment. A fierce wave of bile surged in her throat, clawing its way upward.

'One moment,' she said as she rushed past them, heading for the ladies, flinging the door open just in time before reaching the toilet and heaving into the pan.

Afterwards, she took a few moments to collect herself. She stared into the mirror, the sight of herself with her baby for the last time; she wanted to capture this moment, hold it forever. This was the hardest, most agonising thing she'd ever had to do, and was ever likely to do, but she had to do it.

I can't go on as we are. I just can't.

From that point on, her head took control, while her heart fell into an eerie detachment. It felt as though an otherworldly force had enveloped her, guiding her through the storm of emotions, a supernatural presence aiding her.

She went back to the hotel's reception area where the couple were waiting, joined by a man in a suit and a nurse. Everyone shuffled into a side room. The nurse spoke, the lawyer spoke. Their mouths were moving, their words were muffled as if they were talking underwater. She was in a bubble looking out at them.

The nurse handed her a packet of tablets to stop the breast milk. She stared at them.

'If you could read the contract, please,' the solicitor said, nudging it towards her. 'It's a certificate of surrender.'

She picked up the pen, barely noticing the words, which were swimming before her eyes. "I do agree and promise not to attempt to retake Aisling or induce her to leave any place where she may be found."

Suddenly the couple didn't look kind anymore. She'd signed their papers. This was a business transaction.

That first time she'd met them to discuss the idea, they'd been so kind and understanding of her situation, promising regular letters and photos. "She will always know about you and her Irish roots. Please don't worry, you'll never be a secret," they'd said. But now she didn't believe any of it.

The nurse must have seen panic in her eyes because she came to sit beside her and put her arm around her. 'You don't have to do this, love, it's not too late. The papers can be torn up.'

'I want my daughter to have the best future,' she said through a splitting headache before handing Aisling to the nurse, a simple act that felt as if it was happening in slow motion.

A set of keys were slide across the table. 'These are yours now as we won't ever need to return to Ireland and we've placed a sum of money in your account. It should tide you over the next few years.'

She stood up and through tears shakily said to her baby, 'I'm sorry, pet,' and with that she fled the room, her mind a blur. Everything had happened so fast, as if she was peering through a window at someone else's life. One minute she had her baby in her arms and the next she was back in the taxi on her way home.

CHAPTER 21

The O'Sullivans

Something was wrong, Liam sensed it the minute he walked through the door. The kids were huddled on the sofa, crying. His wife was sitting by the fire gazing into the flames with a haunted expression in her eyes, distant and lost in thought, oblivious to her crying children.

'What's going on, why are you all crying, what's the matter?'

The sobs grow louder.

'Sheridan.' He went over to her. She was still staring, in a void.

'Go upstairs, children,' she shouted. 'Now.'

Now he was alarmed; what needed to be said without them?

She turned and looked at him through angry eyes. 'I've done it, now we can leave this godforsaken place. You can stay here, but we're leaving. Tonight is the last night I'll have to spend in this awful house among people who hate us. Tomorrow can't come soon enough.'

She looked up at him through cold eyes. Her face was vacant, devoid of all emotion. This wasn't his wife, she was like an empty shell. It was as if all the stuffing had been knocked out of her. She wasn't responding.

'What the hell are you going on about, woman? I've had a hard day at work, can't I come home for once without this fuss and nonsense, and have my food on the table? What have you been doing all day?' He glanced round, seeing that the place looked a mess. Something was different though. 'Where's the pram?'

'Out the front.'

'No, it's not.'

'It's probably been nicked, you know what it's like round here.'

'Why leave it there then, are you completely stupid?'

She didn't reply.

He glanced round. The cot was empty. 'Where's Aisling?'

'Gone. Why do you care? That's one thing you won't have to worry about anymore,' she said with a snarl. There was an evil glint in her eyes. 'We're moving tomorrow, you can come or rot in hell, the children and I deserve a better life, so we're going to have one.'

He slumped in the chair opposite her. 'I don't understand, what are you saying, why are the kids crying, why are you so cold, what have you done?'

She stared back into the fire.

'I was really looking forward to coming home tonight, I've got some good news. One of the managers at work, his mother has died and left him a spare property. He doesn't need to sell it right away and is happy to rent it to us cheaply. It's in a safe Catholic area and big enough for all the family. It's about ten miles away. It means at last we can get away from here.'

She burst into tears and broke down.

'I thought you'd be excited, I thought you'd be happy.' He'd been imagining her reaction all day, and this wasn't how he thought it would be.

'And the icing on the cake is, I've been promoted, things will get much easier, see I told you things would improve if we were patient.' He took her hand, but she pulled away.

He looked at her, flabbergasted. 'Aren't you excited, what have you got to say? You still haven't told me where Aisling is?'

Without taking her gaze from the fire she said, 'It's too late. You're always too late. Aisling's gone.'

'What do you mean, gone, she's too young to just go, you're talking in riddles, woman, what did she do, get up and walk out? For the love of Jesus, she's a feckin baby.'

A sudden sense of panic was rising in his chest. 'What have you done, Sheridan, what have you done? He reached out for her hands, but she pushed him away again and returned to stare into the fire.

'I've done what I had to do,' she screeched. 'You're too late. You're always too late, Liam. I've done what I said I'd do. She'll have a life that we can only dream of.'

'What's happened?'

'She's been adopted.'

His heart jolted in his chest. 'What do you mean? You couldn't have. You're winding me up. This isn't funny.'

'I'm perfectly serious,' she said calmly and coldly.

'That's impossible, both of us would need consent, what you are talking about woman?'

'She's gone.'

'Well, you better get her back again,' he shouted. He heard a howl from the stairway. The kids were listening. 'You can't give away my child, over my dead body.'

He stared at her, expecting her to burst out laughing and tell him she was joking.

'We've now got a new home, a new life, you've got what you wanted, can't you be happy for once?' He tried to pacify her.

'She's gone.'

'Well, where is she? I'll go and get her back, where did you take her?'

'She's on her way to America, the flight's already gone.'

'I'll get on the next bloody plane then if I have to,' he screamed.

'No, it's all legally signed off. They've given me the keys to a new house by way of payment.'

He was appalled. 'You've sold our child.' His world was collapsing. He sat there, tears streaming down his face. What the hell was happening? A day that had started out with so much promise, he'd tried so hard to protect his family. He'd known about the house for a week and was keeping it to himself as a surprise.

'I could have told you about the new house a few days ago but I wanted to keep it as a surprise as the property was being cleared out.'

'It's too late, it's done.'

Give the house back, give whatever money they've paid to you back, just get our baby back.' Growing frantic, he rose from his chair and began pacing the room. 'There must be something we can do.'

The door was ajar, and he caught sight of the children huddled on the stairs. They'd stopped crying to listen.

He shut the door. 'What have you told the kids, did you tell them before you told me?'

'I just told them she's gone and won't be coming back. That she's gone to have a better life.'

'You, heartless bitch, how could you do that to my children, their little sister?'

He grabbed his coat. 'I can't stand the sight of you, woman,' he snarled, bending over her. 'I can't take this, what the hell do I do? I need a drink and a smoke. I need to think.'

'Off to the pub again.' She tutted.

'I've got to get out, right now I hate you more than I've ever hated anyone, I don't trust myself not to do anything stupid, like push you into the fire. You've betrayed me, it's like you've stabbed me in the heart. All I've ever worked for. All I've ever wanted was to make you happy. This is how you repay me.' He banged his chest.

She made no attempt to stop him, just turned and continued to stare into the fire.

The damage had been done, the decision had been made. No amount of yelling and screaming would change the situation.

CHAPTER 22

The O'Sullivans

Sheridan tossed and turned all night. She heard Liam come in, in the early hours of the morning, crashing and banging, then silence. She didn't want to go down for fear of a drunken confrontation. The previous day had been a traumatic experience for everyone, and she knew it would be a few days before things calmed down, and right now she didn't want to talk about it to anyone, especially her husband.

After drifting in and out of sleep, she heard the alarm go off to signal it was time to get up for the school run. For the first time in months, she hadn't been disturbed to get up to feed Aisling. She felt surplus to requirements. She was suddenly hit by a cold and clammy feeling, and the emotion swept over her and she burst into tears. Sheer desolation; what had she done? How would anyone ever understand? How would she look people in the eye? She'd always wonder how Aisling was and only time would tell if she'd ever recover from this. Right now, she had to focus on the kids' normal daily routines, if normal was possible.

She padded downstairs and found Liam had already left for

work. There was no message. She wondered what was going through his mind and if he'd find it in him to forgive her and come too.

Still tearful and feeling hollow, she shouted for the kids to get ready for school. She was desperate to get moving. After the school run, she had to retrieve suitcases from the loft and pack. She glanced round; it was sad, but they didn't have many personal belongings and none of the furniture was worth taking. Everything was tatty and worn out. It was a measure of how poor they were. The new house was a fresh start, and they didn't need to buy any furniture, it was provided, plus an income for the next year to help them settle in.

Back from the school run, she made a list and started to pack. Her mind consumed with all the things she needed to do, there was no time to reflect and regret, no time to wallow.

Ready and packed, she glanced round. There were many good memories within these walls. She smiled as she remembered Liam carrying her over the threshold after their honeymoon in Donegal, nearly tripping up and then making love on the front room carpet. He struggled to make love to her these days, especially now that she was a few pounds heavier. She had to admit, she hadn't looked after her figure as she had in earlier years. Her body was going one way, the opposite of what she desired. She was rather partial to a Bourbon biscuit as well as rock cakes. It was how she got through the day.

A wave of sadness washed over her. It was here that all her children were born. This house had witnessed birthday celebrations, magical Christmases brimming with excitement and love. The happy times, though, were overshadowed by the lingering Troubles.

About to lock up and post the key through the door, she realised Liam wouldn't know where they'd gone. She jotted down the new address and said she hoped to see him tonight. "The choice is yours", she wrote.

Turning to the door, she half-wondered whether to pack Liam's clothes and assume he'd join them. She hesitated. Last night he'd been so angry. It was better to give him time. Things were still very raw. In her heart, she knew they'd get through this, he wouldn't leave her, they'd been together for too long. She remembered her mum said once, "Take each other for granted at your peril". Nevertheless, there was a lot of emotion to overcome and maybe one day Aisling would return to find her family.

When it was time to pick the children up from school, she made a phone call from the phone box to order a large taxi and waited outside the house with all the bags. She noticed the slight movement of net curtains in a couple of the houses opposite as neighbours peered out, interested in what was going on. Just then the door across the road opened and a man stepped out, walking across the road towards her.

He looked at her and all her bags and chuckled. 'Going somewhere, are we? A holiday? Surprised you can afford it. Or have we finally managed to chase you off? Took long enough, we knew we'd get to you in the end.'

She stayed quiet, didn't want him to know her business. 'We'll be back soon enough.'

'That's a shame, thought we were getting rid of you finally. Just hope when you get back, your house is still standing.' He laughed and scooted off with a spring in his step.

On the way through, they passed the abattoir. On impulse, she asked the taxi driver to stop while she nipped in to speak to Liam.

'Sorry, love,' the manager said. 'We've not seen him all day. I thought he must be sick.'

She turned away, worried now. Where had he gone? Surely, he wouldn't just disappear? She dashed into the pub; nobody had seen him there either. She got back into the taxi. Liam was old enough to take care of himself, her priority was the children. He clearly had the hump; he'd get over it. The children needed her and in the coming days she was going to be very busy settling them into a new home in a completely new area and arranging places at the local schools. It was a lot of change for them, and she had no idea how they would cope. All she knew was they'd all be so much safer. Getting away from this area was going to be a huge relief. Finally, she could sleep at night secure in the knowledge they weren't going to be attacked.

The children would ask where Liam was and it would be difficult to explain what was going on, but hopefully he'd see sense, swallow his pride, and follow them over. But where the hell was he? He'd never skipped work in all the time she'd known him.

CHAPTER 23

The O'Sullivans

Liam woke early with a throbbing head. He couldn't remember how much he'd drunk but knew it had been a few. He could remember falling over on his way home.

Dragging his clothes on, and splashing his face with water, he knew he couldn't go into work today, there were a few things he needed to sort.

It was still very early, and he slipped out of the house, heading towards the bus stop where he took a bus into the city centre. He dived into the first phone box he saw, flicked through the Yellow Pages, and found the name and address of a firm of family solicitors. The advert stated that the initial half-hour consultation was free. Their offices were a few roads away and he waited on a nearby bench for them to open.

Shortly after nine, Liam stood at the reception while the secretary flicked through the diary. Distressed, he expressed the urgency of the situation. His baby would be lost to another country, he needed to act fast. With a nod, she rose to check if the solicitor could squeeze him in.

'You're in luck, he'll see you now.'

Liam headed into the lawyer's office and extended his hand, thanking him for fitting him in last minute. Knowing he only had half an hour, he nervously hurried through the details, the gravity of the situation spilling out in a torrent of words.

'How can she just sign my baby away? We're married. My name is on the birth certificate.'

The lawyer frowned and tugged at his mouth with his fingers and after a moment said, 'And where is the baby now?'

'On her way to America.'

'That makes things very difficult. They'll have powerful contacts who were able to get her a fast-tracked passport. These are extremely wealthy people. Make no mistake, we'd be up against a top legal team.'

'I don't care what it costs,' he cried. 'I just want my baby back. I'll do anything.'

'It's easy to say that, but do you have the means to fight this?' the lawyer asked, his voice steady but probing. 'What do you do for a living?'

'I work in an abattoir.'

He thought about the desperate struggle to put food on the table and knew this was hopeless. A heavy silence settled over him, as he realised the futility of it all. Before he could even entertain the thought of a legal battle, he knew deep down that he was already defeated. He glanced up at the clock; the time was nearly up.

'I understand how difficult it is to voice this, but there are moments when we must reflect on our blessings. Your wife clearly had her reasons, this was not an easy decision for her. Her family's safety was her ultimate priority. You could spend years battling this, but beyond the financial toll, ask yourself-- do you have the strength to face a fight?'

He left the solicitors feeling completely demoralised, his mind all over the place as he retraced his steps to the bus stop. The streets were filled with a heavy security presence, soldiers and checkpoints at every turn. Graffiti-adorned walls, political messages, the sentiments of a divided community. Barbed wire and barricades. His wife's fears were everywhere, her desperation to escape this troubled city. How could he have missed all these signs around him? Had he been so wrapped up in his Monday-to-Friday life, that he had been oblivious? He wanted his family to be safe too, how could he not want that? But the difference between the pair of them, he wasn't going to cave in to violence, he wouldn't have taken her drastic steps.

Getting off the bus, he sauntered past the abattoir, bitterness consuming him.

Damn work, if I get the sack, do I care?

Without anything to strive for, nothing mattered.

He slipped into the dimly lit pub, the familiar scent of hops and stale smoke filling the air as he ordered a pint and lit a ciggie.

The barman said, 'Hello Liam, where have you been? Your wife was in here looking for you.'

'Bloody woman, she's the last person I want to speak to. Give us the usual, I'll sort her out later.'

He chugged down his first pint. The hours drifted by in a haze as he wallowed in self-pity, until day turned to dusk.

'Come on, Liam, I can't give you anymore, you've had a skinful, drowning your sorrows never solves anything. Believe me, I'm a barman, I've seen it all before. Go home, your family need you. It'll all come out in the wash.'

'Family, huh, who bloody needs them? They're never happy, whatever I do. They don't know how lucky they are. I work my guts out, what thanks do I get? The missus wouldn't be happy if she lived in Buckingham Palace.'

On wobbly legs, one arm on the bar to keep himself upright, he glanced out of the window. It was chucking-out time at the abattoir. He staggered to the loo and as he came back, he heard a familiar voice.

'There you are, lad, you didn't show up today, what's going on? Jesus Christ, you look awful, how many have you had?'

'Too bloody many, if you ask me.' The barman tutted and raised his eyebrows to Liam's dad.

Some of his work colleagues were heading in, straight to the bar in a cloud of laughter and chatter. When they saw Liam, they started chiding. 'You suddenly gone workshy, mate, we've all had to work extra hard today to cover your shift. You becoming a slacker? Think you owe us all a pint.' Laughter rose.

'Come on, son,' Liam's dad said, putting an arm around his shoulder. 'Let's go into the corner and you can tell me all about it.' He glanced at the barman. 'Strong coffee for this one, please, and my usual.'

'It's okay, I'll bring it over.'

Liam filled his dad in on everything that had happened and closed with, 'I feel shit, Dad, what a pile of crap. What the hell do I do now?'

'Get back home to your family. You can't hide in the bottom of a glass forever. Swallow your pride and be a man, make the best of what you've got, they need you now more than ever. A lot of people would spit blood to have what you have. She's a bloody good woman, you'd go a long way to find someone who could hold a candle to her. You need to look after her. Go home and sleep it off.'

'I know, Dad, but I can't believe she'd sell us out, sell our daughter. It's inhuman. What the feck was she thinking?

'Hell, she must have been desperate. Have you not been listening to her? Did you not realise how scared she'd become?'

As Liam stood to go, the alcohol sang in his head. Staggering to the door, he felt giddy, as if he'd been on a fairground ride. His dad trailed behind him, concerned he might stumble. Out on the pavement, he put his arm around him for support as they headed down the hill and across the road to his house. As they approached, the house was shrouded in darkness.

'That's odd, there's no lights on. Either they've all gone to bed, or they've left,' his dad said.

Under the arch that separated the houses, Liam fumbled in his pocket for the key. Never mind his family, his head was hurting. All he wanted right now was to crash out on the settee.

Suddenly, a figure emerged from the shadows, startling them both.

One of the neighbours.

'I thought you'd all gone, or have you just sent the missus away?' As he squared up to Liam, he sneered and forced him against the wall before grabbing him by the scruff of the neck. 'We made ourselves very clear, we don't want you round here.' His face was contorted in a sinister snarl. His manner was so menacing, he sent shivers down Liam's spine.

When the man let go of his neck, Liam was hurled against the wall.

Reeling in shock, Liam watched him stalk off across the road shouting abuse as he went.

'Ignore him, son, it's just hot air.'

'He's a thug, doesn't scare me,' Liam said even though it wasn't true. He swayed drunkenly and with a shaky hand, put the key into the lock and opened the door.

'Hello, Sheri.' He switched on the light and glanced around before calling up the stairwell.

'Looks like they've already gone, son.' His dad went over to the table and picked up a note. 'She's left the new address, wants you to join them.' He slipped it into his pocket.

Liam tutted.

'Sleep on it, son, I'll pick you up in the morning. We're both on the late shift tomorrow, so I'll help you pack your bags and take you over there.'

He couldn't think about the morning, he was going to have the hangover from hell when he woke. 'How can I move there, it's in the middle of nowhere? How would I get to work?'

'There's a brick company out that way, my mate works there. He could put a good word in for you.'

Liam sank down on the settee, nursing his head as his dad gave him a glass of water. 'Get that down you and get some sleep. I'll be over first thing.'

After he left, Liam nestled his head into the cushions, quickly drifting into oblivion.

Sometime later--he didn't know how long he'd been asleep-- he jerked awake, his mind foggy and confused. It was still black outside. What was that sound? A shattering crash. Panic surged through him. What had happened? He stumbled off the settee.

'Shit.' He could smell smoke. His brain played catch-up; had he left any appliances on? Turning, he spotted smoke curling ominously beneath the closed door to the hallway. The air was acrid, and his eyes were already sore. He rubbed them, squinting and nearly collapsing from a coughing fit, just about reaching the door. When he opened it, flames shot through, like serpents blocking his exit and he was hurled back.

My kids, my wife, I must get out of here.

CHAPTER 24

Kathleen

As Kathleen followed Margot across the driveway towards Brodwin Hall, her gaze was drawn to a magnificent Christmas tree in one of the downstairs rooms. Its twinkling colourful lights danced against the backdrop of rich green branches and filled her with excitement about the festive season ahead. Up some stone steps and into the house, she gasped. A golden chandelier sparkled above and illuminated the marble floor. There was a huge ornate gilt mirror on the wall, and she glanced at her reflection as they passed.

She was introduced to the staff manager and followed him up the grand staircase, along a corridor to a door marked 'staff only.' Through the door, she was led past a bucket and mop and various cleaning products and up a dark narrow wooden staircase to a passageway. There were numbered doors, and she could tell this was the staff quarters because it looked long neglected. The walls were grubby, scuffed and painted a faded beige. Dim lights overhead cast a low glow on the worn brown carpet that muffled the sound of hurried feet.

Stopping outside number 5, the manager stepped aside to let

her in. It was a tiny room with a small ceiling window, minimal light filtering in. Two single beds occupied the space, both covered with faded orange candlewick bedspreads, and there was a washbasin in the corner.

'Another lass will be joining you in a few days. Every room has to pay for itself.'

Kathleen wasn't sure how she felt about sharing a room, but this had to be better than sharing a bed with Colin's gran, and anything was better than the laundry's cold dormitory with its creaking metal beds and thin mattresses. She hoped the girl would be nice. The one thing she needed more than ever was a friend. Despite all the girls at the laundry, they weren't allowed to talk––ever––but here it was different. This was her first proper job. She imagined giggling in bed at night, midnight feasts, a best friend like the ones she'd left behind in Liverpool.

Kathleen spent the first couple of days settling in before her first shift. It was a blissful time, and it felt as if she was on holiday. She relaxed on her bed reading magazines she found in the hotel's foyer and took long walks round the grounds. There was so much to explore outside: a lake, a wood, an ornamental garden and a vegetable patch.

She strolled around the lake, the sun filtering through the leaves, casting playful shadows on the path. It was a huge lake and at the other end she could just make out a boathouse nestled in the corner with its own landing stage. She inhaled the scent of pine and earth, her worries easing with each step. The water sparkled like diamonds, and gentle ripples danced across its surface as ducks and swans glided lazily by.

Wandering towards the house, she went to stand by the vegetable allotment which lay dormant under a blanket of frost. Ragged remnants of last season's crops peeked through the soil, their leaves shrivelled and brittle. Raised beds, devoid of life, were lined with icy soil, and glistened in the pale winter sun.

The wooden frames, weathered and worn, stood as silent sentinels, guarding the promise of spring.

Turning to head to the house, she heard someone cough. She swung round, startled; it had seemed so quiet out here, she was surprised to have company. A loping figure dressed in a green jacket and matching wellies emerged from behind the shed. He was carrying a fork and she presumed he was the gardener.

He looked over at her and smiled before pitching his fork in the hard earth. She strolled over.

'I bet this is lovely in the spring when everything's growing,' she said, returning his smile. Drawing closer, she noticed his ruddy complexion, hours spent here in the garden. His looks were deceptive, he could easily pass for someone much older than his years, but she suspected he was less than a decade older than her.

There was an ease about him and a rugged appeal. Maybe it was the way he was leaning slightly on the handle of his fork, or his morning stubble and tousled brown hair.

They held each other's gaze for a beat, and in that brief time, something swooped inside her, disturbing her. She quickly looked away.

She sensed he felt it too because he hurried on, filling the silence with chat. 'It's all frozen over now but there are plenty of other jobs in the garden for me to be getting on with. I'm Fred, the gardener.' He extended his hand.

'Kathleen, pleased to meet you. I've just started here as a maid. I'm not sure what I'll be doing yet, making beds, serving food.' She shrugged and suddenly felt awkward. Maybe she should have asked for a job description.

'You look young to be in work, fresh out of school?'

She was careful what she said. She didn't want anyone to know that she'd escaped a Magdalene laundry, although she doubted anyone would come looking here, not unless Colin had reported her. That was highly unlikely. Why would he help her, then dob her in?

'Yes, I'm from Liverpool,' she replied.

She glanced around her trying to think of something else to say.

'You've got the best job I reckon, until it rains of course.' She laughed.

There was a certain magnetism about him that drew Kathleen in. Perhaps it was the way he enthused about the garden, dismissing bad weather. He was used to the rain and the cold. His hands, calloused from years of nurturing plants, moved gracefully as he gestured, reflecting an easy confidence.

AFTER THE BREAK, Kathleen prepared for bed early, setting her alarm for five. She wanted to feel fresh and alert for her first shift. At five she turned on the bedside light and prised herself from the warmth of the bed. The chill was unbearable and reminded her disturbingly of her time at the laundry where the biting cold seeped into her bones. She pulled back the curtains to see a thin film of ice coating the inside of the window, a shimmering barrier between her and the outside world. She was mesmerised by the patterns illuminated by the moonlight. She scraped her fingernail across the pane and drew a smiley face.

She turned to the wardrobe where her crisp new uniform was hanging, a reminder of the responsibilities waiting for her. With a sigh, she quickly slipped into the clothing, bracing herself for the day ahead.

When she was ready, she stepped into the corridor, joining her fellow staff members, whom she had been introduced to in passing before. They greeted her with polite nods and smiles. They were a mix of ages, men, and women. Silence hung between them as they filed down the rickety stairs and towards the kitchen. Inside, the cook was busy at the Aga preparing steaming porridge for the staff, its starchy aroma filling the air, while the butler meticulously set the long wooden table.

As they sat, the cook dolloped a big helping into Kathleen's bowl. 'Your first day, lass. We don't get much time off here, but nobody goes hungry. Enjoy.'

A jug of milk and a plate of curled butter was offered round. As everyone tucked in, the staff manager looked up at Kathleen, his spoon in mid-air. 'Margot said you enjoy singing.'

Kathleen felt herself blush. 'I enjoy it a bit, I guess,' she added hesitantly, not wanting and be roped into something. 'Just for fun, though. I'm not very good.'

'Nonsense, girl. I bet you sing better than this lot. You should have heard them at the carol concert last Christmas. They sounded like a band of wailing cats in pain. Their voices could scare a flock of geese.' He glanced at everyone round the table and chuckled. 'I'd like you to perform this Saturday evening in the parlour while the guests enjoy dinner. You can play the piano, can you?'

She remembered back to her childhood, singing to tunes that Tony Blackburn and Jimmy Savile played on Radio 1. A distant memory slipped into her mind of sitting on her grandma's knee while she played the piano. That was where she'd first learned to play 'Chopsticks.' Shelling out for her piano lessons was one of the rare thoughtful things her mum had done for her.

Everyone's eyes were fixed on her, waiting for her response. She felt cornered. As this was her first job, she was eager to make a good impression, and the thought of turning down the request made her anxious. Saying no would reflect poorly on her. Feeling the weight of the pressure to prove herself, she quickly said yes.

Later, during her break, she found the parlour quiet, with all the guests out. Seizing the moment, she slipped in to practise on the piano. It was the perfect chance to play freely without anyone listening, just her and the keys. Lost in the music--she'd always loved playing 'Ave Maria'--she didn't notice someone come into the room until she heard them cough. She turned on her stool to see Bert smiling and clapping. 'That was beautiful. Put that on the list for Saturday. You'll get extra pay.' Winking at her, he added, 'and if you're lucky, some guests might give you tips too.'

She couldn't believe it. This was too good to be true. She'd be able to save some money and buy herself some new things.

The next few days flew by, leaving her little time to sit down amidst all the tasks. She learned silver service and how to carry the plates and serve food. In the kitchen she was put to work chopping vegetables, carrying sacks of rubbish outside to the bins and washing up. She was exhausted, scurrying back and forth between the tables out front and the kitchen in the back, balancing plates on her arm and taking all sorts of abuse from the frustrated chef who always seemed to be mad at everybody but himself for choosing his stressful profession. She couldn't help but envy the guests, who were obviously very wealthy; with the hotel's prices, they had to be. They got to relax and enjoy the view over the gardens and towards the lake, sipping wine, sometimes champagne, perusing the menu, making their choices, and filling their tummies with tasty food. As she listened in, she caught snippets of conversation that painted a picture of extravagant lifestyles she could only dream of, filled with talk of lavish yachts and polo ponies, second homes and spontaneous flights to exotic destinations.

Saturday soon came and she woke with a mixture of nerves and excitement. She'd managed to practise her keys when the parlour was quiet, and now she felt more prepared for the evening ahead. She had no trouble deciding what to wear. She rummaged through the bag of hand-me-downs she'd brought with her and slipped into a stunning long purple evening gown with glittery straps. She stared at her reflection in awe, unable to believe how much the dress had transformed her. She looked so glamorous and mature, and it felt wonderful to finally wear something beautiful, such a contrast to the grey, dowdy uniforms worn at the laundry. Her life was on the up and she felt like a new person.

The silky gown hugged her skin and accentuated her curves, making her feel a million dollars. She wasn't used to dressing like this though and felt very self-conscious. Hoping to slip into the parlour unnoticed, she hurried down the corridor but reaching the top of the stairs, she nearly bumped into Bella, one of the waitresses.

'Wow, you look stunning, and what a beautiful dress.' She stood back and gasped. 'If I didn't know you were one of us, I'd assume you were one of them.'

Kathleen chuckled then felt awkward and embarrassed. She wasn't used to people paying her compliments and not knowing how to react, so she downplayed her looks. 'My neck looks bare, but I don't have a necklace, and I've tried my best with my hair, but it's got a mind of its own. I used to have a set of heated rollers but they're back at home.'

'I've got some heated rollers, you're welcome to borrow them. Better still, I'll do your hair for you. I always wanted to be a hairdresser but ended up here.' She giggled before turning to her door. 'My room's just here. It won't take us long.'

Kathleen hesitated; she didn't want to be late, but it was hard to say no.

She stepped into Bella's room. The feeling of being back in Liverpool in one of her friends' rooms hit her like a sledgehammer. She was transported back in time. The walls were covered in posters of David Cassidy and David Essex. She looked down at the carpet, littered with an array of make-up, pots of cream and underwear, and tiptoed around it before perching on the end of the bed. The room smelt comforting, a perfume she recognised but couldn't name.

Just a few minutes in this girl's room took her back to happier times and she soon relaxed. After more than a year living like a bird in a cage or a cornered rat, this was wonderful. The overwhelming relief of finally being free felt like a weight lifted.

It felt normal, ordinary––how life should be––and suddenly she was hit with a wave of emotion. She'd forgotten what it was like to be a teenager.

Once they were finished, she got up and made a dash for the door.

'I mustn't be late.' She was all flustered and her breathing was tight. She then felt anxious, and tears filled her eyes but she quickly recovered. She turned in the doorway. 'I better go. Thank you so much, I haven't worn make-up in ages and the necklace is lovely.'

'Hang on, you need a spritz of something.' Bella grabbed a bottle of perfume from her drawer and handed it to Kathleen. 'Hey, don't cry, you'll smudge the mascara.' She reached for a tissue and dabbed her eyes. 'You're going to be amazing.'

Bella was totally unaware of the profound impact her kindness had on Kathleen. How was she to know her last year had been extremely miserable and she was effectively all alone in the world? Kathleen was determined to make a friend of her. There was something about her that she liked. She reminded her of her own friends, she seemed fun and easy going, the type of person that didn't take things too seriously.

She went downstairs still feeling nervous, this was such a new experience. She'd only sang in the church choir and in a school play. The piano was positioned in the corner of the restaurant away from the guests, and acted as a barrier which made her feel safer and more confident. Her first piece was John Lennon, 'Imagine.' The song created the right mood and had been one of her dad's favourites. Afterwards she sang Frank Sinatra's 'Fly Me to The Moon.' Her focus was on playing the piano and singing. Everyone was busy eating, so she had no idea if they were enjoying themselves.

During one song she looked up to see Bella and the manager gazing at her admiringly, but she ploughed on, lost in the music. She felt totally confident and at ease.

When she finished the session, the whole restaurant turned to applaud. She was suddenly overcome by a sense of appreciation, something she'd never had before and again her eyes welled. She did a little bow, smiled, mouthed a thank you and quickly made her exit. As she passed through reception she was met by the manager and Bella.

'Oh my God, Kathleen, you never told us you were this talented.'

She burst into tears.

'What's wrong, what have we said?' Bella said in alarm. She glanced at the manager. 'Let me take her away.' She put her arm around Kathleen which made her all the more emotional.

'Would you like a complimentary drink in the bar? the manager asked.

After their drinks, Bella invited her to her room for a bit of girly time before bed.

She sat on the spare bed, her back against the wall.

'Why are you sad? You were brilliant. I wish I could sing.' Bella handed her a bottle of Fanta to swig. 'I could offer you a Bacardi, but as we're working tomorrow, I'd better not.'

Kathleen didn't like to confess that she'd never tried Bacardi--or any alcohol for that matter-- apart from sherry and port at her grandma's on a Sunday before lunch.

'I've never had a reception like that. You don't know my life before I came here, I'm not used to the attention.'

'Have you always been able to sing?'

'In the bath.' She laughed.

'What was your favourite song?'

'Soap opera.' She laughed again.

'Ha ha.'

'Used to drive my mum mad all the singing I did, but I enjoyed tonight, it was just so nice to be praised for a change.'

Bella frowned. 'Surely your folk realise you're talented?'

She just wanted to forget about her past and build on her new life here.

'My parents are dead.' She hadn't intended to make the blunt remark and it surprised her. It only applied to her dad, as far as she knew, her mum was still alive.

'I'm really sorry, that must be very hard.'

'You just learn to live with it.'

'It's nice to sit and chat,' Bella said after they'd talked for a while. 'Someone to chat to that isn't old and crusty. The staff are lovely, don't get me wrong, but they are a bit ancient.'

'They're okay, most look like they're in their thirties.'

'I'm a bit apprehensive about the new girl that's coming to share my room next week. I hope she's nice.'

'Someone's sharing with me soon too.'

Bella's eyes suddenly brightened. 'Why don't I ask the manager if we can share?'

'What a great idea. As long as you let me buy you some more make-up when I get paid.'

Bella waved her hand. 'Use what you like.' Her eyes brightened again, and she laughed. 'Actually, there's a room where they keep all the bits that guests leave behind. We're allowed to help ourselves. You'll find perfume and make-up, and all sorts of toiletries. There are no cheap brands.'

'Really?'

She couldn't believe how well her new life was turning out. She had a great job, a lovely place to stay, had made a new friend and rediscovered her joy of music and song. It was a far cry from her recent past, a fresh start, and she couldn't have been happier. Her future was looking bright.

She was totally unprepared for what was to come.

CHAPTER 25

Kathleen

Christmas came and went in a whirlwind of festivity and parties. Kathleen woke on Christmas morning to a blanket of snow and as the sun rose, it cast an apricot hue across the landscape. It was the type of Christmas she'd always dreamt of as a child--a perfect picture-postcard scene, but the reality had always been quite different. It always seemed to rain in Liverpool, casting gloomy shadows over what should have been a fun time. The celebrations centred around church and were austere. The services were always predictable, heavy going and boring and they held little appeal for a child. Their home would be filled with various eccentric aunts and uncles, who would come over for tea and cake. The grown-ups always ended up dozing on the settee and there was nobody for her to play with. Those childhood Christmases, steeped in Catholic tradition, were more about enduring stuffy family interactions than the fun and entertainment she'd craved. Even her brother, Darius wasn't much company. Being older he didn't want to play with her and would take himself off to his bedroom to play with his chemistry set or Meccano. They'd never been close, probably because of the big age gap and she had no idea what he was doing now. He'd left home a long time ago and her mum never talked about him.

Even though she had to work throughout Christmas, she enjoyed every moment. The atmosphere was magical, with the hall festooned with decorations--twinkling lights, vibrant wreaths, enchanting ornaments, and best of all, an enormous tree. The chef and his team prepared huge amounts of food with lots left over from the grand feast served to the guests. The staff gathered in the kitchen towards the end of Christmas Day to enjoy a hearty meal and shared in laughter and party games, making her work feel less like a chore and more like a celebration.

Winter lingered on, like an uninvited guest who had overstayed their welcome leaving behind a longing for the warmth and colours of spring. January passed in a haze, then February arrived, the dullest month of the year when the world seemed dead, and nature appeared to be in deep slumber. She often wondered why February was the month of romance. The hotel was gaily decorated with red hearts. The landscape was draped in muted shades of brown, the earth lay hard and unyielding and above, the sky stretched out in a lacklustre expanse of pale white that seemed to dull the world. Yet amidst this scene, there was a certain stillness, a quiet promise that life would soon awaken once more.

On her days off when she couldn't go into town with Bella, she wandered over to the allotment to chat with Fred. He was always pleasant company and he'd pour her a mug of tea from his flask, and they'd sit on the bench by the greenhouse chatting about life at the hotel.

Valentine's Day arrived and the air was filled with a sense of excitement and romance. Couples had come away to celebrate in style, gazing into each other's eyes. She lost count of how many Mr and Mrs Joneses were staying there. The hotel marketed itself as an ideal break for couples celebrating special romantic occasions, like weddings and Valentine's and featured exquisite four-poster beds in elegantly designed rooms. When Kathleen came down that morning, the restaurant had already been decorated for the evening ahead with candles, red tablecloths, and delicate posies of red roses on each table. Kathleen would be singing and playing the piano. She'd practised a few love songs, among them, Carol King, 'You've Got a Friend,' and The Three Degrees, 'When Will I See You Again'. Amazingly, she had the perfect dress to wear from the bag of hand-me-downs––a long red dress with sparkly straps, cinched at the waist, that hugged her figure perfectly, the silky fabric cascading gracefully to the floor. The back of the dress revealed a modest bare stretch of skin and was crisscrossed with delicate ribbons. The dress completely transformed her.

In the kitchen, several maids were giggling and blushing as they opened their Valentine cards. Kathleen longed to receive a card of her own filled with loving words, and the very thought of it made her heart skip a beat. It seemed so incredibly special and filled her with warmth, longing, and gooey thoughts. She couldn't help but feel a twinge of envy as she watched the other girls open their cards and gifts and imagined how wonderful it would be to feel loved and cherished by someone.

Around five she headed upstairs to get ready for the evening and found Bella sitting on her bed reading a letter.

'Anthony's asked me to marry him.'

Kathleen plonked herself on the bed beside her. 'Wow, did you see that coming?'

'When I went home at Christmas, he hinted at the idea, but I didn't think he was being serious. I'm only seventeen, it feels too young.'

'You don't have to rush into it. Most couples are engaged for a few years before they take the plunge.'

'Yes, that's what I was thinking.' As she folded the letter,

Kathleen saw a twinkle in her eyes and knew that Bella was going to accept the proposal. She felt a sudden ache in her heart as sadness curled around her.

'I bet you really miss him,' she said flatly.

'Yes, I do, that's half the problem.' Bella didn't talk about her boyfriend very often, but Kathleen saw a shadow of pain move across her features as she sat back against the wall and sighed. 'As much as I love it here, I think I need to go back home to Derby and get a local job. There are plenty of hotels I could work in. It's tough being in a long-distance relationship, there's always the danger of breaking up.'

Kathleen looked away but tried to dial down the rising sadness inside her. She was going to lose her best friend and once again find herself facing the world alone.

After this realisation, she didn't have much of a desire to go downstairs and sing. However, she slipped into her red dress and tried to be happy for her friend as she busied herself applying makeup, brushing her hair, and trying to look cheerful but inside, she was already starting to miss Bella.

Descending the stairs, her hand on the rail, careful not to trip in her long gown, she felt the silky fabric billow around her with each step. As she rounded the corner, the front door swung open, and the gardener, in his green Barbour and muddy wellies stepped inside. He stood on the mat, his eyes widening in awe as he gazed up at her, looking completely taken aback.

'Wow, you look so gorgeous.' He froze on the spot as if his breath had been taken away. There was a sparkle in his eyes she'd not seen before and a glowing smile that communicated so much. He wasn't taking his eyes off her, and something seemed to swirl between them as she walked towards him. She'd never considered him in that way before and it caught her unawares. She quickly brushed the thought aside; he was much older than she was.

They spoke for a few moments and afterwards, when she

walked into the restaurant, a man at a table by the window glanced her way. He froze mid-stare and she tried to read his expression. Did she know him or was he simply admiring her? She couldn't tell. Throughout the first session of songs, her eye kept being drawn to him. Something about him unsettled her, his gaze never left her and felt like hot coals piercing into her.

At the interval, he got up from his chair and approached her. She stood to greet him.

'Well done,' he said, drinking her in from head to toe taking in every detail. There it was again, that look, the shadow of an expression, gone before she could make sense of it. 'You have a beautiful voice, and may I compliment you on looking so lovely too?'

She felt the heat rise to her cheeks. 'Thank you.'

'My wife's got the same dress. Where did you get it from?'

Thinking quickly, she lied, 'Only Topshop.'

He looked at her suspiciously. 'No, no, that's not any old dress, that's very exclusive, I bought it for my wife from a boutique in Kensington.' He'd raised his voice and heads were turning. 'It's most unusual, it was supposed to be a one-off. Topshop indeed,' he said with a scoff.

He frowned at her, and she felt like a piece of dirt on his shoe. 'Where are you from?'

'Liverpool.'

'Where did you work before coming here?'

She hesitated, dread washing over her. If anyone discovered her time at the laundry, it could ruin everything. 'Ireland.'

When she saw his eyebrows rise as if something had just dawned on him, panic set in.

'Of course,' he said with a smirk. 'I bet you were a maid at my house.'

'I'm not sure, sir,' she muttered. 'I was a domestic before I came here.'

When her second session began, she found it hard to focus.

The encounter had rattled her and as she tapped on the piano keys, her stomach performed cartwheels with the worry of what might happen next.

At the end of her performance, she bowed and made a hasty exit.

Bella woke her several times in the night by huffing and tossing and turning and in the morning, she sat up, looked over, her hair dishevelled, bags under her eyes and told Kathleen she'd made a decision. She was going to leave to be with her boyfriend.

'I'm pleased for you.' She didn't want to have to think about her friend leaving and the prospect of a new roommate, not when the events of the previous evening were still weighing on her mind, a feeling that intensified when there was a knock at the door summoning her to the staff manager's office.

She dressed and hurried down.

The manager looked up from his staff ledger as she entered. 'Sit down, Kathleen.'

This sounded ominous. She braced herself.

'I have a delicate subject I want to discuss with you, and I'm hoping you can shed some light on a query that's arisen.' He shuffled a pile of papers on his desk and coughed. 'You may recall a conversation with one of our guests last night. It has raised one or two queries. Could I ask you to explain how you came to acquire the dress you were wearing last night, as the gentlemen suggests it was rather exclusive and was under the impression there was only one in existence and that it belonged to his wife?'

His questions made her tense, and she dropped her gaze to the floor. She couldn't think what to say.

'It doesn't seem very likely on your wages you'd be able to afford to wear such a dress.'

She chewed her lip, wondering how to respond, then blurted, 'Actually I was given the dress.'

'That sounds a rather interesting story, tell me more.' His tone was mocking, and he looked at her curiously. She could see that he wasn't at all convinced.

'I don't really want to discuss it. It's part of my past, that's private.'

He peered at her through suspicious eyes. She hated being interrogated, she'd done nothing wrong. 'Tell me, where was it you were employed before you came to us?'

'I looked after an elderly lady in a caravan.'

I'm going to have to make some enquiries to ensure your story is true. I think you need to be a little more forthcoming in your explanation.'

'I haven't stolen it if that's what you're thinking. I'm not like that.'

'I didn't say you had, but I do need to understand the full circumstances.'

'A previous friend was given the dress by one of his customers as she was having a clear out and asked if I'd like them.'

He scoffed. 'That seems rather far-fetched. What's the name of his customer?'

'I don't know her name. I have no contact with her. All I know is, she's the lady who helped me get this job.'

'This is sounding more and more puzzling and less and less convincing.' He shook his head and put his hand on the phone on his desk as if about to make the call. 'This can easily be checked. I'm going to phone the boss. She brought you here.'

Kathleen burst into tears. 'You think I've stolen them. How could you be so unkind? I don't know the man or his wife. I can't give you the name of the lady. I don't want to get my friend into trouble.'

'So, you are admitting they were stolen, just not by you?' He flashed her an angry look.

'I was given them, that's all I know,' she insisted.

'I can make a few phone calls, and if you're in the clear, everything will be fine. If not, we will have to ask you to leave with immediate effect. We have our reputation to think of. I will talk to the guest first and get some more information. Wait here.'

He left the room but left the door ajar. She heard his footsteps retreating along the hallway. She took a tissue from the box on his desk and blew her nose. What would she do if they sacked her? Where would she go? She'd be homeless again with nowhere to turn.

She heard him talking and cocked her head to listen.

'Sir, I'm glad I caught you. I have the young lady in my office. She says she was given the dress.'

'Huh, my wife doesn't just get rid of the dresses I buy her. They're worth thousands. I think the girl stole it. She was very evasive when I asked her where she worked before coming here.' He sounded quite indignant that his wife would even consider giving her old clothes away.

'Do you think you could call your wife? That way we can clear this matter up.'

CHAPTER 26

Margot

Margot was tucked away in her office at the back of the hotel, a sanctuary filled with the subtle scent of polished wood and fresh flowers. It felt like her little kingdom, and she was determined to rule it well. She absentmindedly twirled her pen between her fingers, her gaze drifting to the expansive window that framed the breathtaking view over the beautiful lake. The sunlight glistened on the water's surface, casting dancing reflections that sparkled like diamonds, adding a calming backdrop to her thoughts. As far as office work went, this was the perfect setting.

Her husband was frequently away on business and entrusted her with the day-to-day operations of the hotel. This arrangement suited Margot perfectly. She liked to oversee everything from the front desk to the guest experience and it gave her the opportunity to steer the hotel's direction with her own vision. She took a particular interest in the staffing of the hotel, but her way of doing things often clashed with the staff manager, Bert. His approach to hiring was meticulous to the point of being cumbersome, frequently leading to delays in filling crucial positions.

Margot liked to take control when it came to the recruitment of female staff, but this was becoming more difficult. He kept accusing her of treating male and female applicants differently but didn't understand the challenges women had to go through. She had invested a significant amount of time in establishing connections and guaranteeing the safe rescue of girls in danger. Nothing must jeopardise her operation. It had become more important to her than the hotel's balance sheet and there were girls whose lives depended on it.

She felt a shiver run down her spine, the chilling echoes of that fateful night lingering in the recesses of her mind. Though years had passed, the vivid images still haunted her, woven into the very fabric of her thoughts. The weight of unspoken guilt pressed heavily on her, an unrelenting reminder of choices made, and lives changed forever. She had tried to move beyond it, to stop being her own harshest critic. Yet every time she saved a girl in peril, it felt as if she was piecing together her own fractured past, trying to transform the shadows of that night into a beacon of hope for others. Each act of rescue was her silent vow, a commitment to channel the pain into purpose and forge a brighter path for those at risk.

Bert was becoming a hindrance.

The man's an interfering menace. I'm the boss, not him.

As she contemplated the ongoing challenges, the idea of replacing Bert crossed her mind, but she couldn't think of a single legitimate reason to get rid of him. He was a model employee and always worked by the book. Besides, her husband would never agree to his dismissal and would questions her reasons for wanting him replaced.

There was a knock at the door. 'Come in,' she called.

Bert's face came into view. 'I need a word if you've five minutes.'

She sighed, wondering what the problem was now.

He's too thorough for his own good.

'Young Kathleen. I can't find anything in her file on her background. There's no job application, CV or references. We don't know anything about her. And the girl is being very evasive when I ask about her previous employment, but quite frankly I shouldn't be asking, there should be a complete record on every employee.'

'Is there a problem then?'

He looked exasperated and his arms flew into the air. 'With all due respect, employing people with no record has repercussions.'

She sighed.

'Something's cropped up which is why I'm asking you for clarity.'

'Leave it with me.' The man was such a hindrance. She had things to attend to and he was just a time-waster.

'Don't you at least want to know what's happened?'

'Kathleen is very trustworthy. I picked her up from the docks. Delightful young girl.'

'She didn't come through the usual agency.'

'No, she came highly recommended from one of my friends.'

'One of our guests is accusing Kathleen of wearing his wife's dress. An exclusive dress that's supposed to be a one-off.'

'I think I know the gentleman you're referring to. His wife is the lady who recommended Kathleen.'

'How did Kathleen know the lady? Did she work for her?'

'It's not important for you to know. Kathleen is a valued trustworthy member of our staff. Her privacy is paramount.'

'But I don't understand why you are employing people with no record.'

She stared at him. 'Sometimes in life we have to help those who need help. Have you any reason to doubt her work?'

'No.'

'Well then, you can get back to your work.'

'But this is of great concern.'

'This is something you don't need to concern yourself with,' she said frostily. 'I will resolve the situation. But rest assured, I am absolutely confident that Kathleen did not steal the dress.'

CHAPTER 27

Kathleen

Kathleen waited in the staff manager's office, worried sick about what could happen next. After about ten minutes, she heard footsteps, and he came back into the office and sat down.

'It looks like you're in the clear, young lady, but I shall be keeping a very close eye on you. Something doesn't quite add up, it doesn't make sense and I've been told not to pry.'

Although she was now in the clear, it was interesting how everyone was quick to find fault and put her down. She was pleased that she felt safe and had somebody looking after her but there was the underlying fear that she was always fighting to prove herself. She always felt on the outside looking in. How lovely it would be to have a family around her.

She knew she was innocent but wondered how it had suddenly been so easily resolved. She found out later that evening when the guest came to apologise. His wife had apparently had a clear-out as the dresses no longer fitted her.

'I don't know how you came to acquire it, but you did look rather stunning in it,' he said.

It heartened her that she could continue at the hotel. She loved the guests, particularly the kind older couples, however she still felt intimidated when left alone with single male guests or members of staff, apart from Fred the gardener. The one disappointing cloud on the horizon though was Bella's imminent departure. They had become close friends. She hoped her new roommate would be as nice.

The time passed quickly and soon it was the day Bella was leaving. Kathleen felt desolate. Part of her wanted to go too. As they said their goodbyes, they clung on to each other. This was the hardest part. It was another wrench. Kathleen always looked on the bright side of life though couldn't help feeling apprehensive about the new roommate and doubted they would so easily slot into a comfortable friendship.

A couple of days later, the new roommate arrived. She hovered at the foot of her bed. She was Niamh, and Kathleen had been asked to help settle her in. She appeared completely lost, and her eyes held a haunted gaze. Kathleen had tried talking to her, but the girl had lost her tongue.

She looked defeated, haggard, almost lifeless, yet she couldn't have been much older than Kathleen. Her eyes were underscored with dark circles, and she was painfully thin, with long ropes of muscle in her arms. When Kathleen smiled and tried to be welcoming by putting her at ease, Niamh bent her head and stared at the floor, her arms rigid by her sides. She recognised that haunted look.

She couldn't possibly be one of them. Could she?

Something inside her turned cold like splinters of ice spreading and branching down her spine.

She realised her heart was racing, a measure of the fear she still felt when she thought about The Weeping Lady.

'Come and sit down,' she said in a gentle voice, patting the bed. 'You won't be starting work for a couple of days. They give you time to settle in.'

The girl stood there, still not speaking, so Kathleen chanced a bold comment. 'Looks like you might need a few days to settle in, and maybe some good food to fill you up.'

Despite her best efforts, the girl just wasn't going to speak. Wherever she'd come from, it was clear she'd suffered, and Kathleen found it disturbing to think about what she might have experienced.

'I'll leave you to settle in. Try and rest. I'll be back later.'

Kathleen returned to her duties downstairs but all afternoon she thought of Niamh, unable to shake the uneasy feeling that something terrible had happened to her. How had she come to work at the hotel? She couldn't picture her going through an interview process, not with her shyness and lack of confidence. It just didn't add up. Yet her own situation was unusual, and they had hired her without even meeting her first.

After her shift, she wearily climbed the stairs, yawning and ready for bed. For the past hour she'd forgotten about Niamh, but now she remembered and sighed, feeling mildly resentful at having to share a room. It had been nice to have her own personal space. In the time since Bella had gone, she'd grown used to it and looked forward to the end of her shift, climbing into bed and reading a book before dropping off. It was like being back at home, she valued her time alone and it felt safe. She opened the door. The room was shrouded in darkness, and she switched on the light to find Niamh wide awake and lying on the bed fully clothed, staring at the ceiling, her face expressionless. She quickly turned onto her side away from Kathleen and stared at the wall.

Kathleen leaned down and gave her arm a reassuring touch. She flinched and turned further away. What was going on with this girl? She wished she could fathom it, gain her trust, and get her to talk.

Nothing changed over the next couple of days. Niamh still didn't talk or smile. It was the same down in the kitchen with the other members of staff. The most they got out of her was a nod or a shake of her head, but never a smile. The chef knew better than to start barking orders at her. Everyone was very gentle and patient with her, seeming to know that she needed a wide berth. She soon learned her duties and was very diligent.

A week after joining the hotel, Niamh finally spoke. They'd just got into bed and Kathleen was about to read her book before turning off the bedside lamp.

'It's nice here,' she said, taking Kathleen by surprise. She had a thick southern Irish accent, making Kathleen more convinced than ever that she'd spent time in a laundry or an industrial school.

Kathleen didn't want her to clam up, so she trod carefully, keeping the conversation light. 'Yes, it is, I love walking round the lake and into the woods, it's so beautiful and peaceful. It'll be lovely now spring is here, bit cold out still though.'

She didn't speak again for a few days, but Kathleen was always cheerful around her, chatting away even though she knew she wouldn't get any response. Then one night she woke to hear Niamh quietly crying into her pillow. Worried, she shifted in her bed, wondering if she should say something. Her heart went out to the poor girl, she didn't want her to have to suffer in silence with whatever trouble she was carrying.

'You can trust me, Niamh.' She reached out and touched her arm. She pulled away. 'Leave me alone.'

'Tell me, have you come from one of the laundries?'

She didn't reply but didn't deny it. Her body language and demeanour almost confirmed her suspicions. If this was the case, it would be a long time before Niamh would trust anyone enough to share her past.

CHAPTER 28

TWO MONTHS EARLIER

Niamh

Niamh had been summoned to the front parlour. She'd never stepped inside this room, not even to clean it. She knew this was where visitors were entertained--various members of the Catholic Church, prospective parents coming to The Weeping Lady to choose a baby and very occasionally parents of the inmates. As she stepped into the dimly lit room, she took a moment to register that her parents were sitting at the mahogany table having tea and cake with three of the senior members of the order. It had been months since she'd last seen them, that day when they'd sent her away with that cruel monster Father Joseph, a decision she still couldn't fathom--their shame overshadowing their love. The memory of their cold faces haunted her, their complete silence deepening the ache in her heart--no letters, no phone calls--during all this time.

'Niamh, come in.' Mother Superior's voice was unexpectedly bright and welcoming, a stark contrast to her usual harsh demeanour. Like Jekyll and Hyde, she shifted between two vastly different worlds.

Niamh couldn't find it in herself to smile at her parents because it was still very hard to wrap her mind around the facts. They'd abandoned her, cast her aside with the very man who had robbed her of her innocence, and dumped her here to carry the burden of his actions.

'Mum, Dad,' she said in a quiet, dull voice.

They were in their Sunday best, and she felt conscious of her shabby grey uniform. Her mum was clutching her little black shiny handbag on her lap, and her dad shifted uncomfortably in his chair avoiding eye contact with Niamh.

'Your parents have come here to discuss your future,' Mother Superior said.

About to tell her parents about Luke, she saw the cold expression on her mum's face and stopped herself. Niamh had clung to the fragile hope, convincing herself that once her parents laid eyes on Luke, her precious baby, their hearts would soften, and they'd welcome their grandson into the family. But now, standing before them, she knew better. She had to try though, after all what was the alternative? The nuns would arrange his adoption, taking him from her and she'd never see him again. She felt a surge of desperation and dread at the thought of losing her baby. She loved him beyond words.

'Would you like to see your grandson?' she asked them. 'He's a few weeks old now and he's beautiful. He's got your eyes, Dad. I could run upstairs and ask them to open the nursery and bring him down.'

'I've no interest in seeing a bastard child,' her mum replied. 'There's never been a bastard born into our family until now.' Her tone lacked the anger it had carried all those months ago, instead there was a chilling indifference that sent a shiver down Niamh's spine.

'But he's my baby and I want to keep him.'

'Nonsense, no bastard child is living in my home, and that's the end of it. You'll have to give him up, just like the others.'

Her words were a dagger to her heart. How could the woman who was supposed to love and support her be so cruel and unfeeling?

Mother Superior stood up, a look of triumph on her face. 'You can go now, Niamh, I need to speak to your parents.'

Niamh felt a wave of devastation wash over her and she turned to go. Tears brimmed in her eyes, but she held them back, aware of the repercussions that could follow if she dared to show any emotion in this bleak institution. She felt utterly helpless to stop a course of action that had already been set in motion.

A few days later, Niamh was in the nursery breastfeeding a very hungry Luke when she heard quick footsteps approaching and the clink of rosary beads.

'Hurry up, child, I need the baby.'

She finished breastfeeding and wiped the baby's mouth. Without uttering a word, the nun approached her and lifted Luke from her arms before turning away and taking him down the corridor.

She rushed after the nun with a mix of disbelief and terror. Her breasts were dripping milk and Luke was now wailing. 'Where are you taking him? You can't just take him.'

At the top of the stairs, she screamed after her, 'Please, bring him back. Where are you taking my baby?'

She dashed down the steps and around the corner to see the nun disappear through a door before sliding a bolt into place. She pounded the door with her fists, her breasts still dripping milk and aching, her thin nightdress tangled around her body, until her fists were red raw, and her head hurt from screaming so much. She sank down on the chequerboard floor of the corridor and curled up into a ball with her arms round her knees and her head resting on them. All she felt was utter desolation. The thought of never seeing Luke again was so suffocating, so utterly overwhelming, she'd never come back from this. She was destroyed.

She stayed huddled on the floor rocking back and forth and sobbing before someone came to collect her.

The following day, she was again summoned downstairs. Mother Superior stood outside her office with Father Joseph. The sight of him made her recoil and her stomach twisted in dread. She'd desperately wished never to see him again, but here he was, looming like a shadow. What was he doing here?

'Pack up quickly, we need to get going,' Father Joseph said.

Had he come to take her home? The thought of spending hours in the confined space of his car with him filled her with alarm. Why couldn't her parents have collected her?

Back in the dormitory she gathered her few belongings and wandered back along the corridor. As she passed the nursery, she paused outside to listen to the babies crying, her heart quietly breaking as she thought of all the hours she'd spent in that room with Luke, watching him grow and develop, the joy he'd brought her, the bond they'd formed. Now she was leaving this place without him, and she'd never know what had happened to him. The memories of their short time together were wrapped up in these walls.

'Goodbye, Mother Superior,' she said getting into the car.

'Don't stray from the path of the Lord again,' she replied curtly before turning and walking back into the house.

There was so much rage bubbling up inside her. She wanted to shout at the woman, but what was the point? She thought she was doing God's will, but the truth was she was nothing but a sanctimonious old witch and didn't care about the welfare of any of the girls. A loving God wouldn't allow such suffering and injustice, she was sure of that.

As they set off, her breasts started to ache once more. Her body still thought she should be feeding Luke, and her heart was heavy with the longing for him.

'Couldn't my parents have collected me?' She felt cross and irritated with her parents for not bothering to come. She really didn't want to have to spend more time with this vile man.

'You're not going home, what on earth makes you think your mother wants you back, you little trollop?' he asked coldly. 'We're taking a ferry to England. Then I'll be passing you over to Father Brendan and he'll drive you to his house in Holyhead where you'll be taught respect and humility. Father Brendan needs a housekeeper and someone to warm his bed at night. You will stay for as long as he needs you and undertake whatever duties are required. You should be grateful, many of the girls at the laundry would die for this chance.'

'You make it out that I'm the sinner. You got me in this predicament, you're a disgrace to the church. You should be helping me. If he lays a finger on me, I'll make sure he never sees another day.'

'If you ever cross me, you'll find out just how cruel I can be. Girls like you are worthless. Once a sinner, always a sinner.'

'For a man of the cloth, you're a disgrace, you haven't got a godly bone in your body, you're the sinner not me.' She'd found a voice inside her she didn't know was there and released it like a snake spitting venom. 'You've ruined my life, what's to become of me? You've robbed me. You've made me out to be a slut and you know it. You hide behind the truth, making out you're a nice holy man who people can trust and look up to, but if I told anyone they wouldn't believe me, only I know different, I know the truth of what you did to me. One day you'll get your comeuppance. God works in mysterious ways, isn't that what you lot always say?'

If she could have stabbed him there and then, she would have done.

When she'd finished her rant, she sat there trembling and shivering, tears streaming down her face.

As they drove through the countryside, she tried to calm herself and began to plot her escape. One thing was for sure, she never wanted to be near a man of the cloth again. She'd rather die than serve the Lord's shepherds.

CHAPTER 29

Margot

Margot headed back to the car park after waving goodbye to her friend at the ferry terminal. She reflected on the lovely day she'd had. Her friend had travelled all the way from Dublin to see her. They'd enjoyed a delicious lunch in town, a walk along the coastal path, stopping to gaze at the lighthouse and boats bobbing in the harbour. It had been uplifting to share quality time with a lifelong friend and a welcome break from life at the hotel––a day filled with laughter and shared stories. Margot was always grateful for the time spent with her.

As she approached her car, she noticed a priest and girl wandering around as if they were looking for something or somebody. How curious, she thought, pulling her keys out of her bag, not taking her eyes off them. Something didn't feel right. It seemed odd to see a priest wandering around and with a teenage girl in tow. She knew that the girl wasn't his daughter because priests couldn't marry.

She approached them and put on her best charm. 'Father, you look lost, may I help?'

'I'm looking for a car, I'm meeting my friend here.'

'You'll find plenty of cars here.' She laughed. She was feeling in a silly mood after being with her friend. 'Father, it's unusual to see an Irish priest in these parts.'

Margot looked at the girl standing beside him quickly taking in the shabby state of her. She was wearing a ragged grey dress and battered shoes. She'd seen similar before. The girl looked terrified. Her eyes were dark and sunken and there was a hollowing of the cheeks that should have been blooming and firm.

'What brings you here, Father?'

'We're over here visiting a fellow priest.'

The girl was shivering and looked up at Margot through pleading eyes. 'He's lying.' She spun round and gave the priest a hard shove, sending him tumbling to the ground, his face frozen in disbelief. Without pausing, she bolted away.

Looking shocked, he took his time before scrambling to his feet.

'Bloody girl,' he said brushing himself down. 'She will not do as she's told. She will have to do penance for this.'

'Can I help?'

'Help, you're nothing but a hindrance, lady. You should not have interfered. Now look what you've done. I'm going to have to spend the next few hours searching for her, then take her where she belongs.'

Margot was shocked at how rude he was. A man of the cloth with no manners, that had to be a first. 'She probably needs five minutes to herself.'

'Let her run off, she's not going to get far. She knows what's good for her.'

'Are you sure there's nothing I can do?' She wanted to hold him up, give the girl a chance to get away.

'Don't interfere again,' he shouted as he stormed away.

Margot was a wily old bird, she knew the town, its alleys and cut-throughs, and where the girl might hide. She was conspicuous in her uniform though and could attract attention.

Just then, another car pulled into the car park. The priest dashed over to the car and Margot assumed it was his friend arriving. That would delay his search and work in her favour.

She jumped in her car and drove towards the road that connected to the alley where the girl had run off. The light was fading rapidly, and she feared for the girl's safety out in the cold alone and with no coat. After a while, she spotted her looking in bins. She kept her distance and watched her, not wanting to frighten her. They passed a church and Margot looked up and thought, *she won't be going to the church, that's for sure.*

It was starting to get very cold, and the girl dived into a bus shelter. Margot waited a few moments wondering what she was going to say before slowly peering into the shelter.

The girl was huddled in the corner, shivering, her arms wrapped tightly around her body as if her embrace could shield her from the biting cold.

'Child, it's okay, the priest isn't here,' she said in a soft quiet voice. She sat down beside her. 'I want to help you. Are you a child from one of the Irish mother and baby homes?'

The girl gave a slight nod but didn't speak.

'It's alright, I want to help you. Should you be with the priest or not?'

'I'm not going with him.' She was adamant. 'I'd rather die out here in the cold than go with that horrible man.'

'I know, pet, now come on, we don't have much time. He'll be looking for you. You'll be safe with me.'

She tried to take the girl's hand, but she pulled away. 'How do I know I can trust you? Are you going to take me back to Ireland? I'm not going back to the laundry.'

'You'll just have to trust me. Come quickly.' The girl got up slowly and followed Margot to her car parked a short way off.

'Get in the car,' she said. 'Keep down. There's a blanket in the back, cover yourself up. Don't look up until we reach our destination.'

She started the engine and turned on the headlights. Twin golden spears cut into the darkness as she put the car into gear and drove away. As she drove, her eyes darted over every road they passed, searching for the telltale silhouette of the priest cloaked in his dark attire.

Before long, they had left the town behind, the houses fading into the desolate expanse of Welsh countryside where only sheep roamed. Soon, she found herself driving through the village of her childhood. She hadn't planned to come this way. The village felt eerie in the dark. Even after all these years, the sight of it sent an unsettling chill down her spine, for this was where it had happened. Pausing at the traffic lights, her gaze drifted across to the village hall. She was such a tomboy back then, destined to learn football or another male sport, but if she hadn't taken karate lessons as a teenager, would she have been capable of what she'd done? Was that a blessing or a curse?

Then suddenly, the alleyway beside the cemetery came into view. She eased the car to a stop, her heart pounding as memories of that horrific night flooded back.

The night the local priest assaulted me.

Her training had kicked in, and she had fought back––she had killed him.

The image of him thudding to the ground like a sack of potatoes surfaced sharply in her mind, alongside the chilling sight of blood pooling beneath his head. The investigation into his death had gone on for months, the speculation years. She remembered the headlines in the newspaper. She had never spoken a word to anyone about that night, a secret she wore like a shroud––one she knew she would carry to the grave.

She was reminded of a famous quote. *The grave soul keeps its own secrets and takes its own punishment in silence.* It was a quote that perfectly captured the way she'd lived her life.

CHAPTER 30

The O'Sullivans

Sheridan pulled back the curtains, letting the morning light flood into the bedroom as she gazed at the breathtaking landscape before her. The tapestry of emerald fields rolled away, dotted with isolated farms, barns, and grazing livestock. In the distance she made out the bluey-grey peaks of the Mourne Mountains. A glistening river meandered through the scene. She pictured the boys standing on its banks learning to fish, their shouts of joy echoing in the open air when they caught their first trout.

Below, the unfenced garden blended into the countryside. A chicken pen stood in waiting, empty for now. She thought of clucking hens and the charm they would bring to the property.

An old wooden swing hung from a branch, swaying slightly in the breeze as if beckoning the girls to come out to play. Next to it, a washing line stretched across the lawn. There was something comforting about watching freshly laundered clothes dance in the breeze--a luxury she had never experienced during their marriage. Instead, clothes were dried on airers by the fire or draped over the banister, filling the air with dampness that aggravated the children's asthma.

How she wished they could all share this special moment with Liam, the first morning in their new house. A fresh start. The fear she'd experienced for the past years was evaporating but was tempered by a desperate sadness. One member of the family would always be missing, yet without giving her up, they would still be in that hellhole, their lives in danger.

Her train of thought was suddenly broken by Aidan shouting up the stairs.

'Mum, Mum, come quick.'

She rushed onto the landing. 'What's wrong?' Were they playing up already? They'd only been in the house a few hours. What had they broken? 'Can't I leave you alone for five minutes?' She dashed downstairs, to see the TV was blaring out. They'd never had a television before, she was going to have to control its use, but for the time being it was convenient to keep them quiet while she got on.

As she entered the lounge, she could hear the news. 'What is it? What's so important?' She glanced at the boys, who had pained expressions on their faces.

'Look, Mum, it's our house, it's burnt down.'

A wave of nausea washed through her stomach, a sickening churn. She followed Aidan's pointed finger to the TV, watching in horror. Their house was blackened and charred, the windows were shattered, the roof sagged with burnt beams protruding. Two armed soldiers were guarding it. The reporter was babbling away, but Sheridan's mind was in panic mode. 'Oh my God, Liam, Liam.'

She quickly clocked the girls at the dining table eating cereal, oblivious to the news and rushed to close the adjoining bevelled glass doors.

'Is Dad dead?' Aidan's panicky voice sliced through the air.

'We need to find out.' Sean got up and went to stand in front of the TV staring with a look of horror.

In that moment, Sheridan felt her heart shatter into a million tiny pieces. Watching this spectacle of horror unfold--her sons' youthful faces, their wide eyes of panic mirroring her own dread, the vulnerability of their innocence crumbling away with every second that passed under the dreadful weight of uncertainty--it was like plunging into an icy abyss of despair.

The phone wasn't yet connected. They were miles from anywhere. They had no car. Nobody knew they were here. And the note she'd left, probably long destroyed in the fire because if he'd read the note, he would be here now.

She quickly switched off the TV. All she could think to do was gather them in her arms and hug them tight. It was warmth and comfort in a moment where everything felt so irrevocably broken and so desperately sad.

Just in that moment, the girls burst into the room, asking to go outside to play. She wanted to freeze time, hold on to the last fragments of their happy family, put off that awful moment of telling them their old house was gone. How she longed for the truth to be locked away, to suspend that agonising moment like a bubble where laughter and happiness still danced, and innocence still wrapped around them.

'Yes, you two go outside to play.' She ushered them towards the back door, smiling and keeping her face neutral, not giving anything away. 'There's a swing in the garden.'

'When are we starting our new school?' Maeve asked.

'I need to find places for you all first, but hopefully in a couple of days, pet.'

'Where's our sister, where's Aisling?' Roisin asked.

She'd tried to explain to them yesterday evening what had happened and why Aisling had gone. It had been the most difficult conversation she'd ever had. There was no gentle way to convey to her children the heartbreaking truth of why she had sold their sister. They couldn't comprehend the depths of her decision, nor could they ever fully grasp the pain and complexity behind it. They were young, they were innocent and life to them was simple––families stayed together, families loved each other.

'We talked about this yesterday, pet,' she said gently. 'Have you forgotten?'

Roisin looked up at her through confused and sad eyes. 'Will you send us away too?'

She looked down at her daughters, who were both looking up in alarm. 'No pet, I promise you, that will never happen.' She grabbed their little hands, clasping them together and squeezing hard. 'I promise.'

As she stepped back into the house, the doorbell rang. She had no idea who would be calling. She certainly wasn't expecting anybody. Maybe it was the neighbour from the nearby farm calling round out of curiosity and friendliness. This was the last thing she needed, to put on a brave face and be forced to be polite. She wanted to believe it was just a door-to-door salesperson, someone with a clipboard in hand, but she feared the worst. The police––come to break the news of Liam's death. She paused in front of the hall mirror checking her appearance.

It was Declan, Liam's dad. Everyone called him Dec. He looked ashen. She started sobbing and collapsed into his arms.

'It's okay, love, I've got some news, it's not all bad, it's Liam.'

'I've just seen the news. The house.'

'He's been injured and he's in hospital.'

She gasped in relief. He was alive, thank God.

'We saw the house on the news, and I thought the worst. There was no way of me contacting anybody.'

Her heart raced wildly in her chest, caught between relief and confusion, as the news left her momentarily speechless.

'So he's alive?' Hope soared.

'Yes, but God only knows how. He had a very lucky escape, but he's suffered burns.'

'Can you take me to see him?' She turned in a fluster, rummaging through the coats pegged along the wall rack.

'Of course, that's why I'm here. Will the boys be okay to look after the girls?'

'Oh my God, it could have been all of us.' The realisation struck like a thunderbolt. Her entire family could have perished in that fire, and as for the baby--Aisling would never have made it. In a cruel twist of fate, it hit her then that giving Aisling away might have been the right decision. A desperate and extreme measure, mad, crazy perhaps, but she was safe.

The journey to hospital seemed to take forever. They parked up and headed to the entrance. Before going in, Liam's dad stopped her, his hand on her shoulder.

'I think we're going to be in for a shock, love, but at least he's alive, and that we must be grateful for, but it's going to be a long and painful recovery.'

'How bad is he?'

'I don't know, love, they wouldn't tell me over the phone, only that he's suffered

life-changing injuries. We need to be prepared.'

God, now I've got to look after him as well, he wouldn't listen to me, perhaps now he believes what I was telling him.

This could all have been avoided.

Why are men so stubborn? He thought I was being neurotic.

CHAPTER 31

The O'Sullivans
Sheridan paused just outside the hospital entrance, her heart thumping in her chest like a restless bird.

'I can't do this,' she said, stumbling towards a railing for support, her voice splintering.

Liam's dad took her hand and gave it a reassuring squeeze before leading her inside. The pungent smell of disinfectant hit her making her reel back to the recent memory of little Maeve injured.

She glanced up at the signage, squinting against the stark fluorescent lights buzzing overhead as she looked for the burns unit. They navigated the maze of unfamiliar faces and sterile corridors and with each step that took her closer to his room, she felt a mix of dread and determination as she prepared for whatever awaited her.

They arrived in the burns unit where they disinfected their hands and put on protective coveralls and facemasks before being ushered into a family room to speak with a doctor. Dec had explained to her that Liam was in an isolation room being at high risk of infection due to his damaged skin. This had made her feel panicky; she knew he was in the best place and was in a stable condition, but she was aware of all the complications. Would she be able to hug him? She was still angry.

She'd only been in the unit for a couple of minutes when she started to feel claustrophobic and wanted to dash out for some air, and that was before she'd even seen him. She felt the blood drain from her face and managed to squeak out the words, 'How is he, doctor?'

'Well, Mrs O'Sullivan, I think you should both take a seat, and I will explain the situation.'

Sheridan was glad to sit down. She noticed a jug of water and paper cups. Feeling sick, she reached over to help herself to water.

'I'm afraid I have to warn you that your husband has sustained significant burns across twenty percent of his body including his face. Some are only minor while others are more serious and will require a skin graft. I'm sorry if this upsets you but I need you to know how severe his injuries are. He will shortly be undergoing surgery and unfortunately you will be unable to talk to him as he's heavily sedated. It is likely that his recovery will be long and drawn out. This will mean he will need a lot of support at what will be a very difficult time for him. I cannot emphasise enough how strong you will all need to be as the visual impact on you all will be significant. I do need to prepare you both for what at first may seem a horrendous sight, but his wounds will heal in time although he will never recover to his former looks. We have specialist staff who will be able to support you. He will need you to be strong for both him and the rest of your family.'

She stared at the floor.

'Do you have children?'

'Yes.'

'The hardest impact will be on your children, as he will be unable to play with them for some considerable time due to the ongoing pain he will experience, and his appearance may frighten them. I'm sorry to be the bearer of this news but we will do everything in our power to care for him until he is released from the hospital. If you wish to see him, I can take you to the viewing screen but I'm afraid you can't go in, as he will soon be going into surgery. As you will appreciate due to the nature of the incident, the police are keen to interview you in case you may be able to shed any light. There is a female officer waiting in the reception area when you are ready to speak. Have you any questions, although the information I can give you is limited at this stage? I shall know more after we've operated. Please take as much time as you need. We will of course keep you updated.' The doctor closed his folder and led them along the corridor.

Sheridan felt shaky, as if her legs might give way at any moment. Dec put his arm around her as they came to the window, where beyond, Liam lay.

When she saw him, her breath caught in her throat, and she let out a howl. That once handsome familiar face, transformed into a harrowing image, would be carved into her mind forever.

Shaking and with tears pouring down her face, she quickly looked away. 'Why's he got a drip?' she asked the doctor.

'He's receiving large amounts of intravenous fluid because of tissue swelling and capillary fluid leakage. Please don't be alarmed by all the machines. They are monitoring his heart and vital organs.'

'Come on, love, let's get you home, we can come back later, after his surgery.'

'But the kids, what am I going to do? And I still need to find them new schools.'

'Don't you be worrying. Vera will come and look after them. Everything's going to be okay.'

She staggered towards the exit with Dec supporting her and offering reassuring words. She didn't know what she'd do without her in-laws, they were a godsend. But she knew one thing––everything was not going to be fine. Life was going to be hard for all of them especially Liam. Looking after her husband and the children, dealing with the fallout of everything that had happened. Her mind flashed back.

Thank God I don't have a baby to look after too.

She felt guilty for thinking this, but right now others needed her more.

CHAPTER 32

Father Joseph

After Niamh sent Father Joseph crashing to the ground, he lay there, momentarily stunned before scrambling to his feet, angry and embarrassed. He brushed the dirt off his robes, his hands trembling, a mixture of shock and outrage coursing through his veins.

Never in his years of service had he encountered such defiance from anyone, let alone a woman, a young girl like Niamh. A storm of thoughts raged inside him.

I'm a priest, a shepherd of the community, a conduit of God's will. I deserve respect. How dare she challenge my authority.

'Damn girl,' he mumbled under his breath, his fists clenching at his sides, his legs shaky. The audacity of her actions, he couldn't let this act of disrespect go unchallenged and Mother Superior wouldn't be impressed in the slightest if she found out. Niamh had to be taught a lesson on the importance of obedience. The scriptures emphasised submission to authority, a principle that had been upheld for centuries. It was his duty to guide her back to the Lord. With that mantra bolstering his sense of purpose, he muttered, 'I will find her.' But as he glanced round, he couldn't see where she'd gone. There were a couple of alleyways, she could have gone down either. And what had happened to the interfering busybody? She was nowhere to be seen. Had she followed Niamh or driven off?

Just then, a woman hurried over, her expression filled with concern. 'Are you okay, Father? I saw what happened. Margot should have helped you. I'm really surprised at her. She's usually so caring.'

'Margot?' Father Joseph asked, confusion wrinkling his brow. 'Who's Margot?'

'The woman you were talking to. She owns a hotel a few miles away. I thought you knew her.'

A flicker of irritation flashed through him. *Margot.* She was just a passerby, but now suspicion crept in––was she helping Niamh to escape? Where could they have gone? Was she out there looking for Niamh, aiding her in this defiance?

He felt his grip on the situation slipping away. Who did the little tart think she was? Father Duncan would be here any minute. How was he going to explain himself? He was supposed to be delivering Father Duncan's new housekeeper.

'What's the name of this hotel?'

'It's the Brodwin Hall Hotel, a converted castle set in beautiful grounds. Take the road out of town towards Conwy, you can't miss it.'

Father Joseph thanked the woman, and as she walked away, he noticed Father Duncan pulling into the car park. He hastily made his way over to him.

'Hello, where's the girl?' Father Duncan's robes swished as he walked, the fabric casting a sombre shadow as he approached.

'That's a good question. The insolent little wench assaulted me and bolted a few minutes ago, but goodness knows where she could have gone. She has no money, she's only recently delivered a baby, and if she has any sense, she'll come back.'

Father Duncan glanced round. 'Must admit you do look rather pale and shaky, are you alright? I don't have time to waste chasing a girl round Holyhead. If she doesn't want to work for me, we can't make her. Your Mother Superior can find me a more appreciative girl– one who understands the value of this position and how lucky they are. I mean, she's getting free room and board in exchange for a few light duties. I have no interest in employing someone who shows nothing but ingratitude. It's disrespectful and quite frankly exhausting. I need someone who is keen and values the opportunity.'

'She was speaking with a woman––Margot, I'm told her name was, by a passerby. You might know of her, she owns the large hotel out of town.'

'Ah yes, I think I saw a hotel on my way in. What on earth would she want with the girl?'

'I can't shake the feeling this woman may have helped her slip away. We could drive up to the hotel, we can't just abandon the lass, we're responsible for her.'

Father Duncan looked thoughtful. 'I don't think we should be too hasty. Let's walk into town, grab a coffee. We might find her wandering the streets. It's not a big place.'

As they sipped their steaming coffees, sitting by the window in a greasy spoon café, every now and again glancing up and down the road, Father Joseph said, 'I think you're right. I don't think we should be too hasty. If we just show up at the hotel, we'll spook them. I propose we wait a bit––maybe even a few days––then show up unexpectedly to catch them by surprise.'

'Chances of that woman helping her are probably miniscule but worth a try, I guess. Not as if she knew her. Let me know when you're back over this way and we can head out there.'

'In the meantime, we could drop into the local police station.'

'I'm not sure, they might start asking difficult questions,

considering her background, least they know the better, let's hold fire for the moment.'

A fortnight later, the priests met in Holyhead. They climbed into one car and set off towards the hotel. Arriving at the top of the long driveway, they decided to walk the rest of the way. They took a moment to collect themselves, glancing at each other with silent understanding. With a shared nod, they stepped out of the car, the crunch of gravel underfoot punctuating the stillness. They started their walk down the long drive, the looming hotel coming into view, shadows stretching ominously as evening approached. Each step felt heavy with purpose, the weight of their mission pressing down on them.

The front door was propped open for a group of guests who were gathering their bags and suitcases and heading out to the car park. Cheery after their stay, they smiled and said good evening. Father Joseph reached for a copper bell on the hall table displaying an array of leaflets of local places to visit. He picked it up and the sound of its tinkling rang through the house.

A man appeared from an office behind the reception. He was wearing a dark suit and there was a badge pinned to his lapel. He was the staff manager. 'Gentlemen, I'll be with you in a moment, I'm just taking care of a few guests, if you could kindly wait.' He showed them to a settee across from the reception. 'I'll be with you as soon as I can.'

As they waited, Father Joseph looked around. It was a classy hotel, probably very pricey, not the sort of place he was used to staying in. His eye was drawn to the gleaming Moroccan-style tiled flooring which added an elegant touch. To one side, a neatly arranged rack held pairs of wellies and umbrellas, suggesting that even the most refined guests were prepared for unpredictable weather. Above them, a stunning chandelier hung gracefully, its crystals catching the light and casting shimmering reflections around the hall.

Soft murmurs of conversation floated from the lounge area where guests were sipping coffee and chatting. Just then, there was a loud screech and the sound of females giggling. For some reason he thought of Kathleen. It sounded like her.

Leaning forward and about to get up to investigate, Father Duncan put a firm hand on his shoulder. 'Let's do this properly, remember who we are.'

The man reappeared. 'Sorry to have kept you. How can I help you gentlemen? Do you have a reservation?'

They stood up and Father Joseph spoke. 'We're here on a delicate matter. We're concerned about the welfare of a young girl who is supposed to be in our care. She ran off a couple of weeks ago. She's only recently been in hospital, she's vulnerable and we really need to find her.'

'Oh.' The manager frowned. 'Have you reported her missing to the police?'

'We don't want to alarm her by getting the police involved, she's a fragile lass and needs protecting.'

'What makes you think she might be here? What's her name?'

'Niamh. She was last seen talking to the owner of your hotel, Margot, in the car park by the ferries over at Holyhead. We were wondering if Margot might have brought her here. If we could speak to Margot that would be very helpful. We just need to find her, but it's probably a long shot that she's ended up here.'

Father Duncan pulled out a small photograph of Niamh from his pocket. 'This is the lass.'

As the man peered at the photo, Father Joseph tried to gauge his reaction. His expression was blank and if he recognised Niamh, he wasn't giving anything away.

'I'm sorry Father, face doesn't look familiar. How old is she? I can get the owner to speak to you. Would you like me to get her?'

'Yes, that would be most helpful.'

The manager walked away down the corridor and knocked on a door. Father Joseph could hear whispering, and strained to hear what was being said but it was too far away.

Margot walked towards them. 'Father, didn't I meet you a couple of weeks ago in Holyhead, how may I help you? I understand you're looking for a girl called Niamh, is that the young lady you were with? The one who pushed you over.' She chuckled. 'Sorry, Father, I did have to laugh, she was such a small girl and you being rather large.'

'Yes, it was and after your interruption she ran away, and we can't find her. We're very concerned.'

'Can I ask, why did she run away? Isn't it unusual to run away from a priest? What makes you think I might be able to help? I have to tell you, I run a very reputable hotel here, she's far too young to be of use here, why would she come here?'

'I thought she might have asked you to help her.'

Margot laughed. 'Have you reported her as a missing person? The police are in a far better position to help.'

'Well no, it's rather a delicate matter with her family, we thought it's better we deal with it.'

'Well Father, I'm a very busy person, I think the police are your best port of call. You can phone them from here if you wish.'

'Oh no, no, we'll continue our investigations and hopefully find her before she comes to harm.'

The priests looked at each other and Father Joseph said, 'We'll call the police if we can't find her, thank you for your time, we'll trouble you no further.'

They returned to their car and Father Joseph turned to Father Duncan and said, 'Well she's either a good actress or she's keeping it close to her chest, but she gave nothing away. I think we need to keep our ears close to the ground for a few days to see if any clues turn up. If we can't find her, she's no longer our problem.'

Father Duncan laughed. 'The thought of you rolling around on the floor does fill me with mirth. You have to admit, it is rather funny. Reminds me back to the days when we were boy scouts together.'

CHAPTER 33

*K*athleen
　　　Kathleen was descending the stairs when the priests were leaving. Just as she reached the landing where a huge leaded light window overlooked the drive, she stopped in her tracks and froze. One of the voices in the hall sounded familiar. So familiar it cut right through her. A chill ran down her spine as she strained to listen, her heart pounding, her legs suddenly wobbly.

Father Joseph.

What was he doing here? The front door opened, and she heard Margot saying goodbye. Quickly, she ducked behind the heavy velvet drapes and peered out the window as she waited for the person to come into view and her worst fears to be confirmed.

She found herself staring down at the top of Father Joseph's head. As he walked away, she was left in no doubt that it was him. She felt physically sick. He was the one person she never wanted to see again. The air thickened around her, anxiety building inside her as the terrible memory of what he'd done to her came crashing back.

Had he come looking for her, and how had he found out she was here?

She waited a few moments watching them disappear carefully keeping out of view before heading down the second set of stairs and hurrying down the hall towards Margot's office.

'What did those priests want?' She was shaky and on the verge of tears and Margot, quick to sense something was wrong, offered her a chair and reached out to touch her arm.

'They were looking for Niamh.'

'How do they know Niamh?' Kathleen asked in alarm. Everything now made sense. So, Niamh was connected to the laundries. She'd guessed as much. She suddenly felt uncomfortable.

'It doesn't matter, miss, I better get back to my work.'

As she got up, Margot frowned, took her hand and looked into her eyes. 'I understand, Kathleen,' she said in a gentle tone. 'I'm not going to pry, but I think that priest caused you and Niamh a lot of harm. Don't worry, you're safe here--for now anyway--as long as he doesn't come looking again. You were both lucky you weren't around.'

Kathleen was too scared to speak. Her heart was in her throat. She slipped out of Margot's office and hurried upstairs to find Niamh.

Back in their bedroom she found Niamh sitting on her bed sobbing. She'd completely broken down. 'They suspect I'm here. I've seen them, the priests.'

'What do you mean?'

'They're looking for me, they want to take me back, I'd rather die than go back. I can't go back.'

Kathleen sat down on her own bed and faced Niamh. 'Can't go back where?'

She started shivering and shaking. 'I can't tell you. I'm too ashamed. There's no point, no one would believe me, don't you know priests are sacred, they can do no wrong?'

She swallowed her own inner torment, pursing her lips and forcing herself to stay quiet about her own situation. Even though she desperately wanted to share her story with Niamh, she knew she couldn't, and this was about Niamh not her. Everything Kathleen wanted to say gathered on her tongue and the effort of holding it all back almost choked her. Back at the laundry, the girls hadn't been allowed to speak to each other, their names were changed to make it difficult to trace each other and for their adopted children to trace them in years to come. It had been drummed into them to be careful who they trusted.

When Kathleen woke the following morning, the early light was seeping into the room, and she got up, stretched, and craned her head to look out of the small dormer window. The sky was painted in soft apricot hues. She turned, surprised to see Niamh's bed was empty. It had been made, suggesting she wasn't in the bathroom.

There was something unsettling about Niamh's absence. She wasn't scheduled to work until the afternoon. She hadn't heard her get up, but these days, Kathleen was a heavy sleeper and not easily woken.

She noticed a note on her pillow with the letter K on it. When she opened the note, the writing was scrawling and there were smears of ink.

I'm sorry, there's nothing for me here, I know you tried to help me and be my friend.

Had she ran away?

Dressing quickly, she headed downstairs. The usual clanging of pots and pans echoed from the kitchen, but it was just Cook and her assistant and they hadn't seen Niamh. Back in the hall, she glanced at the grandfather clock, realising she had twenty minutes to find Niamh before her shift started. Perhaps she was being overly anxious, but as she pulled on her coat and wellies, an unsettling thought crossed her mind.

What if Niamh has done something silly?

She stepped outside into the chilly morning air her feet crunching over the gravel, looking around and trying to work out where Niamh might have gone. It was a big garden with a wood and lots of ground but in the short time that Niamh had been here, she'd taken to wandering round the lake and seemed to like being close to water.

As she made her way towards the lake, a light mist swirled over the water making it look ethereal, romantic in the early light, breathing up from the dark water like a monster's sigh.

She stopped in her tracks, something catching her eye.

A dark figure stood at the end of the jetty on the far side of the lake.

Niamh.

What was she doing there and only dressed in her thin nightie and boots? Had she lost her mind?

She called out and Niamh briefly glanced round before plunging into the cold water. Kathleen panicked and screamed before dashing round the lake as fast as she could, her heart banging in her chest. The path was muddy and slippery which slowed her down. Reaching the jetty, she gazed out across the water shouting. There were no ripples, she couldn't see Niamh swimming, there was no motion at all. The water was completely still. She suddenly froze. Had she imagined it? Suddenly she was aware of the pounding of feet on the jetty and turning, her heart lifted when she saw Fred the gardener.

'What's the matter, why are you making such a racket?'

'It's Niamh, she's jumped in.' She scanned the water, willing Niamh to appear. She had no idea if she could swim.

'Why would she do that, it's bloody freezing in there, are you sure you weren't imagining it? It's very misty out here, the light can play tricks.'

She stared at him. 'Of course I'm sure.' Her voice wobbled with tears and panic.

He grabbed her arm coaxing her away from the edge of the jetty.

Something floating on the lake a couple of feet from the jetty caught her eye. It was the plastic hair slide she'd given to Niamh a couple of days ago. 'She's down there,' Kathleen screamed, pointing to the hair slide and a flurry of bubbles.

'Come on, we need to act fast,' Fred said. 'I'll get the boat out. You go back to the house and get help.'

Kathleen dashed back into the house and raised the alarm. After what felt like an eternity the distant wail of sirens pierced the heavy air and soon the hotel grounds were a flurry of activity, guests peering from windows and doors, murmuring amongst themselves.

Kathleen was back at the water's edge watching Fred rowing frantically, desperately scanning the water for any sign of Niamh.

A police car skidded to a halt on the gravel, its flashing lights reflecting off the surface of the lake. Kathleen rushed over as two officers got out. 'She jumped in, the water's freezing and I don't know if she can swim.' Her voice trembled and tears welled in her eyes.

'Stay here,' the female officer instructed Kathleen before turning to the male officer. 'Call for backup and get the rescue team on site.'

The sound of the boat's oars splashing echoed across the lake as Fred continued his search, calling out Niamh's name, his voice strained and frantic. Meanwhile, the officers began setting up a perimeter, directing onlookers to stay back.

The female officer put a reassuring hand on Kathleen's shoulder, 'Let's go inside and get you warm. I'll need to ask you some questions and where's the manager?'

Inside, they went into Margot's office and were joined by Bert the staff manager.

The officer took out a notepad and pen and sat down. 'I need to take down some details.' She scribbled notes as Kathleen spoke, before looking up to ask, 'Is there any reason why you think she might have jumped into the lake? What was her state of mind yesterday?'

Kathleen explained that she'd been sharing a room with her since Niamh arrived a couple of weeks ago.

'You must have got to know her very well then,' the officer said.

'No, not really. She hardly spoke. She didn't sleep well, something was clearly tormenting her, there was a sadness in her eyes, and she'd often cry herself to sleep. And then this morning she got up before I woke and left a note on her pillow.'

'A note? Can I see it, please?'

Margot stared at her, and Kathleen knew she was in the doghouse for not mentioning the note before the police had arrived.

She went upstairs and came back with the note. The officer read it out. 'I'll need to keep this.' She then turned to Margot. 'Where did Niamh work before? Where's she from? I'll need to see her file.'

Margot and Bert looked at each other awkwardly. Was she mistaken, or were they hiding something?

'We don't really have a file as such, Niamh hasn't been with us long,' the staff manager blundered.

'Oh? You must have her National Insurance number and next-of-kin details, I assume.'

'No, we don't have those details yet. We're waiting for details from Ireland. That's where we believe she came from.'

The police officer frowned. 'How are you paying her?'

Margot and the staff manager glanced at each other before dropping their gaze. 'So far, in cash, but we will need to set her up on the payroll.'

'How many other staff are you paying in cash?'

Bert shifted awkwardly in his chair and rubbed his ear. 'We're all above board, I can assure you.'

'That as may be, but I'd like to return tomorrow to look at all your staff files and I might need to make some enquiries to the tax office, and we will also check the missing person files. Someone is bound to have reported her missing.'

After the officer left, Kathleen returned to her duties but struggled to concentrate. Her mind was filled with dread and worry. If only she could have stopped Niamh--she was to blame--she could have found the right words to reassure her that life was going to be okay, she could have been a better friend. She kept glancing out of the window down to the lake. The longer the search took, it was less likely she'd be found alive. Her thoughts spiralled into a dark place. What if they never found her? The thought of her lifeless body rotting at the bottom of that dirty cold lake twisted like a knife in her heart. It was just too awful to contemplate.

A short while later Margot marched into the room and called her to her office. Her manner was brusquer than normal. This wasn't the caring, soft woman she'd grown used to. She seemed on edge, and this made Kathleen wary and, on her guard, as she followed her down the hallway. Was she in some kind of trouble?

Margot's hands were on her hips, the type of posture adopted when someone meant serious business. 'Why didn't you tell me about the note?' she asked as soon as the door was closed. 'You should have come to me. This could get us into a lot of trouble especially when the press find out.'

'I was very upset, I still am. Sorry but I wasn't thinking straight. They haven't found Niamh yet. Do you think she drowned?'

Margot's face softened and she sat down, her elbow on the edge of the desk as she began kneading her temple with her fingers. 'I'm sorry, yes of course, we're all very worried about

Niamh. If you want to take a couple of days off, I'll understand. It's hard to work when you're worried sick. There were two priests that turned up yesterday to see her, did she know about this?'

Kathleen didn't know what to say, but she was suddenly panicked. What if Father Joseph came back?

Her fear must have shown on her face. 'I hope they won't be coming back, I'm not going to pry, Kathleen, but I do know where you came from and I'm sure you fear anyone linked to the Catholic Church after what happened to you. That's why I wanted to help you. I don't know if Niamh told you, but I got her out of a difficult situation with the priest. That's how I met Niamh, at the ferry terminal. She was obviously very scared of him and I'm not sure quite where she was being taken. She wouldn't say much. Did she talk about this to you? Do you know why she was scared of him?'

'I couldn't get anything out of Niamh. But she seemed deeply traumatised about something in her past.'

Margot sighed. 'I've tried to help some of you girls, but I can't risk getting into trouble. I think you need to get away from here for a couple of weeks, until things settle down. The police will want to see your file for a start and that could put us both in a difficult situation. I've been paying you in cash too. Besides, it will be very upsetting for you once they find...' She turned away, a haunted look on her face and didn't finish the sentence, but Kathleen understood. She was referring to Niamh's body.

A sickening shiver swept over her as tears started rolling down her cheeks. She flopped down into a chair, all her strength suddenly gone. How much more sadness in her life could she cope with? So many awful things had happened. Each one pierced her heart like a shard of broken glass. Her daddy's death in the Troubles. Raped by the priest. Pregnant. Her baby's death. Now Niamh, another victim of the cruel and inhumane laundry system.

She looked up at Margot through misty eyes. 'Where am I supposed to go? I have nowhere, no one.'

Margot reached out and squeezed her hand. She was businesslike and efficient but also warm and caring and Kathleen saw that warmth now shining in her eyes. She'd miss the hotel, she was used to being here and this was where she'd felt safe, she had friends, a cosy room, a job she liked.

She patted Kathleen's hand. 'I have a friend who's offered to take you in for a while. It's all organised. Pack your bags and be down in reception in twenty minutes. You're going on a long train journey. Ask Cook to make you some sandwiches and cut you a slice of cake. You'll have a great time, enjoy, and we'll see you very soon.'

Confused, she panicked. 'Are you sacking me?'

'No, of course not, you're one of our best workers, you've been nothing but hardworking, diligent and trustworthy and if you choose not to come back, you'll get a glowing reference from us.'

CHAPTER 34

VIRGINIA, SUMMER 1976

The Granvilles
Eighteen months had passed since Aisling arrived in America. Her second birthday was fast approaching, and a big party was planned. The Granvilles had hoped the baby would settle down and bring them the joy they so desperately desired, but the reality was, anything but. This wasn't what they'd signed up for. It felt as though an F4-level tornado had arrived and decided it was fine to cause this much destruction.

Life before Aisling's arrival had seemed blissful by comparison, but now they wondered why they'd wanted a child so badly. It wasn't the dream they'd thought it would be. A kind of monotonous fatigue that somehow came with parenting was beginning to get to them and affect their work. On reflection they wondered if they'd made the right decision to adopt. Friends were always wittering on about how delightful and adorable their children were. They had made it look so easy.

They were totally unprepared for what was to come when they took baby Aisling on. Their lives had been turned upside down. It was impossible to work, the romantic weekends away were gone, socialising was impossible, and they were onto the twelfth nanny in eighteen months. How could so many nannies not cope? All they had to do was cuddle her. Afterall, it was only a baby. How difficult could that be? These young girls, they had no idea how lucky they were. The pay was significantly higher than the going rate, they had a luxurious bedroom with a private bathroom in their beautiful mansion with use of the swimming pool and sauna, as well as a car and all their food paid for.

At her wits' end, Janie sat one morning in front of the doctor pouring her heart out, Aisling fidgeting on her knee and tugging at Janie's hair at every opportunity. Sometimes she wondered if the child just needed a damn good smack to snap her into shape and show her who was boss, but as yet she'd not had the courage to start smacking. It felt abusive, but God knows she'd wanted to.

'I've run every test available, but I can't find anything wrong with your child,' the doctor said in a weary tone, making Janie feel that she was taking up too much of his time. She was paying good money, he'd come highly recommended, but what had he actually done to help her?

'And what about the CT scan? Has she got developmental delay or is she retarded? Surely there's something wrong because her behaviour can't be normal. None of my friends have the problems I have.' The child was a complete nightmare most of the time.

'Everything is perfectly normal, but child physiological issues don't normally present at this age.' His tone became cheerful. 'Which is good. I think it's just her age, the toddler stage can be very trying, but it will get easier. In a few years, you'll look back and smile. It'll all be forgotten.'

Janie felt irritated. She wasn't thinking about the future, her focus was on the here and now and keeping her job and marriage. The child was jeopardising everything. 'She throws a fit every time she can't get her way, she has multiple meltdowns, and she screams all night.' She was like an unguided missile that could fly off in any direction at any time.

'It could be teething, her cheeks are a little pink, or growing pains. I did run food allergy tests, nothing came up. She's not dairy intolerant. And she's not in any obvious pain. She probably just needs more of your attention and a routine. Children thrive on routine.'

Rattled, Janie went to stand up. She didn't want to listen to any more of his lame advice. He was a crusty old doctor, what did he know about bringing up a child?

After the doctor's appointment, she rushed home to prepare for a call with the film director of her upcoming movie. She was about to enter a very busy filming period, requiring short absences from home to work on location over in California. Arriving home, she sighed in relief at the prospect of handing Aisling over to the nanny. Fortunately, this nanny showed no signs of wanting to leave, handling the child's tantrums well. As she turned the key in the front door and went inside, balancing Aisling on her hip, her handbag weighing heavily on her shoulder, something didn't feel right. She heard thudding footsteps coming from upstairs and a door slamming. She lowered Aisling to the floor and dumped her bag beside her. The child burst into tears, then went for Janie's handbag and started pulling everything out.

The nanny appeared at the top of the stairs and Janie knew immediately what was going on from the way she was dressed––in drainpipe leathers and stilettos, her duffel bags packed and slung over her shoulder.

Not again, this can't be happening.

And at the worst possible time. These nannies certainly knew how to choose their moments.

The nanny marched down the stairs and into the hall. 'I can't do this anymore, sorry.' Anger and frustration simmered behind her words.

'You can't just leave without giving notice. I've got an important meeting shortly.'

'I can do what I like, and I will do.'

'Don't expect a reference then. And I don't see why I should pay you either. You've broken your contract.'

She dropped her bags on the floor and clamped her hands on her hips. Janie noticed she was defiantly chewing gum, a habit she despised and forbade in her house. 'Right now, I really don't care, there are plenty of other jobs. I'm not surprised the other nannies left.'

As she went to pick up her bags, exasperated, Janie grabbed her arm, forcing the girl to look at her. 'I know she's not an easy child, but please, I need you, don't leave. I'll pay you extra.'

'Nope, sorry. I don't have the skills to look after a little monster because that's what she is.'

All the pleading in the world wouldn't make the girl stay and after she'd gone, Janie stood with her back to the door, staring down at Aisling before sliding to the floor and sobbing. She was very tempted to have a drink, enjoy the alcohol dancing through her body, grabbing her by the hand and dragging her into the well of oblivion. But she knew she couldn't hide at the bottom of a glass. It would wreck her career and besides, she had responsibilities, she was a mother.

She looked down at Aisling who'd now stopped crying. The entire contents of her handbag were scattered across the floor, and she was biting one of the leather straps.

'Jesus, child, that's a two-hundred-dollar designer handbag you're about to rip to shreds.' Exasperated, she gathered all the bits and put them back in her bag before taking Aisling into the kitchen diner where she plonked her into her playpen. The child started howling. She'd never liked the playpen despite all the colourful toys that filled the space. It was supposed to be a playground, not a prison. But what else could Janie do? The nanny had left without warning, and she couldn't cancel her business call. Achieving this role in the film was the pinnacle of her career, the child was not going to jeopardise that, she would have to amuse herself. With Aisling still howling, she slipped into the next room, gently closing the door behind her while she dialled the director's number.

'Janie, I can't be too long, but we can chat when you get here tomorrow.'

'Tomorrow?' Had she missed something? The first session wasn't for another week.

'Yes, tomorrow. Had you forgotten?'

'I've got next Thursday in my diary.'

'We definitely said tomorrow. I don't know what's happened since you've had a baby, but your mind's gone all mushy.' He let out a laugh. He was half jesting and half serious, but she knew he was right. With the lack of sleep and the constant changes of nanny, it was very hard.

What the hell was she going to do? She couldn't keep letting them down every time a nanny left. She was in high demand, but even actresses were replaceable. There was no time to book flights and finding a replacement nanny was going to be impossible. Robert would have to look after Aisling. He'd have to work from home until they could find another nanny.

Coming off the phone she rushed back into the kitchen, where Aisling was still howling, her little face flushed and streaked with snot, her wails piercing the air with a desperate intensity. Janie knelt and gently lifted the toddler from the confines of the playpen.

As she bounced the little one on her hip, she paced up and down trying to soothe her while her mind raced with thoughts of flights to California and looming work issues.

The chaos of her mind clashed starkly with the chaos in her arms. Aisling was wriggling in her arms like a sackful of eels. It was hopeless, she'd really tried, but motherhood was painful, like indigestion and she was failing miserably. She felt as if she'd been thrown out of a car travelling at high speed. The door flung open, a gust of wind, a mean forceful shove and here she was face down on the tarmac.

Looking at the child's tear-streaked face, her heart went out to her, and she realised that all the money in the world couldn't give this child what she most needed--her time and love.

And there it was--that thought that kept returning.

Motherhood isn't the dream I thought it would be. That's the brutal reality. Do I really have time to fit a child into my life?

Why did it feel wicked to feel this way?

She loved her career, much more than motherhood. Acting was the most wonderful experience, it filled her with such excitement, stirred her senses and elevated her to the highest pinnacle, stardom, an accolade that made her feel privileged. Now that she had a child, she knew it was wrong to think like this. It was like an ugly blight on her character setting her apart from other mothers who all oozed such devotion to their little lambs.

She went to sit at the messy kitchen table, strewn with breakfast dishes the nanny hadn't cleared and bounced Aisling on one knee while shifting through papers to find the travel agent's number. The sooner she booked a flight the better, then she could get the ball rolling in terms of finding a new nanny. Robert would have to interview them.

It happened so fast.

As if in slow motion.

Too fast to stop her. Just like all the other recent incidents. Aisling made a grab for the pepper pot and shook it in Janie's face. The cloud of spice was thick and made her sneeze and cough violently. It stung her eyes, made her gasp for breath.

Bloody child, how much more of this can I take?

CHAPTER 35

IRELAND SPRING 1975

The O'Sullivans

As Dec and Sheridan returned from hospital after visiting Liam, they drove into the lane to find cars strewn haphazardly across the driveway with reporters milling about, cameras and microphones at the ready. There was even a TV van parked across the verge.

'Jesus, Mary and Joseph, would you look at that.' Sheridan gasped in horror.

'For the love of Jesus, how the hell did this filthy lot find you?' Dec got out and stormed over, pushing his way through the crowd.

The reporters flocked towards him like seagulls to chips, thrusting their microphones like beaks in his face, hungry for an interview.

'You must be Liam's father, is it true your son burnt his house down for an insurance claim?'

Dec was incensed. 'No, it is not true, you vultures. Leave us in peace.'

Another reporter rounded on Dec with more questions.

In an angry voice, Dec shouted, 'You lot are good at kicking up the dirt, making up stories and mud sticks even if it's not true. You ruin lives. Clear off, the lot of you.'

Sheridan saw her children huddled together at the lounge window peering out in horror. What had she done, dragging them into this?

A woman reporter rushed over to the car as Sheridan got out, trying to offer kind words to elicit a story. 'Mrs O'Sullivan, how is your husband, is he going to be okay? It was lucky the children weren't in the house.'

Before she had the chance to answer, somebody in the crowd shouted angrily. It didn't look like he was a reporter. Was this man from down in the village or had he come all the way from Belfast to taunt them? 'Why have you moved here, Mrs O'Sullivan? How come you suddenly moved? Is there something you're hiding? You had five children, are you the woman who got rid of her baby? Why would you do that? Why didn't your husband move here at the same time? You should be guilty, leaving your husband behind to burn in that house.'

How did they know so much about her? Suddenly, it clicked. The original newspaper must have leaked the information--the very publication she'd first contacted.

And then she noticed a fella from the abattoir, a man who'd caused Liam some bother on a number of occasions. Before the Troubles, they had been friends. He was Catholic. 'People like you bring us all down,' he shouted.

She remembered seeing him confront Liam in the street after work and the words he'd shouted. "You're either with us or against us, you're a soft touch, man, and it's time to step up". She had known it then, and knew it now, he wanted Liam's involvement in the struggle, he wanted to drag him into the depths of the IRA.

For weeks, a relentless swarm of reporters gathered outside their home. The once peaceful road was transformed into a chaotic media circus. Camera flashes lit up the dim morning light, while the incessant chatter drowned the pleasant countryside sounds that Sheridan had long yearned for. Every time they attempted to step outside, they were met with a barrage of microphones, journalists clamouring for a comment, their questions overlapping in a noisy frenzy.

'Mrs O'Sullivan, we've spoken to your old neighbours. They think you deliberately set fire to your house.'

'Mrs O'Sullivan, your neighbours said your sons are little troublemakers.'

'Mrs O'Sullivan, your neighbours said you used to leave your kids on their own and that you're unfit to be a parent.'

'Mrs O'Sullivan, what sort of mother sells her child?'

The lawn felt like a stage with onlookers and cameras capturing every movement, turning simple errands into stressful confrontations. Privacy seemed like a distant memory, leaving them feeling trapped in their own home.

A couple of days later, Sheridan was interviewed by the police at the police station. They bombarded her with a flurry of questions. 'How did you afford to move house, Mrs O'Sullivan?' 'Why didn't your husband come with you?'

When the fire report arrived, it revealed that a petrol bomb had caused the blaze. The police once more called her in for an interview. 'Did you have anything to do with the bomb that was posted through your door? Mrs O'Sullivan, did you try to kill your husband?' 'Was he ever violent towards you? Are you running from his blows?' 'Mrs O'Sullivan, you used to have five children, now you have four. Were you worried about your baby's safety?' And with that question, everything tumbled out.

It took a couple of weeks for the CPS to make their decision and when it came through, that she and Liam were not going to be prosecuted, the relief she felt was enormous.

Sheridan eventually found a local school for the children, but it wasn't the village school and was a bus ride away. The difficulty in finding places had to stem from the suspicion that lingered around her. People recognised her in public, making it difficult to strike up relationships. She felt isolated. Neighbours ignored her, or stared from their windows as she passed, and some even crossed the street to avoid her. "That's the woman who sold her baby to fund a better lifestyle", she overheard in the supermarket as she walked down the frozen food aisle.

They were supposed to be happy in their new home, but her dream had turned into a nightmare. It was difficult enough for her to cope, but the impact on the children truly broke her heart.

The boys were always glued to the TV or down by the river fishing. The girls increasingly isolated themselves in their room, playing upstairs the minute they returned from school. She felt like an outsider in their lives, as they hardly engaged in conversation with her. When they did speak, their remarks were often dismissive and curt and there wasn't the warmth they once shared, however hard Sheridan tried. The worst thing was the whispering behind her back. It was rude, and she was constantly having to tell them off, but the truth was it hurt her to the core.

This way of life partly suited her though. No one made demands on her. Nobody cared. She could retreat to her own room, pull the covers over her head and cry into the pillows without interruption and clinging to Aisling's a hand-knitted duck, like a crutch. Would the past haunt her forever?

Every day she asked herself the same question. What if I hadn't given up Aisling? And not a day went by when she didn't think about her daughter. How she longed to hear from the Granvilles––anything to know how her daughter was doing. A few lines, a photograph. How she hoped that one day her child would want to discover her Irish roots and come and find her. Until then, all she had were the memories but even they were rapidly fading. She thought about all the usual milestones and tried to imagine what Aisling looked like. As she visualised the child crawling and babbling, her eyes would fill with tears and a dull ache would spread across her chest. And then she'd try to pull herself together by trying to stay positive and thinking about all the opportunities Aisling now had, otherwise the pain would overwhelm her. But it was hopeless. One minute she was positive, the next she was back in that pit of despair. The little girl had taken root in her heart and would remain there until the day she died.

The girls pushed her away if she tried to hug them, they no longer wanted a bedtime story or a run around the park with her. It was debilitating and lonely. She might as well not be a mother. Her fun, lively children seemed to have vanished, replaced by distant and aloof versions of themselves. Remarks were churlish and derogatory, the type of behaviour she might expect from teenagers.

One day she went upstairs to call them down for tea. She could hear them talking and with the door ajar, she paused, hovering outside the room as she listened to their animated chatter.

'You've got to tell Mum,' Roisin was saying in a stern voice.

'I can't, they've already said what'll happen if I do.' Maeve's voice was all squeaky and immediately Sheridan knew that something was very wrong.

'I'm surprised Mum hasn't noticed your bruises.'

'Why would she? I don't let her in the bathroom. She wouldn't care anyway. She didn't care about Aisling. If she could sell us too, she would do, but we're too old, people prefer babies.'

'She didn't sell Aisling. She swapped her for this house. I don't even like this house. I prefer our old house. Who cares about fields of cows and sheep.'

'That's what they keep saying at school. "Your mum sold your sister".'

Sheridan felt blotches of heat rise from her neck suddenly ashamed of her childish need for reassurance. Her children were being taunted. She was the adult. She was to blame for their sullen behaviour. It was all a pitiful cry for help. It was up to her to make amends, to unite this broken family. But how? The damage was done.

Her legs seemed to sway weightlessly beneath her, and black dots swam in front of her eyes as reality hit.

Her child was being bullied.

That meant a trip up to the school. With everything else happening, this was the last thing she needed, but she was worried. If her child was being bullied, she had to sort it.

Just then, the phone started ringing. It was the hospital. Liam was being released from hospital. He'd finally be coming home.

CHAPTER 36

IRELAND SPRING 1975

*T**he O'Sullivans*
The move to the countryside was supposed to improve all their lives, but the thought of Maeve having such a miserable time at school made Sheridan feel miserable too.

She stood at the school gate watching her daughters disappear into the throng of children heading into the building. There were groups of mothers gathered around the school gates for their daily dose of gossip and lingering long after their children had gone into class. These women were no more than acquaintances, the worst breed of humans that you could meet-- primary school mothers,--the playground mafia. She wasn't a part of any group and suspected she was the topic of conversation, malicious comments, and speculation, given some of the glares she had received during their short time here. Chatting in the playground and being invited to coffee mornings was how she'd imagined it would be in this rural setting, but this lot were a different breed. They drove Range Rovers and tried to give the impression they were something special, constantly trying to outdo each other with their fake Gucci handbags and false nails. It was a competitive world in the school playground and

Sheridan hated the smugness on their faces. They'd seen her in the papers, and they were quick to judge. What would they have done in her situation? she wondered.

As soon as the children were safely inside the building, she headed towards the reception and as she passed one of the groups of mothers, they stopped talking and glanced round to stare at her before whispering something. It crossed her mind to confront them but instead she delivered a quick smile and hand wave, determined to rise above their cattiness, but her heart was hammering, and she tried to bat down the humiliation welling inside.

'I'd like to see the headmaster, please,' she said marching up to the reception desk where the secretary had just come off the phone.

'So many children off today, must be the winter flu.' The smartly dressed woman muttered looking flustered. 'Sorry.' She had her attention now. 'You'd like to see Mr Wilson? Do you have an appointment?'

'No, I don't.' She hoped she wasn't going to be sent away. She couldn't go through this ordeal again.

'Is it urgent, because he's about to take assembly?'

'Yes, it is, I'm afraid, but I don't mind waiting.' She glanced round. The reception area resembled a doctor's waiting room, with rows of chairs and a coffee table piled with magazines. For a moment, she felt a pang of sadness thinking about her wonderful doctor back in Belfast and how supportive he'd been over the years, even as just a listening ear.

As she waited, she flicked through every magazine on the table and read the school newsletter pinned to the noticeboard above her chair. She suddenly felt the secretary's gaze on her, but when Sheridan looked up, the woman quickly glanced away. Was this how it would be, always recognised as the mother who gave her baby away?

Forty minutes later, she was called in. The headmaster sat at a large desk decorated with framed portraits of his smiling family. The walls were adorned with various certificates, and a glass case displayed silver trophies.

He leaned towards her, fixing her with his hazel eyes. 'How can I help you, Mrs O'Sullivan? Your daughters are new to the school.'

She sighed, as if breathing out months of tension. 'Maeve's being bullied.' Her voice was thick with emotion, and she stifled a tear.

He gave a half smile, a flicker of pity darting across his eyes for the briefest of moments. 'What makes you say that?'

She wondered if he was going to deny the school had a bullying problem, but she went on to tell him everything she'd overheard.

'But have you spoken to Maeve yourself? Perhaps it's a misunderstanding. Maybe they knew you were at the door listening in. Children make things up, it's generally a cry for help. Your children have been through a lot. I read the papers, Mr O'Sullivan.' He let his comment settle in the air before continuing. 'Have you seen the bruises she referred to?'

'Well no.' She paused, feeling muddled. 'Not exactly. She's hiding everything from me. She's become sullen, not the happy child she was.' The conversation wasn't going to plan. She'd hoped for sympathy, but above all, action, and this didn't seem likely.

'As a first port of call, I shall book the girls to see the school nurse, separately though. The nurse will explain that they are having a routine inspection for nits and to check how they're getting on here. She'll likely ask them to strip down to their undies and get them to step on the scales. She's usually very good at finding out if children aren't settling in.'

'That would be helpful.'

'And in the meantime, I'll alert the teacher, she's very experienced. She'll spot anything that's going on.'

'Thank you, it's a huge worry, I just want her to be happy.'

He hesitated. 'That won't be easy, given your circumstances. I appreciate it's a delicate thing to ask, but did you prepare the children before you did what you did and what was their reaction?'

'Surely, Mr Wilson, you must understand the hell we were living in, stuck in the middle of a Protestant community as an isolated Catholic family, taunted and threatened every day, houses in Belfast fire-bombed daily to get their occupants out. I had to take them away for their safety. Tragically not soon enough to prevent my husband suffering from significant injuries. The parents who live here have no idea, they always believe what they read in the press, they don't know our full circumstances. Maybe if they did, they'd treat us differently. We just want to be treated like a normal family.'

'Sadly, that's very unlikely due to you giving away your child, and in this close family- orientated community I don't think you'll get the support you might expect. Tread cautiously and in time people may grow to understand your situation.'

The elastic band inside her snapped and she crumpled into tears. He was right, she'd handled it so badly. The countless mistakes she'd made, and now her children were the ones paying the price. The weight of her actions pressed heavily on her heart, and a sinking feeling grew inside her. They'd never forgive her.

The thought of living with their resentment was almost too much to bear. Most of all, she hoped her children would understand her actions. After all, Liam was the living proof that her deepest fears had been realised.

CHAPTER 37

CORNWALL, SPRING 1975

Kathleen

Kathleen stood waiting on the edge of the station platform staring down at the tracks, almost in a hypnotic state. So many troubled souls had chosen to end their lives this way, hurling themselves in front of a train. Gone in an instant. A traumatised train driver, whose sleep would be forever broken by nightmares. And then she was back to thinking about Niamh.

The train slowed, its wheels squealing against the tracks as it pulled into the station. Sucked into a small crowd of passengers, she was propelled onto the train and found a seat in a quiet carriage.

Closing her eyes, she pictured Cornwall with its rugged cliffs and wild coastline, cobbled pathways down to quaint bustling harbours, fishermen unloading their daily catch, a row of whitewashed cottages with thatched roofs. The images in her head were conjured from photo albums and books. She'd never been there herself. As a child they'd holidayed in Blackpool or Lytham St Anne's. She looked forward to the endless sunshine. Wild and windy days watching the sea crashing against the rocks and the seagulls circling above. It was a far cry from Liverpool. She could almost smell the salty sea air. What an adventure it was going to be, but it would fly by and before long she'd be back at the hotel. It was a shame, it would be so lovely come the summer, not that it wouldn't be now. Even with the rotten weather, Kathleen knew that it was a beautiful part of the country. She could picture herself in the summer, swimming in the sea, strolling round the gift shops, chatting to the fisherman.

She wondered what Sophie would be like. She was excited yet nervous and hoped she'd understand the local dialect.

After a couple of changes, the train pulled into Truro. She alighted and gazed down the platform before heading towards the exit and handing her ticket to the member of staff. She spotted a rather rotund lady, her hair tied into a bun and wearing a skirt that was far too tight around her bulging middle. She realised that she hadn't been given a description of Sophie, she didn't know who to look out for, but this lady looked like a stereotypical café owner and clearly enjoyed a cake or two herself. Dashing over and about to introduce herself, she saw the woman dart towards a man and greet him.

She looked around and suddenly a young woman came bounding over. 'You must be Kathleen.'

Instantly, Kathleen liked her. Sophie was not at all what she expected. She looked so young, not much older than her, too young to be a café owner. Her long hair was the colour of well-brewed tea and tumbled in messy curls around her petite pear-shaped face. She was wearing slim jeans, a polo sweater and a simple gold chain, everything put together so effortlessly.

'Do you like being called Kathleen or are you a Kathy?'

'Call me Katie, Kathleen's so fuddy-duddy.' She hadn't intended to change her name, but Katie sounded pretty and modern. Right in that moment she knew that a fresh start was exactly what she needed, and it felt liberating from the Irish and Catholic associations tied to the name Kathleen.

They got into Sophie's small Fiat and headed down to St Mawes.

'How do you know Margot?' Kathleen asked.

'I don't, she's a friend of my grandmas. They knew each other a long time ago, but they're still in touch. My grandma owns the café, I'm just helping out before I go to college in September. Grandma ran the cafè for thirty years, but she's getting too old and can't stand on her feet for long. I'm sure you'll get to meet her though. She's a sweetie, still got all her marbles.'

'I'm happy to help in the café, I haven't just come for a free holiday, I do intend to muck in.'

'I was hoping you'd say that. We always need extra hands.'

It had been such a long journey and Kathleen's body ached. She gave a loud yawn and tried not to nod off.

St Mawes lay at the end of a peninsula. They wended their way down winding roads and through pretty villages before slowing and trundling down a hill flanked with low pebbled walls and into the small town. A quaint sign greeted them telling them that St Mawes was twined with a town in France, not that she could even take a wild guess at pronouncing it. In the fading light she saw the outline of a bedraggled group of granite buildings and then they turned right and drove along the seafront, only a path and a metal railing separating the narrow road from the sand itself. The white of the waves caught the moonlight as they crashed onto the beach. She hadn't been to the beach for years and had forgotten how wonderful it was.

Sophie swept into a parking space overlooking the harbour. An ancient stone wall ran alongside the harbour, and on one side was a row of mainly white properties and a large white hotel that looked as if it had been extended and added to over the years. Out of the car, Kathleen walked over to the railing to gaze across the harbour, breathing in the briny smell and listening to the halyards clinking against the masts, hinges, and chains creaking.

She looked down, noticing how much litter was strewn around the car park. The wind had sent a couple of crisp packets whirling off the ground. One of the dustbins had fallen over and its bin bag had been half-dragged out, by greedy seagulls no doubt. It had been ripped open and the contents had spilled everywhere. It wasn't the best first impression of the town.

'Well, this is it,' Sophie said, swinging her car keys in front of her with a beam on her face.

Kathleen turned away from the harbour and saw the café for the first time. It was on the corner of one of the roads leading down to the front. It sat there like a place of refuge. The premises had been painted a pastel shade of blue which made it look odd, crouching at the end of a row of white buildings. Kathleen read the signage which looked as if it had seen better days; the paint was flaking, and a wooden panel had splintered but she could make out the name in pink lettering.

Mawe Cake.

She smiled at the play on words. Standing under the small porch, Sophie dug the key from her coat pocket and twisted it in the lock. There was a sign to the right of the doorway declaring dogs were welcome inside.

A small amount of pushing, and the door creaked open and led into the café. The walls were a bright sunshine yellow and there were white wooden tables and chairs throughout. Some of the tables were covered in pink and white chequered tablecloths. The café had closed hours ago but still smelt of freshly baked bread, and she picked up a hint of cinnamon and cheese. Maybe they served cinnamon buns and cheese scones. The smell was divine and made her mouth water. Her packed lunch was long since eaten, and her stomach growled.

'You must be ravenous,' Sophie said, helping to carry her

bags up the wooden stairs to the flat , where she was shown to her room. It was a small room with freshly painted white walls with sloping eaves and a gauzy curtain. She gazed round, noticing the bedding, a print of tiny daisies that looked like it had been bought in Laura Ashley. There was a shelf with a sweet collection of seaside treasures: an enormous conch shell, a beautifully carved wooden seagull, vibrant coral pieces, and a glass jar filled with smooth pebbles.

A starfish hung on a hook above the bed, and on the opposite wall an embroidered picture of the harbour. She peered at the detail. 'Did your grandma do this?'

'Yes.'

'She's very clever.'

'She's a creative old stick. She worked like a Trojan in the café, now she spends her day jam-making and pottering round the garden.'

Kathleen thought about her own grandparents, suddenly hit by a wave of sadness. They must have found it strange, their granddaughter vanishing midway through the school term, months away from her O levels. What lie had her mother spun to cover the shame of her daughter's pregnancy?

'I'm in the room next to you,' Sophie said, cutting into her thoughts.

Realising she'd been staring at the starfish, she twirled round and followed Sophie who had been chattering the whole time.

A quick glance into the bedroom opposite and then the tiny kitchenette.

'I hope you like fish and chips.' It was more a statement than a question. 'There's a great chippy across the way.'

They headed across the road where the window of the chippy was all steamed up and it was busy inside. There were a couple of lads at a nearby table and they looked up and smiled. Kathleen felt herself blush.

'We don't get many customers this time of year,' Sophie

explained after they'd ordered cod and chips. 'But the bakery does well all year round and in the summer there's a continual queue for our ice creams. We serve the finest Italian ice cream, it's to die for.'

Kathleen couldn't remember the last time she'd eaten fish and chips. Her mouth watered. The chips were just how she liked them, fat and long and greasy. She smothered them in lots of salt and vinegar. It was a habit she'd picked up from her brother Darius.

Darius.

It had been a long time since she'd thought about him. She had no idea where he was, but with ten years between them, they weren't exactly close. He'd left home to go to university when she was about ten and he had only made fleeting visits back to Liverpool. He always seemed to complain about coming home, as if it was putting him out of his way. They had very little in common, apart from their shared DNA. He was a boffin, she remembered him spending hours down in the garden shed making batteries and simple gadgets. He had a hot temper and often argued with their parents. He always had to be right and seemed to look down on his own parents as though he was better than them. She didn't miss him and doubted he thought about her either.

'Hey, Sophie,' one of the lads called over. 'Who's your pretty friend?' He winked at Kathleen.

'Mind your own business,' she called over playfully before turning to Kathleen.

'That's Kenny Lowen, and his mate, Bryn Thomas. You'll get used to the fellas round here. They're as bold as brass. With it being such a small, isolated place, any newcomer attracts attention.'

'And there was me thinking it was my great looks,' Kathleen said with an awkward laugh before dipping her head in embarrassment.

'Why don't you bring her to the Legion on Friday. There's a disco,' Kenny piped up as he speared a chip.

'That's a funny name for a nightclub,' Kathleen said with a laugh.

'It's the British Legion.'

'Oh my God, I thought that was only for old codgers.'

'We'll think about it Lenny. If you two aren't going, we might consider it.' Sophie giggled, then turned to Kathleen with raised eyebrows. 'Lads, they think they're so special.'

Leaving the chippy and out into the chilly evening, Sophie linked Kathleen's arm, and they headed back to the café. It was such a simple act, it felt special, a friendship stitching together, a bond being formed. She had imagined this moment with Niamh, but it hadn't happened. She glanced across the harbour wall, fixing her gaze on the inky water. She shuddered to think once more about poor Niamh at the bottom of that cold lake.

She quickly pushed her dark thoughts aside. Even if her stay here was brief, she was going to enjoy her time in this quirky Cornish town. A smile crept across her face. The Friday disco awaited, and with it a chance to dance, let her hair down and embrace the fun she'd almost forgotten. Her future was uncertain, but for now, the excitement of being here felt like everything. It was exactly what she needed right now--a dose of happiness.

CHAPTER 38

VIRGINIA, SUMMER 1976

The Granvilles

It had been a tiring day of difficult meetings, and as Robert Granville arrived home he was looking forward to kicking his shoes off and fixing a bourbon on the rocks. Close to clinching several important deals, he felt very pleased with himself.

Heading into the kitchen, he gave Janie a peck on the cheek, loosened his tie and dipped his finger into the food bubbling on the stove. She batted him away with a tut and reached into the cupboard for a crystal glass, handing it to him before going over to the freezer for ice. He smiled. She knew exactly what he needed at the end of a long day.

He glanced round. What a mess it was. He hated seeing the kitchen in such a state, as if a bomb had hit it. An assortment of cereal and biscuit packets littered the counter. It didn't look as if the place had been touched since breakfast. Why hadn't the housekeeper been in? And where was the nanny? She was supposed to keep on top of things when the housekeeper wasn't around. Aisling was sitting in her playpen whingeing and reaching to be picked up. The last thing he wanted was baby puke down his shirt.

'Why's she not in bed yet?' he asked pulling out a chair and slumping down.

'Don't get too comfortable, you're looking after Aisling, I'm flying to California tomorrow and I'll likely be away for several weeks.'

He spun round. 'What are you on about, woman?' Where *was* that damn nanny?

'And while I'm away, you better get a good nanny that can do the job. Perhaps you can ring that contact of yours.'

'You can't just up and go, you've got responsibilities. You've got a bloody baby for God's sake.'

'The nanny's left.'

'Again? What the hell is happening, why do they keep leaving?' He pushed his chair back angrily, stood up and wheeled round to face her.

Janie took plates from the cupboard and began to set the table. 'You tell me. She just quit out the blue, no notice, no goodbye. I'm as hurt and confused as you are.'

'I don't know how these nannies think it's fine to screw us over. How can she stand to leave our daughter without a goodbye, the little girl who's given her heart to that selfish bitch, who asks for her every morning and every night. All those special moments they've shared, and they think nothing of walking out. We've been generous, kind, we always treat them like a member of the family from day one.'

'Come on, Robert, you know as well as I do how difficult a child she is,' Janie said wearily. His wife looked completely exhausted, like a deflated balloon the day after a celebration. And she was about to take on a new assignment. Good luck with that one, he thought.

He glanced over at Aisling. She'd exhausted herself with all the whining and had fallen asleep on a heap of soft toys, her thin hair fanned across a giraffe. She looked so cute with her thumb in her mouth, like an angel, so why did she turn into a monster the minute she woke? It would be far better if she slept for twenty-three hours a day. Surely Janie could cope for one hour. It was a woman's job to look after the children.

'Can't you just forget about work until she starts school?' He swept his fingers through his hair, feeling exasperated. 'Why have a child if you're just going to carry on working? It doesn't make sense.'

'No, it wouldn't make sense to you, Robert. For starters, I need my sanity. Bringing up a kid is lonely and stressful.'

'You should find it a joy to be a mother after everything we've been through, the endless hospital appointments, every month having our hopes dashed. Otherwise, what was it all for? You wanted a baby, you thought of nothing else, talked about nothing else. You were completely obsessed.'

She wheeled round, her face hard and cold. He'd never seen her like this before and it shocked him. What had happened to his loving wife? 'The child's a handful, a total nightmare at times. You've seen what she's capable of.' She was referring to the embarrassment of Aisling's behaviour at their friends' house a couple of weeks ago when the child had toppled a vase of flowers, thumped another child, and rubbed chocolate into the cream settee.

She poured herself a large glass of wine, her shoulders slumped. 'This wasn't what I signed up for.'

'It was never supposed to be plain sailing. Ask your friends. They manage.'

'None of my friends have the problems we have. I don't know what we're doing wrong.' Her voice softened and she looked thoughtful as she sat down opposite him. 'Do you think she senses that we're not her real parents? Maybe she's suffering adoption trauma, is that a thing?'

'Don't be ridiculous, you just need to give her more attention and do all the things mothers do, and that means putting a hold on your career till she's older. I definitely will not become a househusband. My job is far too important.'

'Don't you dare patronise me. My career is just as important as yours. Maybe there's something that couple didn't tell us, and they were just keen to get rid of her?'

'You're overthinking and making excuses,' he said, but maybe she had a point.

'You'll have to work from home, darling.'

'How am I supposed to do that? I've got meetings all over the place and I need to be in the office.' He glanced over at Aisling. 'What the hell do I know about babies?'

'Good time to learn. I'm going to be rather busy over the next few months with a punishing filming schedule.'

'For Christ's sake, I've told you so many times, we don't need your income.' He put his hand over hers. 'They can find someone else to fill the role.'

She pulled away from him. 'No, I'm not doing that and letting them down. Besides, this isn't just a job, it's a career. This film is a fantastic opportunity. It's not about money. I'd do it even if I wasn't paid.'

'That would be daft. Those directors, they run you ragged.'

'I love my job.'

'How am I supposed to run the business with you galivanting all over the place? Do you have any clever ideas?'

'You'll have to ring round all the agencies, find a replacement and try and get one that can handle children.'

'You just wanted a baby to keep up appearances. You've got no interest in her, you never spend any time playing with her. What sort of mother are you?'

Janie stared at him with a pained expression. Tears sprang to her eyes. 'Oh, I see, you're blaming me now, are you? I knew it was a mistake to go to Ireland. You and your bloody contacts. Maybe we should give her up, find some new parents. A better fit. A couple with medical and professional training that know what they're doing. Maybe we're just wrong for her.'

'You mean give up, just like that?' He snapped his fingers. It seemed so simple but now that she'd said it, he felt an inner torment begin to lift, rather like the relief he'd once felt as a teenager when his parents didn't need him to babysit his kid brother. He was able to go off fishing for the weekend with his mates and they'd had an amazing time. That was one of the penalties of having a brother who was ten years younger. He remembered the unfairness of it, having his childhood robbed by two selfish parents.

'I don't like to hear myself say it, but yes.' She had a resigned look on her face.

He reached out and took her hands. They were silent for a few moments before he spoke. 'We were happy enough without her, weren't we? These days we seem to just bite chunks from each other. I hate it.'

Her eyes were filling with tears. 'I never wanted to be in this position, I tried to get her help, she needs more than we can offer. Perhaps I'm just not cut out to be a mother. We've had all the tests, they say there's nothing wrong with her, but they don't have to put up with her tantrums.'

'Hey, it's okay,' he exclaimed.

Her mouth twisted and she seemed to digest this for a moment. 'Something's always felt a bit…off?'

He blinked at her. 'Really?'

She shrugged and glanced over at the peacefully sleeping baby, as if the child understood the importance of this conversation. Normally she disrupted their evening. 'I don't know. Maybe in hindsight we shouldn't have taken her.'

'We didn't take her, they offered their baby to us. They were desperate for the money. Some folk will do anything for money. We've got nothing to feel guilty about.'

'It does seem odd how desperate she was. I thought a mother's love was all-consuming. But those Irish women, it's like shelling peas. They pop 'em out like aspirins.'

'Perhaps it's just not meant to be. Afterall, we spent long enough trying to make one of our own.'

'You make it sound so matter-of-fact, like baking a cake. Put all the right ingredients in and it pops out. Life's not like that.'

She looked so lost, he wanted to lean over and kiss her beautiful mouth. He didn't. They just sat there, holding hands across the table, a quiet acceptance settling between them. Something had to give.

CHAPTER 39

IRELAND SPRING 1975

The O'Sullivans

It was a bright Saturday morning in spring. Sheridan and the kids stood at the lounge window watching Dec help Liam get out of the car. As he came into view, plodding down the path like an old man and clearly struggling with each pace, they all gasped and instinctively moved closer together. Sheridan put her arms around the girls and for once they didn't resist.

'It doesn't look like Daddy,' Roisin muttered.

'Why's Daddy like that?' Maeve said with a shudder.

The children hadn't visited their father in hospital because Liam hadn't wanted them there, but Sheridan had tried her best to prepare the children. There was no amount of warning though to ready them for this. The change in Liam was immense. It was jarring. This wasn't their dad. He was an imposter. He'd morphed into someone they didn't recognise. A knot coiled in her stomach with the sudden realisation that nothing would be the same again.

She watched him tottering, that swagger that had first attracted her to him, gone. He looked like a newborn foal taking its first tentative steps and the pain was visible with every move he made. His dark, bushy eyebrows that sometimes gave the impression of sternness, had gone, as had his toothbrush moustache. She remembered him saying, "a kiss without a moustache is like beef without mustard." His eyes were panda-like and the scar on one side of his chin, a dent like a fingerprint in plasticine, and the creases around his mouth and eyes were gone.

His face was a canvas of destruction, a patchwork of red blotches after a battle with fire's fury. He'd survived, and inside he was the same man, but did she still love him, or was her commitment to him now merely duty?

Dec arrived at the door first, stepping over the threshold with Liam's bags. Through the hall and into the lounge, Sheridan immediately picked up on Dec's deliberate diversionary tactic when he started complaining about the journey from the hospital. Several roads were closed, the sun obscured his vision and there were potholes along the lane.

Liam didn't rush to embrace the children. It was as if he hadn't registered their presence. He went to straight to the patio windows, gazing out across the fields with a vacant look in his eyes and then he gave a heavy sigh. She wondered what he thought of the view, but he didn't say.

After five minutes of Dec's nervous chatter, Sheridan glanced at the children willing them to give their father a hug. Whatever her struggles were with Liam, he deserved a hero's welcome from his own kids. But they were holding back, stiff, and uncertain. She knew he'd missed them––he'd told her enough times––and he'd be hurt by their awkward stares. But they weren't moving, their eyes wide as they took in the sight of their dad. The dynamics had changed, all the warmth had leached away like the end of a summer's day, replaced by this painful distance that nobody knew how to bridge.

Maeve was now clinging to Sheridan's legs and Roisin was

hiding behind the settee, refusing to come out, like she did when there were Daleks or monsters on *Dr Who*.

Maeve looked up at Sheridan, clearly troubled by the sight of her father. Her little face was all scrunched up and her lips were wobbling. 'That's not my daddy,' she whined. 'When will Daddy look normal?'

After Dec had left, Sheridan turned to the children, coaxing Roisin from her hiding place and freeing Maeve's grip from her legs.

Roisin was staring at Liam in the way that children often stared at disabled people in the street.

'Why don't you all go outside to play, give your father a chance to settle in.' She'd waited long enough for Liam to reach out and for the children to do the same, but it hadn't happened. The air hung heavy, charged with unspoken words, the tension thick enough to cut.

The boys turned and stomped off with long faces, the girls scampering after them. Sheridan and Liam stood in uncomfortable silence at the window, their arms stiffly at their sides as they watched the girls push each other on the swing while the boys kicked a ball. The children seemed oblivious to their watchful parents, as if their father's return hadn't happened at all.

'We've got two indoor loos, so we have,' she said.

'There's nothing wrong with an outside toilet, except on an aeroplane.'

She smiled. He hadn't lost his humour.

'What do you think of the view, beautiful isn't it?' He'd never been one for country life, finding it too quiet. Born and raised in the heart of Belfast, he was a city lad through and through. She remembered him saying a long time ago while they were holidaying in Donegal that the countryside made him restless, and he preferred the hustle and bustle of the city. He had a saying, she remembered. "A pint on every corner, and a chippy for after".

'Huh, if you say so. You'd rather have a pretty view than our daughter.'

'Stop it, you make me look cold and callous.'

'That's exactly what you are. The woman I married has gone.' She glanced up at him feeling the shame of what she'd done. There was real loathing in his eyes, as well as a deep sadness, something she'd never seen before.

She turned sharply, her eyes filling with tears. 'It's more than just a view, Liam, it's a fresh start for us, and for Aisling, a new life.'

'A new life for who? What goes on in your head, woman? What planet are you on? How is a house supposed to replace a child?'

She rounded on him, defending herself, not letting him tarnish her as cold-hearted.

'Just remind me, Liam, what did you do exactly? Where in all of this did you put your family first? If we hadn't left that night, we'd have burned in our beds and been carried out in coffins. All those warnings, you never took heed. Aisling would not have survived, so don't you dare turn this on me,' she spat. Her heart was racing, and she felt anger swirl through her like the first gust of a brewing storm.

'I'm going to bed, where am I sleeping?'

It was only ten in the morning. Maybe he needed time alone. It was a lot for him to take in. She was prepared to give him the benefit of the doubt. She turned and headed to the stairs. 'Our room's at the back, the one with the view.'

'Isn't there a spare room?'

She glanced down at him. 'For goodness' sake, you're still my husband.'

'I'll keep you awake,' he said matter-of-factly.

'Your snoring's never been a problem before.'

'That'll be the least of your problems.'

She continued up the stairs, confused by his comment but reluctant to ask, and led him across the landing to the small room overlooking the apple orchard.

Much later, when they were all tucked up in bed, she lay there watching the hands on the clock tick by. Thoughts raced through her mind. His disfigurement was overwhelming, their marriage was fragile, and his expression showed he no longer felt the same. Then there were the children. How would they accept their disfigured father, especially the girls who were frightened by his appearance?

Midnight passed, she still hadn't dropped off and it was then that she discovered what Liam had meant by his earlier comment.

A blood-curdling scream pierced the air.

Frantically, she scrambled from bed and ran to the spare room, peering round the door, trying not to wake Liam from his nightmare. The curtains were open and the light from the full moon illuminated sweat beading on his forehead. He was thrashing in his sleep, and it was scary to watch. Her first thought was to wake him, but it might be the wrong thing to do. He screamed again. She heard the creak of a floorboard and turned to see Aidan standing on the landing in his pyjamas. She hushed him with a finger to her lips and pulled Liam's door to.

She crept across the landing and guided Aidan back into his room where she perched on the end of his bed. He sat down beside her, rubbing his eyes and yawning.

'What's up with Dad, do the burns hurt?'

'I expect he's very uncomfortable, the burns will be sore and itchy, but it's the mental scars that will be harder to heal.'

'How do you mean?'

'When someone experiences something really scary like a house fire, there are burns you can see, but emotions we can't.

It's the trauma of what your dad's been through, it's giving him nightmares, making him shout out in his sleep.'

'What if he does it every night? I don't want to be woken up, I've got exams coming up'

She patted him on the knee. 'You need your sleep, love, you've got football practice in the morning.' She pulled the cover back and tucked him in before padding across the landing back to her own room.

The rest of the night she just lay there thinking. The panic had set in, and she just did not know what the future held. The perfect life was already starting to crumble. What if Liam didn't stop screaming at night, he might never recover and what if the children couldn't cope with the change and worst still, *I can't cope with him in my bed again. What if I can't cope, full stop? So many what-ifs.*

It was now about survival but at what price?

CHAPTER 40

CORNWALL, EARLY SPRING 1975

*K*atie (aka Kathleen)

Katie woke with a start. At first she didn't know where she was, then she remembered. She must have overslept because it was already light, and the sun was pushing through the curtains casting an amber glow across the room. The bed was so cosy she could have slept for hours, but noise rising from the café below and outside in the harbour had woken her. She hauled herself out of bed, padded across the floor and threw the curtains open.

As soon as she looked down on the harbour, at the little boats bobbing on the water, the fishermen busy at work hauling in the nets, a surge of happiness and excitement rushed through her. She couldn't wait to get out there. How lucky she was to be here. It felt like a fresh start, away from everything bad that had happened, a new beginning, which in a way it was because she'd changed her name to Katie.

Katie.

She rolled the name around her tongue. It would take a while to get used to. People would call her, and she'd ignore them before realising they were talking to her. Maybe she'd revert to Kathleen at some point in the future, especially if she wanted her family to find her, but for now, that was the last thing she wanted.

She hurriedly dressed, eager not to miss a moment of her time here and headed downstairs straight into the cafè. There was a determination about her, she was happy to get stuck in but when she looked across the tables to the corner, her heart skipped a beat.

It was Kenny and he was perched on a metal chair at an oval table by the far window with toast and coffee. He looked scrubbed clean and his cheeks glowed, his dark cropped hair damp and shiny around his face as he hungrily munched through his breakfast.

He glanced up and smiled at her, crumbs of toast around his mouth.

'Want to join me, I'm sure it'll be toast and coffee on the house for you.' He glanced over at Sophie and winked at her before brushing his hands together, and for the first time she noticed the unusual colour of his eyes––a deep cornflower blue.

Katie didn't want to be drawn into a conversation without talking to Sophie first. As far as she was concerned, she was here to work and didn't want to come across as a shirker. She was ready to take whatever orders Sophie threw at her and prove herself an asset.

Sophie was busy serving customers. 'Relax, Katie, I'll bring brekkie over in a minute, I know you're keen to help out, but you've only just arrived.'

Kenny took a sip of coffee. 'You heard what the lady said, sit.' He patted the chair next to him. Sitting down, she noticed a twinkle in his eyes, casting over her the way one might admire a dress in a shop window.

'What brings you to these parts?' he asked. She spotted a damp, rolled-up towel on the table by his coffee cup.

'I work at a hotel in North Wales, I'm only here for a few

weeks for a short break. I've just arrived, but I already I love it––I could easily stay forever.' She surprised herself by saying this.

'Once the place gets under your skin, it stays with you.'

Sophie brought coffee and croissants over. She looked the part wearing an apron, a tea cloth draped over her shoulder.

'Don't tell me you've been for a swim?' Katie said nodding at his towel.

About to serve her next customer, Sophie glanced over. 'He's one of the mad ones, swims in the sea most of the year. There's a club that meet on the beach.'

Katie pretended to shiver. 'Rather you than me.'

'Don't knock it, girl, till you've tried it. It's a great way to start the day, wakes the brain up.'

'I bet it does, and a few other bits we won't mention.'

They laughed and Katie blushed. 'So, what do you do?' He looked sharp and polished, like an office worker.

'I work in the bakery, that's why I'm here, delivering trays of bread and cakes. Which reminds me, I best get on.' He stood, grabbing his rolled towel and clutching it under his arm. Then he leaned down, and lowering his voice said, 'They're hiring more staff if you're interested. There's a notice in the window.' He pointed to a small card pinned to the café window. 'No harm in applying.' He chuckled heartily. 'Be great to see your face around.'

She watched him leave the café, a fizz of excitement bubbling. He was somebody she wouldn't mind getting to know. And as for working in the café, the fact they were looking for staff felt like a sign. She glanced around, a smile spreading across her face as she imagined herself fitting into this friendly and welcoming atmosphere in this adorable little town.

Despite Sophie's protests, Katie was keen to make a good impression, especially now that she'd seen the advert. She'd broach Sophie later about it. Without asking, she found the broom cupboard and started to sweep the floor before clearing and wiping tables. Sophie and another girl were trying to do everything themselves, serving customers coming in for bread, cakes and pasties and serving food at tables as well as clearing. They were rushed off their feet.

Towards the end of the day, the queue petered out and there were just a few bread rolls and a jam doughnut left behind the counter. Katie wondered how on earth they'd managed to cope with the volume of customers before she'd arrived. It didn't seem possible.

'Thank you so much,' Sophie said, taking her apron off and beaming at Katie. 'I don't know how we would have coped without you today.' Katie was delighted with the praise; Sophie wouldn't even need to interview her, she'd proved herself already. The job was hers, she didn't care about going back to the hotel.

'I saw your notice in the window. I'd like to apply for the job.'

'Notice?' Sophie looked confused until she realised what Katie was referring to, her expression shifting as the lightbulb went off in her mind. 'Oh, that notice.' She headed towards the window. 'It should have been taken down last week, we've just filled the job, a lady's starting on Saturday. Can you help until then if you're happy to?'

Katie's heart sank but she tried not to show how disappointed she was. She forced a smile and said, 'Yes of course, it's the least I can do.'

So much for this being a new chapter, or a fresh start, she felt a heavy sense of resignation wash over her. Deep down she knew she'd be back at the hotel with the ghost of Niamh and the priest lurking in the shadows waiting to pull her back. With one girl found, the alert was out––the hotel was a haven for escapees. A sense of dread settled over her, her past it seemed could not easily be shrugged off. It felt as if every time she took two steps forward, it was one step back.

Ireland

August 1976

The O'Sullivans

Sheridan had been working part-time as a cleaner at a local hotel but today was her day off. The job was okay, it wasn't difficult cleaning rooms, but she hadn't made any friends there. Not long after starting, she'd overheard two of the cleaners gossiping about her. "That's the woman who sold her baby". "What sort of mother does that?" Of course they'd seen her picture all over the newspapers. She would have left there and then, but with Liam not working, she needed the money. The Social Security payments just weren't enough. She'd learned to knuckle down, ignoring the snide comments, and tried to tuck in her pain like a shirt that was too long.

Today was her day off. She woke to the birds chirping. The sun was pouring through the window, casting a warm golden glow across the bedroom. It was the kind of summer's day that felt magical. The sky was a brilliant blue, dotted with fluffy clouds.

Her heart jolted.

Aisling would have loved this, what a beautiful day for her second birthday.

There had been no news at all, but she hoped to receive something today.

The past eighteen months had been very difficult. Liam was still waking at night, his interaction with the children was limited. She'd tried to get him out into the garden, but he'd shown no interest in going out, not even to venture down to the village pub. He spent most of his time in his room gazing out with a vacant look in his eyes. He hadn't returned to the marital bed, but she was quite glad about that. She couldn't imagine his charred skin rubbing close to hers, the thought made her retch. It was so sad. She no longer felt the intimacy towards him. They'd barely even hugged since his return which was unheard of. His moods were often dark, he found the kids an irritation most of the time, and therapy didn't seem to have any effect.

She padded down the stairs, her gaze drawn to the doormat where a single brown envelope rested. She recognised the logo of the electricity board.

Her heart sank. How she longed for a photo, a lock of hair, a handprint. Anything. Just to hear how her daughter was doing. Had she been kidding herself all along hoping they'd remember their promise to her? They'd got what they wanted. She wasn't on their minds. They'd moved on, long forgotten her.

After getting the children's breakfast and waving them off, she sat down with a coffee before clearing the kitchen and making their beds. As she was about to take her first sip, the phone rang. It was her closest friend, Jean. They had grown up together, attending the same schools and living across the street from each other. Jean was ringing because it was Aisling's birthday, she was her godmother and had been there for Sheridan this past eighteen months. She hadn't judged or condemned her and always offered a listening ear.

They chatted for a few minutes, soon engrossed in a conversation of what might have been.

'How are things with Liam?'

'Just awful, Jean. It's hard to deal with his dark moods. He's sullen and the children seem frightened of him. He doesn't play with them, and it's as if he's a scary monster.'

'And what about your relationship?'

'We're still in separate rooms. And quite honestly, I'm glad. I can't bear the thought of him lying next to me, the thought fills me with horror, makes my skin crawl, and as for sex, I find it hard to look at him, let alone do that.'

'Poor you. But you're not missing much. If you ask me, sex is overrated, like going on a cruise. Ninety percent of the time you're just staring at the sea. That's why they have so much onboard entertainment.'

'Maybe that's exactly what we need, a holiday. He's just not the person he used to be, Jean. I don't know if the old Liam will come back, and if he doesn't, I don't know if I can stay with him.' Her voice was all wobbly and her eyes filled with tears.

'Where is he now?'

'In his room. He hardly comes out. He's turned into a bolshie teenager. I just seem to be his carer now and I didn't sign up for this. I know I should honour my wedding vows but I'm finding it difficult. And I know it's impacted the children. It breaks my heart seeing other dads playing with their children. Liam used to be a devoted father.'

She finished the call and strolled into the lounge, stopping in her tracks, horrified to see Liam sitting on the settee within earshot gazing out of the window.

'Oh, hello, dear. How long have you been sitting there?'

'Long enough,' came his sharp reply.

She saw tears rolling down his cheeks.

'So much for loyalty. I don't think there's anything left to say.'

How much had he overheard?

He didn't look at her. She noticed his hand was shaking. 'I can see I'm not wanted here. I'd hate to stand in your way.

Perhaps it's time for me to find somewhere else, lock myself away like Quasimodo, a freak of nature. I didn't ask for this.'

'Stop feeling sorry for yourself. If you'd listened to me in the first place, but you've done nothing to help yourself. You've a wife and children that still love you.'

'Oh, how generous of you to stick by me. What a true martyr you are.'

'You're not helping yourself, moping around all day. It's time to get up and grab life, be appreciative you're still alive, make an effort with your family. It's a nice day, we could go out for a walk.'

'I'm not romping round the countryside breathing in all that stinky manure. I've told you before, I don't like it. How little you know me. I'm a townie and always will be.'

'You should be happy to be alive.'

He turned and glared at her. 'How can I be? Today of all days. My daughter's second birthday. Our family is not complete. There'll always be one piece of the jigsaw missing. You sent her away as if she doesn't matter. You care more about a nice house in the country. I've lost everything, you don't give a damn. How do you expect me to feel?'

'What do you want me to do? Things are as they are, we need to make the most of life.'

'There is no *we*, Sheridan, not anymore. What I have is a body that's no use to me. I'm scarred for life. People recoil in horror when they see me. I don't want glares and sympathy. I'm handicapped. It would have been better if I'd died in that fire, that way I'd be no hindrance to anybody.'

'Would you just listen to yourself? You used to be so cheerful.'

He gave a sharp intake of breath as if he were seething. 'When I married you, I never dreamt you'd do the thing you did. I thought you adored our family, always put them first. How wrong was I.'

'That's exactly why I did it, to protect everyone.' She was tired of explaining herself.

'Kids should grow up learning to defend themselves. We don't go on the run, we stand up for our beliefs.' He stood up and faced her. 'I could join the paramilitaries and hide behind a balaclava. Only thing I'm fit for, paying these murdering bastards back for what they've done. I need to be back in Belfast to fight the cause. I'm going to make them pay for what they've done. That's my life goal now. I'll go back to me dad's for a while. I've been speaking to Dad. I can move in with him. I can't cope with this poncey life in the country.'

'You're talking in riddles.'

'I now know what my mission is, it's better you and the kids aren't involved.'

'I don't know what you're talking about, but I don't like what I'm hearing.'

'I've been having a chat with a young fella.'

'What young fella?'

'Nobody you know. Name's Martin McGuinness. His mates think I could be a significant benefit to the group. About time we drove those Prods out of Ireland once and for all. They're not welcome here. Oliver Cromwell had a lot to answer for.'

'Oliver Cromwell. He died centuries ago, what's he got to do with anything?'

'Have you forgotten your history, woman?'

'I don't want any more problems.'

'Don't worry, you're safe out here, I'm off to Belfast, that's where all the action is.'

He'd been in bed for too long, months of festering and plotting revenge and this was the result.

He stomped back upstairs and distracting herself from her worried thoughts, she switched on the TV to listen to the lunchtime news. To think what she'd be doing now: baking cakes, making sandwiches, and preparing games for Aisling's second birthday. This house was a storybook childhood home, roses round the door, a swing in the garden and plenty of places to play hide and seek. She imagined a group of two-year-olds charging round the garden having so much fun. Then she corrected herself. They were only here because of Aisling. Picking up a cushion, she clutched it tight against her chest and let out a sob. The anguish in her heart tore at her, breaking through in a great rush that swept her beyond all control. This was happening frequently but there was no one to comfort her. Liam must have heard her cries, but he remained upstairs wallowing in his own self-pity.

Sheridan was so lost in tears that she nearly missed the news reporter's words between her gulps. A famous actress was rumoured to be giving up her adopted Irish child, now two years old. Through her teary eyes, she looked up at the TV.

Janie's picture filled the screen.

'Oh my God, Liam, get down here quick, it's the baby,' she screamed.

She was shaking uncontrollably. From behind her, she heard Liam's feet on the stairs. 'What's wrong?'

Horrified, she could barely speak as she continued to stare at the screen.

'According to a close source, Janie Lee has given her child up because it doesn't fit in with her working regime. The source told our news network that Janie and her husband have been struggling with the child since they adopted her and in addition, she is rumoured not able to keep nannies for long, due to the child's behaviour.'

Janie's sister was interviewed. 'Things haven't gone well for my sister and her husband. They feel they're not the best parents for the child. Janie mentioned that the fit is all wrong, and the child needs more qualified parents.'

The reporter asked, 'Do you think the child has a condition like autism?'

Janie's sister replied. 'No diagnosis has been given, but it could be adoption trauma, if that's real. Children understand, don't they?'

Sheridan let out a howl and sank to the floor. 'My baby, my baby, I want my baby.'

'This is the last straw,' Liam screamed at her. 'I've gone through all this pain, and they don't even want our daughter. What's this been for? I told you no good would come of it.'

He picked up a fancy vase with flowers she'd picked from the garden and in a fit of rage, hurled it against the wall.

Oblivious to the shattering glass and damp sprigs nearby, she howled uncontrollably.

'It's no use you getting upset now, because it's too late, you broke this family up needlessly. This will never be my home, the home I've made. I tried to make a life for us, but it wasn't good enough. Why couldn't you just be happy with what you had. Loads of people have bigger families than us and manage to cope. Don't ask me for any sympathy.' He was all snarling and the look on his face shocked her. She saw the hatred in his eyes.

Clutching the pillow, she rocked back and forth sobbing. 'I thought I was doing it for our good, it was a sacrifice I was prepared to make.'

'Did you ask me or the kids what we thought, before you handed her to those rich Yanks as though you'd just delivered a bag of shopping?' He leant down, his face close to hers. 'I just don't know how anyone could do that, let alone my own wife. I don't know if I'll ever be able to forgive you, or if I'll ever get over this.'

A COUPLE of days later while the children were at school, Sheridan was in the kitchen washing up when she saw Liam's dad's car pull up on the driveway.

She dashed to open the door. 'Hello, love, this is a nice

surprise, I didn't know you were coming over. Liam could do with the company. He's been very down in the dumps lately. I can't get him out the house. I keep telling him, he'd enjoy a nice walk.'

'I've come to pick Liam up.'

'Oh good, where are you taking him? He needs perking up. He still hasn't tried the local pub.'

'He's coming to ours for a while.' It took her a moment for her to react. She hadn't believed him when he said he'd go back to his parents, but just then, as she turned, Liam was standing at the bottom of the stairs, a suitcase at his feet.

'What's going on? Why are you going to your dad's?'

'We talked about this two days ago. Did you think they were idle threats? I don't make idle threats. You should know that.'

Why would he want to go and live with his parents when he had his family and a lovely home here?

He was really planning to leave her. It didn't feel real. It felt so final. She stared at him unable to take it in.

He straightened his body, and she noticed a look of triumph in his eyes. 'I'm going to do something that will make a difference to our country, our people. I'm going to join my comrades in arms.'

Her jaw dropped and she glanced from Liam to Dec in horror. 'Don't be such a bloody fool, you'll end up dead. Dec, you've got to stop him,' she pleaded.

Dec just stared at the doormat.

'I'm already dead, love, might as well do what I can while I still can.' As he passed her, he leaned in and gave her a brief kiss on the forehead.

'Aren't you going to say goodbye to the kids?'

'There's no point. I don't have a family anymore,' he said coldly. 'I can't live here anymore. I need to get away. I'm going to do something that will change many people's lives. I'll sort out the people who did this to me, you mark my words.' There was a chill in his eyes as he looked at her one last time.

Dec went out to the car leaving them to say their goodbyes, but Liam didn't turn around to look at her and with his hand on the doorframe about to head off, he said, 'I have a mission, I have a purpose again, and I have a job to do.'

'What job?'

'I'm joining the IRA.'

He stepped outside and headed off.

CHAPTER 42

CORNWALL

Katie (aka Kathleen)

Friday evening arrived, and Katie was exhausted after a week of hard work at the café. She'd been kept on her toes, but now she couldn't wait for her well-deserved Saturday off. She planned to wander around the town and enjoy a walk along the beach and up onto the cliffs. And the thought of exploring the castle perched on the hill, it felt like a big adventure.

She removed the rollers from her hair, then gave it an extra spritz of Silvikrin to keep it in place, knowing how breezy it was by the sea. After applying blue eyeshadow and thick mascara to make her eyes dazzle and a touch of powder to her face, she stepped back to admire her reflection. She was wearing a French-cut skirt with a slinky top and was just slipping on her denim jacket when Sophie called out to ask if she was ready.

'Wow, you scrub up well,' Sophie gushed.

She laughed. 'A girl's got to make the effort, never know who you might meet.'

'I think I know who you like, it's that Kenny. He's been lingering in the café every morning after making his delivery.'

'Doesn't he normally then?'

'Does he heck.'

'You look stunning, by the way.' Sophie was wearing a pair of black flares and a strappy red top. 'With your figure, you'd even shine in a bin liner.'

They gathered their bags and Sophie linked arms with Katie, pulling her into the chill of the evening air. They made their way around the harbour wall to the British Legion club, where the disco awaited. Laughter and pop music spilled out as they opened the double doors, their eyes dazzled by the flashing lights and strobes. The disco ball was spinning, and fractured shards of light were turning the floor into a kaleidoscope. They bought their tickets and headed to the bar.

Katie hadn't felt this happy in a long time. To think how far she'd come, escaping the laundry, landing a great job at a posh hotel, now this holiday and best of all, making a friend, the fun they were going to have. Finally, she'd turned a corner, she could enjoy her youth and she couldn't believe how much she'd missed out on. But her newfound happiness was tinged with sadness. There wasn't a permanent job for her here. And even if she found another job here in this town, where would she live? On her wages, she'd never afford the rent.

Sophie pulled Katie towards a table where her friends were sitting, a group of girls between Katie's age and mid-twenties. The hall was crowded, and she glanced round hoping to see Kenny and his mate, though she was not quite sure why she was poised for his arrival, he probably already had a girlfriend. Not that he'd mentioned anyone, but he was bound to have a string of admirers, good-looking bloke that he was. Anyway, why would she want to be getting close to someone when she wasn't here for long? It was just nice that there were friendly people in this town.

Her eyes were drawn to the DJ, an old geezer with long sideburns, all trussed up wearing tight yellow trousers with a t-shirt and multi-coloured tank top. She wondered if he was an old war hero. She thought of Tony Blackburn and listening to the radio in her friend's bedroom back in Liverpool. Then she was on a nostalgic path, in her mind trotting out blasts from the past: Paul Gambaccini, or the Great Gambo as people called him, John Peel, Dave Lee Travis, and Noel Edmonds. And that odd wacky DJ with the big cigar, Jimmy Saville and he now did a show, fixing kid's dreams. If only someone could fix her life.

Sophie pulled her up to dance when 'Mamma Mia' came on and the other girls joined them. She smiled at the collection of white handbags dumped in the middle. They were nearly the same but distinguishable by the different bows and buckles. When the song finished, the DJ went on to play Mud's 'Tiger Feet', Suzi Quatro, 'Devil Gate Drive' and David Essex, 'Going to Make You a Star'. As she spun around it was then that she noticed Kenny standing in a line of fellas leaning against the wall chatting and watching the girls dancing. Catching her eye, he gave her a little wave.

Towards the end of the evening the music slowed, and the crowd thinned as couples shimmied to the floor for a smoochy. Katie smiled as lads darted off in different directions looking for girls to dance with. She felt a tap on the shoulder and Bryn was standing there and asked her to dance. She felt a stab of disappointment hoping that it would be Kenny. but didn't want to be rude so allowed him to pull her out to the floor as 'Nights in White Satin' blasted out over the music system. She looked at the DJ who looked particularly cheesy. As they twirled in a circle, she caught sight of Kenny looking at her with a disappointed frown on his face. Bryn was trying to make conversation, but she wasn't listening. Her mind was elsewhere. When the song finished and before the next one started, she made a hasty retreat to the toilets and on her way back deliberately passed Kenny. He quipped, 'I wish that had been me, I would have loved a dance with you.'

'You should have asked me then.'

The next slow dance started. He quickly said, 'Come on then,' as they made a dash to the floor before the song ended. He put his arm around her, and she felt her heart flutter. It felt so good to be close to him and their bodies folded into each other so perfectly. She breathed in his scent, a hint of Brut. She smiled and thought of the ad, Henry Cooper, 'splash it all over.'

Towards the end of the evening, he suggested stepping outside of the hot and stuffy hall for a breath of air. They perched on a low stone wall, gazing up at the night sky, a vast canvas painted with shimmering stars, twinkling like diamonds scattered across a velvet tapestry.

'That's Orion,' Kenny said. 'You can see his belt right there.'

She was impressed that he knew the constellations and remembered how much she'd loved watching the night sky at the caravan, even though no one had shown her the stars then.

He leaned closer, his breath catching as he traced the outline with his finger. 'And there's Taurus, the bull.'

'Do you think there's life out there?' she wondered aloud, her mind sparking with curiosity.

He turned to her, their faces close enough that she could feel the warmth of his beer-infused breath on her cheek as he gently tucked a strand of hair behind her ear. A shiver fluttered down her spine. She looked at his handsome face, overcome by a desire to kiss him. He took her hand and a million sparks shot through her.

'Perhaps if you're free tomorrow, I could give you a tour of the town.' His lip grazed her ear as he spoke sending shivers down her.

'I'd love to, that was my exact plan for tomorrow. Now you can show me all the secret places.'

He laughed. 'At least in this town you'll never get lost.'

. . .

THE BABY HUNTERS

THE NEXT MORNING when Katie came downstairs, she found the new lady had already arrived. She wondered how she would get on in the busy environment but watching the woman putting on her apron and tying her hair, she thought she seemed flustered and a bit old for this type of work.

Kenny was waiting outside for her, hands deep in the pockets of his donkey jacket, collar turned up, hair slicked back. Her heart did a little pirouette, she felt suddenly shy and self-conscious. It was always this way when she liked someone. As they walked up the hill towards the castle, he quickly put her at ease, telling her how he and Bryn had moved here five years ago from Manchester. They'd come here on holiday to go surfing and loved it so much, they'd decided to stay. Bryn worked on the fishing boats bringing in the catch for the local restaurants. 'I don't miss Manchester, it's a grim place, all that smog and rain and miserable people. I don't even follow the footie. So, whereabouts are you from?'

'Liverpool, can't you tell?'

'Blimey, I wouldn't have guessed, you don't have much of an accent.'

'You saying I'm posh?' She laughed.

'Sophie said you're a singer.'

She blushed and looked away, embarrassed. What had Sophie been telling him? She didn't consider herself a singer, it was merely something she'd been asked to do in the evenings at the hotel to entertain the guests. However, she enjoyed it and found it to be a release.

'What can you sing for me?' he asked with a laugh.

For a minute she didn't know if he was mocking her and suddenly, she felt shy and conspicuous.

'I was only teasing you, putting you on the spot, you don't have to, not out here on this wild cliff, but there is a karaoke evening coming up in town. Do you want to go with me?'

'I'd love to, I won't be shy in front of a bigger audience.'

It was easy chat, and she could have gone on to talk about her background, but she was keen to avoid further questions about her past. She hated keeping up a pretence and wasn't sure how she'd deal with direct quizzing. She wondered how much to tell him about her life. Everything came back to that fateful night in January 1974, the night of the Hawkwind concert. It was hard to believe it was only last year, now it felt like a lifetime ago, probably because so much had happened since. But it still crouched there, in the recesses of her mind, left a mark on her, a stain that subtly shifted how she saw herself and would haunt her forever.

And then they moved on from their family backgrounds and as the talk returned to music, it struck her how much their tastes coincided, and how easy he was to be around.

Up on the cliff they looked down, watching the sea pounding on the rocks, seagulls wheeling and squawking above. Kenny pointed to a group of shags perched on the granite. She smiled; they looked like a cluster of old gentlemen.

The chat was constant, and she soon found herself relaxing and forgetting about her troubled past. They walked for miles all around the peninsula, stopping briefly to look at the view, up a pathway towards the castle, along the headland and back towards the harbour. It was an obscenely beautiful day, the sky baby blue, but it was bitterly cold as though the air was made of broken glass.

He gazed out to sea. 'I came down here in the summer and the first time I walked along this pathway, I spotted dolphins. You don't tend to see them in the winter and only on calm days. They like the warm water.'

'Wow, that must have been amazing. I've never seen a dolphin.'

'You will. I guarantee. But not yet, it's too early.'

'Tell me about your job. Do you just do the deliveries, or do you get involved in baking the bread too?'

'Deliveries in the morning, then I bake the cakes in the afternoon.'

She couldn't imagine him baking cakes.

'It was my dream job even though it involves getting up at the crack of dawn. To be baking, the thing I'd always loved as a kid. My grandma taught me to bake. I love kneading dough and batch cooking all my favourite foods: farmhouse loaves, crusty rolls, fluffy croissants.'

'Stop, right now.' She laughed. 'You're making me hungry.'

'One day I'll make a wife very fat.'

They both laughed.

She wished she'd worn a hat and scarf and was quite glad when they eventually headed back to the café for hot chocolate and tea cakes.

Stepping into the café Katie immediately noticed that Sophie wasn't her normal relaxed, happy self. She looked flustered and agitated.

'Thank God you're back,' she said, relief washing over her face. 'Would you mind clearing a few tables, we're rushed off our feet.'

Katie glanced round. The new lady was nowhere to be seen. The place was heaving, there were no free tables and poor Sophie was barely coping.

Kenny looked from Katie to Sophie. 'Give us a pinny, count me in.' He took an apron from the hook and a tray and wove around the tables to begin clearing crockery.

'Where's the new woman?'

'She left halfway through the lunch rush, couldn't hack it, she kept getting orders muddled up and making mistakes on the till. One of the locals jumped in to help me for an hour but she had to go. The washing up is stacking up in the kitchen and we're running out of crockery.'

'You had to sack her?' Katie was shocked but not surprised. When she'd seen the woman, she had wondered how she'd cope.

'No, thank goodness, she realised it was too busy for her. I hate telling people they're not good enough. But she was chasing customers away, it wouldn't have worked out. So many people just don't have a clue.'

'So now you've got to look for someone else?' Katie glanced round at Kenny who gave an encouraging smile as if to say, *go on, girl, the job's yours.*

'I've found someone, but I need to ask her if she's interested.'

Katie's heart sank. 'Oh? That was quick.' She felt tears wobble in her voice and was surprised at how hurt she felt.

'She's perfect for the job, is a real hard worker and great with the customers.'

Kenny flashed a conspiratorial look at Sophie as if they were sharing a secret that Katie wasn't party to, and suddenly she wanted to escape upstairs. What was the point in helping? There was nothing in it for her.

There was a lull in the queue and Sophie turned to Katie. 'I'm looking right at her. Are you up for it?'

'Who me?'

'Well, yes, I can't think of anyone I'd rather have working with me.'

'I'd love to but I've got to go back to the hotel soon and besides, where would I live?'

Kenny said, 'You can stay with me.'

'No, we're having none of that here, if you want to date Katie you do things properly. If you're happy with the room you're in now, you can stay there.'

'What about the hotel, they need me?'

'Leave it with Grandma, she'll sort things.'

A warm glow washed over her. A job. *And* a place to live. It felt like her birthday and Christmas all rolled into one and without hesitating she accepted the offer.

'Okay,' Sophie said clapping her hands. 'That's enough, back to work.'

Within the hour all of the tables were cleared, and order had been restored. Kenny had done wonders in the kitchen and cleared up all the mess without breaking a single plate.

'Coffee and cake for the next week for you,' she said to Kenny.

'It's okay, Soph, I don't like cake.' They both chuckled.

When the café shut, Sophie said, 'You've done so well, you can have the evening off.'

'Oh, that's jolly decent of you, and am I entitled to a pay rise yet?' She laughed.

'Stick with us, kiddo, and you'll be just fine,' Sophie said.

The following morning when she strolled past the newsagent, her eye was drawn to the row of Sunday papers, Niamh's face staring out, and below, the headlines. Her heart thumped in her chest. 'Girl found in lake at exclusive hotel,' one of them read.

She bent to pick the paper up and quickly glanced over the story. A few sentences caught her eye. 'Several prime ministers and famous actors have stayed at this luxury hotel.' 'The owners are embroiled in a police investigation into false accounting,' and 'claims have arisen that the owners were sheltering escaped prisoners and vulnerable girls who'd suffered abuse at the hands of the Catholic Church.'

A chill swept through her, and she shivered. How fortunate she was to have escaped; it wouldn't have been long before the laundry and the priest had discovered her whereabouts. And then what?

Smiling to herself she strode along the cobbles and up the hill. She had all the tools to start a new life, new home, new job, new friends, and things were beginning to look bright. For once in her life, she was starting to look forward to the future.

THE END

Author Note

Thank you for purchasing 'The Baby Hunters,' which I hope you enjoyed. If you have a moment, please would you kindly post a short review on Amazon. Reviews are always appreciated.

'The Baby Hunters' is part of a series called 'Every Family'.

The series is about Kathleen's life in a Magdalene laundry and her later struggles. You can read the books in any order. Here is the link to the complete series:

UK : My Book
USA : My Book
Australia: My Book

OTHER BOOKS BY JOANNA WARRINGTON

To stay up to date on my latest releases, please follow me on Amazon. Here is the link:

https://www.amazon.co.uk/stores/Joanna-Warrington/author/B00RH4XPI6

My most popular series is *Every Parent's Fear* inspired by the thalidomide scandal

Link to series: UK: My Book

USA: My Book

Australia: My Book

Today, the word thalidomide immediately rouses sympathy for the ten thousand children who suffered from its effects—in the fifties, it was simply the best new wonder drug for expectant mothers.

Sandy is one of these mothers, even if she isn't so sure she wants to be. The aspiring model had a one-night stand with a journalist that resulted in her current predicament. Shunned by her family, Sandy quietly checks herself into a maternity home to wait out her pregnancy and prepare to have the baby adopted.

Rona, one of the home's employees, finds it hard to see Sandy and the others expecting. She and her husband have been trying for years, but Rona is unable to conceive. When Sandy delivers a child disabled by thalidomide, Rona makes a life-changing decision that will have dramatic consequences.

Meanwhile, Sandy's journalist lover stumbles upon the scoop of a century. As he investigates corruption entrenched in the company that developed thalidomide, he is surprised to reconnect with Sandy, the one who got away. He and Sandy feel drawn to each other, but both will have to confront old wounds if they want to be together.

The first part of a hugely popular series (over 100,000 copies sold)

You might also enjoy reading about four modern women and their messy lives in:

Can We Sync Or Will We Sink?

Link to series: UK: My Book

USA: My Book

Australia: My Book

A collection of four novels (**which are also sold separately**) about the grubby reality of marriage, family and romance. Tender, funny, entertaining, life-affirming and at times heart-breaking. Can each family confront, forgive and heal? Will they sync or will they sink?

Printed in Great Britain
by Amazon

59955310R00160